Marital Privilege

Marital Privilege

Greg Sisk

NORTH STAR PRESS OF ST. CLOUD, INC.
St. Cloud, Minnesota

ISBN: 978-0-87839-739-6

This is a work of fiction.

Lest any person with a criminal motive believe he or she might gain any advantage from reading this novel, please know that the descriptions of explosive materials, the use and storage of explosives, the making of illegal bombs, forensic techniques for identifying the source of explosives, and regulations governing explosives are incomplete, used in a fictitious manner, and in some respects purposely misleading.

While the author has strived to be generally accurate in describing the state of the law of evidentiary privileges and criminal procedure, this novel is not intended as legal advice and should not be relied on as such. Moreover, even in the narration of legal doctrine, elements of literary license have been introduced into the storyline.

While the non-residential places in this novel are often real locations, they are used fictitiously. The incidents, names, and characters are the products of the author's imagination and any resemblance to actual events or to actual persons, living or dead, is entirely coincidental—with the exception of Tucker the cat, who is quite real.

Printed in the United States of America

First Edition: June 2014

Published by:
North Star Press of St. Cloud, Inc.
P.O. Box 451
St. Cloud, MN 56302

northstarpress.com

Acknowledgements

At each stage of planning, writing, and revising this novel, I have been blessed by the patience, encouragement, and generosity of many people, including my law school colleagues here and elsewhere: Julie Oseid, Patrick Garry, Mark Osler, Jerry Organ, and Father Dan Griffith; my current and former students, Liz Malay, Alyssa Schaller, Michelle King, Alicia Long, Caitlin Drogemuller, Catherine Underwood, and Nicholas Lebbin; my mother, Roberta Sisk; and, of course, my loving, patient, and artistic wife Mindy and my bright-eyed and bright-minded daughter Caitlin.

"Society has a deeply rooted interest in the preservation of the peace of families, and in the maintenance of the sacred institution of marriage; and its strongest safeguard is to preserve with jealous care any violation of those hallowed confidences inherent in, and inseparable from, the marital status.

"Therefore the law places the ban of its prohibition upon any breach of the confidence between husband and wife, by declaring all confidential communications between them to be incompetent matter for either of them to expose as witnesses."

~Supreme Court of Florida, 1898

"Society has a deeply rooted interest in the preservation of the peace of families, and in the maintenance of the sacred institution of marriage, and it seems to me expedient to preserve a wild felicity any violation of those hallowed confidences unheard of in, and insepar-able from, the marital status.

"Therefore, the law places the ban of its prohibition upon any breach of the confidence between husband and wife, by declaring all confidential communications between them to be incompetent matter for either of them to expose as witnesses."

—Supreme Court of Florida, 1898

~Prologue~

ITTING ON HIS BRONZE CHAIR with his back to the burnished brown brick arches and stark white columns of Bascom Hall, Abraham Lincoln holds vigil over the quadrangle at the center of the University of Wisconsin campus in Madison. As the long sloping field withers from the burnt brown of summer into the blanched bone white of winter, the martyred president waits serenely for the green resurrection of spring.

The undergraduate who comes to Lincoln on his pedestal prematurely, so the legend goes, will never graduate. But, according to university tradition, the graduating student who abides until commencement day and then confides in the Great Emancipator will realize the fulfillment of her aspirations.

On a Saturday morning in late spring, Candace Peterson joined the line of cap-and-gown-wearing graduates that stretched down Bascom Hill, which now was a luxuriant greensward. Each one waited to climb into the great man's lap and declare hopes and dreams into his bronze ear. When her turn arrived, Candace gripped the statue's platform and hauled herself up until she was perched high above the quadrangle on Lincoln's right leg. Whispering into his ear, she wished for a satisfying career and a loving family, which she frivolously requested be "sweetly tied together in a bow."

Before climbing down, she leaned over to kiss Lincoln's metallic-green cheek—and, with her right foot slipping on the metal base, toppled off the pedestal. She avoided a hard landing by grabbing the edge of the statue's platform with her right hand and by the fortunate presence of the two young men waiting below who eased her descent to the ground. Escaping the fall with nothing more than grass stains on her commencement gown, Candace surrendered her place to the next graduate in line.

On Sunday afternoon, the very next day, Candace was married to Bill Klein. She had returned to her childhood parish in Golden Valley, Minnesota. In the simple sanctuary of Good Shepherd Catholic Church, before a prominent crucifix on an otherwise un-adorned wall and beneath simple dark wooden rafters, Candace pledged her love for Bill until "death do us part."

After the priest had blessed them and pronounced the mar-riage, while her family and friends applauded, she kissed the man who was now her husband—and would be the father of her child.

~1~

SHE LOVED HIM. God knows, she really did love him. Still. Why, then, did she have to reacquaint herself with that manifest truth yet again this morning? Why had her waking routine come to include a recitation in her mind of the same mantra of true love, before she could face him at the breakfast table?

Hearing no answer to her self-directed interrogation, Candace Klein rolled out of bed.

Most people loathed Monday mornings, as the pleasures and relaxation of the weekend commuted into the toil and grind of the work-week. For Candace, the close of each weekend—with its long hours spent side-by-side with Bill (or, increasingly, spent in the same house but in separate rooms)—was becoming something of a relief.

Returning each Monday to a busy and minutely scheduled daily agenda made it easier for Candace to suppress her personal disquiet. Everything seemed normal when she could scan through her computer planner and see each portion of each day parceled out in a series of classes to teach, committee meetings to attend, appointments with students, and time reserved for scholarly writing projects.

Yes, of course, she loved him. They were a happy family. Until next weekend.

CANDACE HAD PASSED her thirty-fifth birthday a couple of weeks earlier. She was an attractive woman, much prettier than she thought (when she bothered to think about her features at all). Her wide and inquisitive eyes and her easy smile long had captivated anyone fortunate to see her, even when she had made only a limited appearance.

Once, that enchanting smile had played across her face without need for rehearsal, touching an audience ranging from the barista filling her coffee order in the morning to the suit-wearing office worker waiting next to her for the light to change at the crosswalk. Now, while that genial flash of teeth still made a regular appearance, the stage had first to be set with friends, faculty colleagues, her students, and, especially, her beloved boy.

Still, the warm light of intelligence that illuminated her capacious eyes had not faded. Even now, at least by the end of each morning, that penetrating radiance could burn away the lingering fog of melancholy. As she returned each week day to her professional world, where her bright mind would be bathed with the sunlight of scholarly thought, distractions could be banished into the darkness . . . at least during the work hours.

Like many girls, beginning in middle school, she had been convinced her nose was too big or her hair too plain in color or her hips too wide. When she reached her junior year of high school, she experienced a sudden boost in personal confidence, that she had to admit had more than a little to do with the fact that boys began to notice her. As more time passed—as the high school years wound down and she entered adulthood—Candace had become increasingly comfortable with herself as a person, not as an object of cosmetic evaluation by others.

At her seventeenth birthday party, she had announced to her close circle of friends that "my face has finally grown into my nose," as she laughed self-deprecatingly. Although she had meant the remark as a joke among girlfriends, she found as time went by that she had come to believe it. She decided for herself that she had matured into a "not so bad looking" young woman. She had come to accept herself as reasonably attractive. But she couldn't quite think of herself as *pretty*.

To be sure—even after she had escaped the cruel and minute examinations and appearance rankings imposed by teenage peers—she remained perpetually disgruntled with her hair. It wasn't light enough to be called blond. And it wasn't dark enough that brunette was fully descriptive either. She thought of it as plain and colorless. But by the time she had passed from high school, she had become too impatient with an emphasis on superficial looks to bother with artificial coloring for her hair.

At the end of the day, Candace's bright eyes were the one physical trait that perfectly reflected what was inside her head—an energetic and stimulating mind.

From the time she could remember, the world of ideas had been her personal world as well. When other kids had lavished their free time on television and video games, Candace had read—no, devoured—books. Sure, she had read her share of silly teen fiction novels. But she had read the "Great Books" as well—and not only when assigned in high school English Literature class. Before high school graduation arrived, she had turned increasingly to non-fiction, frequently on political and historical themes.

The fundamental questions of the ages on the meaning of life and liberty and justice, the ancient discourses on the nature of humanity and human society, the historical events that had set the stage for the modern world, the political debates of the present day—all had found welcome passage from books into her inquisitive mind through the open portals of her wide eyes. As she moved through college and into professional school, she discovered that the study of law wedded together the philosophical inquiries with a practical means for the deliberative resolution of problems.

For more than thirteen years now, Candace had directed those bright eyes and applied that bright mind to the study and practice of law.

And now she had become a Professor of Law (well, an Associate Professor of Law—not tenured yet), a blessing and a privilege she could hardly believe had come her way.

In her work life, she was one of the lucky ones. She had found her calling, had found happiness.

Now, she could not help but think, if only that were still true of her personal life.

◆　◆　◆

LOOKING TO THE OTHER SIDE of the bed, Candace confirmed that, again this morning, she had been left alone in the master bedroom. As usual, Bill Klein had risen before her. He undoubtedly was already at his favorite chair in the kitchen nook downstairs, eating his bowl of Honey Nut Cheerios, drinking his first cup of coffee, balancing the newspaper on his knee, and flipping through the channels on the television parked at the corner of the kitchen countertop.

Candace could hear the sound of the TV wafting up the long curving stairway from the kitchen area at the rear of the house on the first floor. The faint but discordant noise echoed down the second floor corridor to the master bedroom near the front of the house.

The Klein house was in Eden Prairie, a small city to the southwest of Minneapolis. The face of this suburb was speckled with lakes, ponds, and puddles of varying depths, sizes, and shapes, like freckles on the cheeks of a red-headed child.

The Klein's Tudor Revival style house at 3732 Dunnell Drive lay to the east of small and kidney-shaped Eden Lake, to the north of the larger but thinly stretched Neil Lake, and to the west of the shallow and meandering expanses of the Anderson Lakes.

Is J.D. up yet? Candace wondered, as she stretched next to the bed.

Probably not.

Their nine-and-a-half-year-old son was staying up way too late for a third-grader. But now that he had taken so joyfully to reading, she found that she just didn't have the heart to insist that he put his book away and turn out the light when the clock reached 9:30 p.m. After all, J.D.'s teachers had not reported that he had been tired or grumpy at school.

6

Until a couple of months ago, J.D. had always been up before Candace. In those days, she would find him sitting downstairs, eating cereal, and watching TV with his dad. But the habit of early rising had been broken when J.D. had discovered that books could transport him to another place each night. It may not yet have affected his school work, but the later sleep time and delayed waking certainly was generating a morning rush to get ready for school.

Because the master bedroom was the one closest to the stairway, she stepped to the top of the passage and listened carefully. She could hear that the TV was on to the Fox News "Morning Edition." That meant J.D. had not yet arrived at the breakfast table. If J.D. had gone down earlier, Bill would have switched over to the Family Channel or Nickelodeon.

Candace walked down the hall to J.D.'s bedroom. Sure enough, she could see his little form under the blankets, his round head covered over and near the foot of the bed. Only one foot was sticking out from under the covers, pointing toward the headboard. J.D.'s body routinely made a 180-degree turn during the night.

A little "meow" issued from a small lump next to the larger shape under the blankets, telling her that Tucker had spent the night with J.D. again. Tucker was an orange tabby cat, with a pure white belly. The white fur colored half of Tucker's long slim front legs, resembling boots, along with a snowy daub on his lower jaw.

Candace liked Tucker, but she didn't adore him. The cat would tolerate a minute or two of petting, if she came across him in the house and leaned down. But he wasn't much for snuggling or jumping up to sit on a lap. In fact, she was a little leery of the cat, because he might well nip her on the hand if she caught him in a disagreeable mood when she reached down to stroke his back.

But not with J.D. If he leaned over to caress the cat or even pick him up for a petting, J.D. never came away with a bite on the back of the hand or a scratch on his cheek. Tucker was more than willing to cuddle next to the boy in bed. J.D. never brought out Tucker's cantankerous side.

"James Daniel," she said lovingly but firmly. "It's time to get up. The bus will be here at 7:45."

"Okay, Mom," J.D. said, and slowly sat up in bed, rubbing his eyes.

She pulled out clean underwear and socks from the chest of drawers in his bedroom. She reached into his closet and took his uniform blue pants and button-down shirt off the hangers. That J.D. was required to wear a uniform at St. Gregory's Catholic School made it simple and easy to lay out his clothes each day. No arguments about what to wear in this household, she thought with a satisfied smile.

RETURNING TO THE MASTER bedroom, Candace washed her face and applied her makeup. She sat back on the bed to slide on her jeans. Casual dress would become her daily style now that the law school semester had concluded.

The jeans had been pulled up only to her knees when Candace found herself sliding back into second-guessing the choices she had made in her married life.

If only her father had been a baker or a plumber or a doctor, maybe things would have unfolded differently. Maybe they'd be somewhere else now, living different lives, happier lives. Or at least Bill wouldn't be working for her father.

She knew this rueful self-reproach was an unhealthy habit, but one that she was indulging more and more often in recent weeks. She tried to be stern with herself. She should clear her mind of negative thoughts, arrange a smile on her face and march downstairs to be with Bill and J.D. for a few minutes before she drove into downtown Minneapolis to her office at the University of St. Thomas School of Law.

Although this particular Monday morning fell in the middle of May, Candace already was on a summer schedule at the University of St. Thomas. Law school classes had ended at the beginning of May, followed by two weeks of exams and then commencement ceremonies for the graduating third-year students, which had been held just last weekend. Starting today, Candace could trade her professional dress, which she always wore to class, for her summer jeans. For her, this was the day on which she could turn her thoughts full time to writing projects for the next three months.

But summer had not yet come for her boy. J.D. had about three more weeks of school, with St. Gregory's Catholic School letting out for the summer at the end of the first week of June.

So Candace knew she could afford only a few more minutes to commiserate with herself before she had to get J.D. out the door and to the school bus on time.

Yes, coming home to Minnesota three years ago after nearly a decade with Bill in Chicago had been a big, big mistake. Oh, the problem was not the Twin Cities, which she liked very much and was perfect for raising a family. Nor was there any problem with her work as a law professor at the University of St. Thomas School of Law, which she adored.

Indeed, she reprimanded herself, *it's really not Minnesota*. It was the foolish, stupid, asinine, insane decision they'd made to accept her father's invitation to take Bill into the family construction business.

It was more Bill's decision than hers at the time. And they both had thought it would be an interim step in his career. But she should have realized it was a recipe for familial disaster.

Candace found herself staring at her own image in the full-length mirror hanging next to the dresser. She looked tired, she thought. She looked sad. She wasn't so drawn or forlorn in appearance that anyone else would notice, but she could see weariness on her face and melancholy in her eyes.

Collecting herself and banishing depressing thoughts with an exercise of sheer will, she found the strength to go through the bedroom door and walk to the stairway.

When Candace came downstairs, Bill glanced up briefly from the newspaper and TV. "Good morning, Candy."

No one called her "Candy." Not even her own father. Only Bill.

When Bill adopted that nickname shortly after they started dating during college at the University of Wisconsin some fifteen years ago, it had been endearing. Now she found it irritating, like when a casual acquaintance affects an improper intimacy. Of course that reaction made no sense when the person in question was her own husband. The problem undoubtedly was hers, not Bill's.

She hadn't said anything to him about her discomfort with being called "Candy." But it grated on her again this morning.

"Hello, Bill."

He nodded as he returned to his reading and watching.

That annoyed her as well. Had they become that comfortable or distracted? Couldn't they at least acknowledge each other with more than a gesture in the morning? Why did every interaction with Bill have to be so awkward?

THREE YEARS AGO, the family had been ensconced in Chicago and assumed they would remain there always. When she had embarked on a search for a position as a law professor after several years in law practice and two years as a teaching fellow at the University of Chicago, Candace had assumed she would take a position with one of the many law schools in the Chicago area.

That had been "The Plan." It had always been understood between them. Although they had never explored it in any depth, both of them had assumed she would lock in a full-time law teaching job at a Chicago area law school. Their Chicago-centered life would sail forward on an even keel, at a safe speed, and in familiar waters.

And she had been invited to join the faculty at two law schools in Chicago.

But the place that most intrigued her during interviews was a new Catholic law school that recently had been founded in Minnesota at the University of St. Thomas. The school had a faith-based mission and emphasized professional formation. The faculty envisioned the practice of law as not just an occupation for personal success but as a vocation for the common good. And the faculty was committed to scholarly prominence, intending to build the new law school into a national institution. It would be a chance to get in on the ground floor of something big.

Candace came away from her visit to the St. Thomas law school in Minneapolis with heightened enthusiasm about law teaching and with a stronger belief that she could make a real difference with a new generation of law students. No other school had touched her in the same way.

She had made up her mind to approach Bill and earnestly make the case for taking the chance and moving the family to Minnesota, where both she and Bill had grown up. She had planned her whole argument out, point by point, just as she had diligently prepared a legal argument to a judge during her years in practice in Chicago. Fearing that Bill would be resistant to leaving his established position with an engineering firm and upsetting their settled life in Chicago, she rehearsed and revised and re-rehearsed the argument again and again. As a finale, she was going to remind Bill that she had arranged her professional life around his engineering career at times in their shared lives and straightforwardly submit that it was his turn to make a sacrifice for her.

As it turned out, she didn't get very far into her appeal to Bill when it became apparent, to her pleasant surprise, that Bill needed less persuading than she anticipated. As soon as she opened the door to a move, Bill had looked at her with a smile and allowed that maybe it was time for a change of setting. Indeed, he was relieved that she had raised the subject. He'd been holding back in recent weeks. He hadn't shared with her just how frustrating his work at the engineering firm had become in recent months.

They had talked through the night, weighing the advantages, as well as the risks, of making the move. They shared their hopes and dreams for their family life and their careers. Candace and Bill confessed their hidden fears to each other and openly acknowledged their previously suppressed anxieties. In so doing, they saw those worries fade away in the incandescent light of a newly discovered optimism.

In that moment, Candace had felt like they were more than a married couple. They were partners in building their own future. They were fully committed to each other in every way. They would take this big step together.

Candace had tried to convey how excited she was about the prospect of joining the new law school in Minneapolis, about how her faith and her idealism had been captivated by the mission of the University of St. Thomas. Bill seemed genuinely intrigued by her story and expressed unreserved support for her desire to undertake this new challenge.

In turn, Bill had revealed that things had been going downhill at work, beginning with the economic downturn. The state government in Illinois had been on a spending binge for more than a decade. When the recession hit and raising taxes was no longer a viable political or pragmatic answer to everything, it looked more and more likely that the state would fall into insolvency.

Funding for public construction projects had already collapsed. It was doubtful that Illinois would be able to generate much revenue or find willing lenders to finance new projects. Bill's own engineering firm worked on few government-funded projects. But as public projects disappeared, competing construction and engineering firms were chasing fewer and fewer private building initiatives.

Moreover, Bill had just gone through one of the most disappointing and discouraging episodes of his career. For several months he had been preparing plans for renovation of an historical warehouse building in south Chicago, converting it into a neighborhood grocery store. Every historical building renovation presented unique challenges in negotiating the line between creating a usable space for a viable modern business and protecting the historically significant features of a building constructed for another purpose in another time.

On this occasion, however, the city historical landmark commission had become dominated by a purist clique. They had no practical appreciation for the situation—or maybe they just didn't care. The commission insisted that no alterations be made to the edifice of the building. Then its members declared that no changes could be made to the interior that could be observed from outside. Such restrictions made no sense for a grocery store, which had to provide some marketing of its nature on the outside and inside of the structure. This was especially true on an arterial street with a high speed limit where possible customers would have only seconds to recognize that they were driving by a grocery store. Eventually the historical commission's enduring intransigence caused the client to lose the financing necessary to continue the project.

So a neighborhood would be left without a grocery store. Badly needed jobs in a difficult economy and in a depressed urban area would not be created. An historical building would be left vacant, likely leading to further deterioration, vandalism, and perhaps occupation by squatters.

Everyone was a loser. Including Bill.

He hadn't lost his job, but he had lost his spirit for historical building renovation work . . . at least for now. Yes, he had enough seniority at the engineering firm and was sufficiently valued that he almost surely could weather the economic storm. Yes, "The Plan" would still work. Yes, "The Plan" was still the safest path to take. But, Bill said, he was ready professionally and emotionally to set out on a new course.

By the time Candace and Bill had talked all the way through to a mutual decision, the sun was rising. When then-five-year-old J.D. woke up, they walked down the street to a local café for breakfast. They talked animatedly about what it would mean to leave Chicago and how they could build a new life in Minneapolis.

Everything looked bright. They were in it together. They held nothing back. The words flowed easily between them.

WHY NOW, COMPLAINED Candace to herself, was every conversation so flat? And did Bill feel the same way, or was this just a phase she was going through? God knows, she really did love him. Right?

It had been months now since she'd felt even a little passion for Bill. She knew marriage was a commitment between two people through good and bad, not an ecstatic passage of unending marital bliss. Still, how long could a dry spell last before you couldn't deny to yourself any longer that something was wrong, really wrong?

◆ ◆ ◆

J.D. RAN DOWN the stairs and leaped into a seat at the breakfast nook next to his father. That little boy may be slow to get started and leave his bed in the morning. Once he was up, though, Candace marveled, he opened the throttle all the way.

Candace poured him a bowl of cereal and a glass of orange juice. "It's almost 7:30, kiddo," she said, "so eat up quickly. The bus will be here in just ten minutes."

J.D. scarfed down his cereal, put the bowl in the sink, gave Candace a hug (she was delighted that he was still willing to do that), said goodbye to his father, and ran out the door to catch the bus to school.

◆ ◆ ◆

"HEY," SAID BILL, as Candace picked up her briefcase and moved toward the door leading to the garage. "Take my car today, and let me take your mini-van."

That brought Candace up short. Her husband Bill's car was, well, his. He didn't like anyone else, including Candace, driving it. When he'd purchased the car two years ago—a fire-engine red, two-door coupe, with a "moon-roof" and optional "rear wing spoiler"— she'd jokingly called it his "mid-life crisis car."

She still called it that. But she wasn't joking any more. (She rarely joked with Bill any more.)

It wasn't really a sports car, nor anything expensive. It was a Honda Accord coupe. But it looked sporty, especially with the accessories and the shocking red color.

In any event, Bill was quite possessive of his red coupe. If she ever drove it, even on a short errand, he complained that she'd moved the position of the seat, or adjusted the mirror wrong, or changed the station on the radio. If she were keeping score—and she realized just by thinking about Bill's past reactions that she apparently was keeping score (not a good sign)—this possessive and obsessive behavior about a stupid car was getting on her nerves as well.

"What?" she asked, startled by his suggestion.

"I need to stop off at the furniture store today and pick up those new dining room chairs. I need your mini-van to haul everything home."

"Okay," Candace replied, shrugging. Even though she rarely drove Bill's car, she did keep a copy of the key to the coupe on her key-chain.

Walking into the garage attached to their suburban Minnesota house, she hit the button on the electric garage-door opener. She got into the driver's seat of the Honda Accord.

Whether Bill liked it or not, she had to move the seat forward if she were to reach the pedals, and she had to adjust the rear and side mirrors. She could always move them back when she got home. If she remembered. If she wanted to remember.

Before she could start the car, Candace saw a small hunched shape trudging back up the long driveway. It was James Daniel.

She rolled down the car window, and said, "What are you doing here, honey?"

"I missed the bus, Mom."

"Didn't I tell you you were staying up too late? You've got to be able to get up and get going on time in the morning. Starting tonight, J.D., you're getting to bed on time."

"Well, get in the car," she sighed. "St. Gregory's isn't too far off my route to the law school. And, anyway, we've got to get you to school. If we start off right now, we might even beat your bus to the school."

J.D. opened the door, folded the front seat back, and climbed into the back seat of the two-door coupe.

"Why are you driving Dad's car? Does he know?" Even J.D. understood that his father didn't like others driving his car.

"I guess your father needs the mini-van to haul some furniture home, today. So he made an exception to his rule that only he gets to drive this car."

She turned on the ignition, pulled out of the garage, shut the garage door by the remote, backed up to the side of the driveway, turned the front of the car around, and started to coast down the long curving driveway.

"Darn it," she said aloud. "I've got my briefcase here on the front seat. But where's my purse? Do you see it there in the back seat, J.D."

"No, Mom."

"Well, I'll have to go back in the house. If I pop in quickly and get it, we can still get you to school on time."

She backed up a little, parked the car about twenty yards from the house, and stepped out.

Walking toward the front door, she pulled her house key out. Now, she thought, where did I leave that pur—

SHE WAS LYING face down on something hard, something rough.

Her face hurt. Her back hurt. Her knees hurt.

It felt like that time, way back in middle school, when she'd been pushed down hard from behind on the playground by a bully.

Something wet was running down her cheek.

Where am I, she thought? *What am I doing here?*

And everything was so quiet. Well, not quiet exactly. There was a painful ringing in her ears. No other sound.

She scrabbled up to her knees, wincing at the pain. Her knees were badly scraped through her now-torn jeans.

She touched the wet spot on her face and looked down at her fingers. Red. Blood.

She saw a few blood drops down on the asphalt in front of her, where she had been lying. Her blood.

Looking up, she saw the front of her house.

The big picture windows along the living room were gone. She saw broken glass sparkling in the morning sun.

She sat back on the blacktop. *What's going on?* she wondered. *How did I get here?*

An acrid smell assaulted her nose.

Smoke stung her eyes.

And then she looked behind her.

Black smoke and orange flames enveloped a deformed object in the driveway.

What is that? The car?

THE CAR! OH MY GOD! J.D.!

The front door of the house flew open, and Bill ran out. "Are you all right?" he yelled. To Candace's injured ears, it sounded like he was talking underwater. "What the hell is going on?" he shouted, as he stared wide-eyed at the burning car in the drive.

"J.D.!" she screamed. "Oh, dear God! J.D.!"

"It's all right," Bill said. "It's all right. J.D. is already off to school on the bus. It's all right."

But it wasn't all right. It would never be all right again.

"No," she sobbed, "no, no, no. He missed the bus. He was in the car. He was in the car."

"What?" cried Bill, horror now creasing his face. "J.D. was supposed to be on the bus. He was supposed to be on the bus."

~2~

L IEUTENANT ED BURTON stood on the front porch of the Tudor-style house, surveying the scene at 3732 Dunnell Drive. He was in his late forties, with a full head of dark-brown hair. He liked to think of himself as medium build, and he did work out (on occasion), but his belly was starting to hang over his belt. If he wasn't careful, he had told himself many times, he was going to get fat.

After confirming that Candace Klein had not suffered any serious injuries beyond a possible mild concussion and seeing her off in the ambulance, Burton had asked Bill Klein to remain behind in the house for a short while to answer some immediate questions. Klein had asked for a few minutes alone to compose himself. So Burton had stepped out on to the front porch.

The patrol officers who had initially responded to the emergency calls walked over to Burton. They reported that they had made a quick canvas of the area, careful not to disturb the immediate car bomb scene itself, looking for anything out of the ordinary. The only thing they'd found, which wasn't really out of the ordinary in this suburb, was that the small side door to the Kleins' garage had been left unlocked. Not surprisingly, theft from unlocked garages was one of the most common crimes in Eden Prairie.

Burton had been with the City of Eden Prairie Police Department for a quarter of a century. Even in this usually sedate suburban setting, homicide was not unknown. But a car bomb was something very

18

different. And Burton knew that meant the case likely would be taken away from him very shortly. Federal jurisdiction almost surely would be asserted, probably before he left the crime scene this morning.

Many cops are the sons and daughters—and even the grandsons and granddaughters—of cops.

Not Burton. Burton's father had been a dentist.

When Burton decided to get his bachelor's degree in "Law Enforcement" at Minnesota State University in Mankato during his sophomore year, his father had been disappointed. He had hoped his son would follow in his footsteps and become a "true professional."

Burton senior would have been most pleased to see his son pursue a career in the medical profession, but even a law degree would have been enough to satisfy his father's dream of having another "professional" in the family.

Burton had graduated from "Mankato State" and taken a job as a junior police officer in the southwestern Minneapolis suburb of Eden Prairie. One evening, he invited his father to ride along with him in the squad car. Burton's father watched his son deal firmly but politely with a drunk driver, skillfully defuse a neighborhood dispute that threatened to turn into a fist fight, and respond to the call of an injured man who had fallen off a ladder in his house, where Burton also had offered comfort to the man's distraught wife and young children.

At the end of the evening, his father had said to him in a quiet but clear voice, "I guess you really did become a professional after all."

Burton's father had been dead for more than ten years now. But Burton still felt a thrill of pride go through him whenever he thought of those words from his father on that night more than two decades ago.

Nonetheless, years and years of responding to calls on just about everything under the sun (and after the sun had set for that matter) had not prepared him for his arrival at the scene of an apparent assassination attempt by the means of a car bomb. And it wasn't just that such an episode was rare in Eden Prairie. It was rare anywhere in the United States.

There was no doubt this had been a car bomb. Contrary to the typical Hollywood car crash scene in which the vehicles explode into flames, Burton knew that cars rarely detonated, no matter how devastating the crash. Cars involved in an accident could catch on fire and burn—he had seen that a few times—although flames were hardly a common aftereffect of a vehicle accident. Almost never would a car explode.

This car, however, plainly had exploded. The blown out front windows of the house, the shredded lower branches of the large oak tree in the yard, the pieces of the vehicle flung here and there throughout the driveway and the yard left no room for doubt. This had been an explosion.

And it had been no accident. This was a homicide.

Dispatch from the police department headquarters told Burton by radio that some television reporters were already speculating as to whether this was a terrorist incident. Sadly, Burton thought, the leap by some in the media to that assumption probably was because of the large population of Somali immigrants in Eden Prairie, nearly all of whom were Muslims. To be sure, there had been a group of Somali teenagers who had been enticed from Minnesota back to Somalia to fight for an extremist Islamist group in that nation's civil war, which in turn had generated considerable news attention. But, as the Eden Prairie police well knew, while there were a few bad eggs in the Somali community as with any other group of people, you could hardly find a more law-abiding and hard-working set of people anywhere.

And, in any event, it was clear to those on the scene that this outrage had been targeted at a specific person or persons—not some attempt to stoke fear in the general public. And terrorists certainly wouldn't carry a bomb with them to attach to a car at the scene.

The car was no longer burning. Burton had told the firefighters to use as little water and fire-extinguishing foam as possible and simply make sure no flames continued to erupt. He wanted to disturb the scene as little as possible, so as not to damage any forensic evidence that might remain in the now wet but still smoldering mess of metal and plastic.

The medical examiner was slowly pulling a gurney away with a small body bag. The medical examiner must have noticed Burton's tight lips and doleful eyes, because he stopped for a moment and called to Burton on the porch, "If it makes you feel any better, the kid didn't suffer. I can already tell that the initial force of the explosion killed him instantly. He never felt the flames."

Burton replied, "Actually, hearing that does make me feel a little better. A little. Thanks."

"If you think it would help any," the medical examiner said, "feel free to let the parents know as well."

"I will," Burton nodded.

He continued to watch as the gurney bumped down the long curving driveway to a waiting van.

In an episode of terrible timing, Bill Klein stepped outside on the front porch next to Burton just as the gurney was being loaded into the medical examiner's van.

For a brief second, Burton thought Klein had mercifully missed the transition. Then he watched Klein's eyes travel down the driveway, move back to the burned car, go back down again to the gurney and the van, and then come to a stop at Burton's face. Burton could see in Klein's eyes that the significance of the event had not been missed.

"If it's any comfort, and I know it probably isn't," Burton said, "the medical examiner told me that death was instantaneous. He didn't suffer."

Klein's lip trembled, and he nodded. "You can come inside now to the kitchen if you like," he said to Burton. "The living room is a mess, with broken glass from the front windows thrown all around the room."

Burton followed Klein back into the house, where they bypassed the living room and proceeded down the hallway that led directly back to the kitchen at the rear of the house.

Klein slouched into a chair next to a breakfast nook. He looked wrung out. Burton remained standing.

"I know you're eager to get to the hospital to check on your wife," Burton began, "so I'll make this brief. This should only take ten or fifteen minutes. I'll then see that you are taken directly and rapidly to the hospital. We can follow up with further questions later."

Klein nodded again, as he looked at the floor.

"If you haven't realized already, you should know that this plainly was not an accident."

Klein looked up for a moment, and his eyes grew wide. But he didn't seem surprised. "I figured as much," he said in a low voice. "I've seen explosions before. This looked like one."

Well now that's interesting, thought Burton. "You've seen explosions before?" he followed up.

"Yes, we use explosives—TNT specifically—in our construction work."

"Tell me about your line of work. How are you employed?"

"I'm a construction engineer. But I don't do much of that any more. Now I guess I'm a glorified foreman watching over work crews on construction sites."

"And where do you work, Mr. Klein?"

"For Insignia Construction. My father-in-law, George Peterson, owns it."

"So, you say that you use dynamite in the company."

"TNT, actually," corrected Klein. "Most people think they're the same, but TNT's a different chemical compound than dynamite and more stable, better suited to construction work."

"In what way does your company use TNT?"

"Is this really necessary now?" asked Klein. "Couldn't this wait?"

"I promise I'll keep this brief. When something like this happens, we need to jump on the investigation right away and collect as much information as we can from the start. Please bear with me for just a few more minutes."

Klein looked distracted. "I'm sorry. What did you ask me?"

"You told me that your company uses TNT. I wanted to know how it's used."

Klein hesitated, but when he began to answer, drawing on his expertise in this field, he appeared to pull himself together and became more articulate. "Well, parts of central Minnesota are underlined with granite, which originally was buried very deep in the earth. Through uplift over the eons and erosion of the softer material on the surface by the glaciers in the last ice age thousands of years ago, the granite comes up close to the surface in several regions. We sometimes need to use TNT to blast away boulders or break up rock ledges to make room for roads or foundations for buildings, especially in some of the new subdivisions near St. Cloud."

Hmm, thought Burton, *so this guy is no stranger to explosives.* But he turned the questions in a new direction.

"So," Burton continued, "can you think of any reason someone was trying to kill your wife . . . or your son?"

"Actually," Klein said, "Candace was taking my car for the day. I'm usually the one driving the Honda coupe."

"Perhaps then you were the target," suggested Burton. "Can you think of anyone who would want to kill you?"

"To kill me?" repeated Klein with what appeared to be genuine bewilderment. "I can't imagine that anyone would hate me so much as to want to blow me up in my car."

"Have there been any problems at work, anyone who's angry or might have a grudge?" followed up Burton.

"Well," Klein said, "we did have to fire this fellow, Olin Pirkle, recently. We caught him stealing supplies. He was a longtime employee too. He was pretty angry about it. He left a couple of nasty messages on my phone when he learned I'd reported him to the police for theft."

"That's probably a good place to start then," said Burton. "It wouldn't be the first time that a disgruntled employee . . ."

"Former employee now," interjected Klein.

"*Former* employee then. It wouldn't be the first time that a disgruntled *former* employee acted out his anger. To your knowledge, would this Pirkle have had any access to explosives, such as the explosives you use?"

"Well, Pirkle was one of those in the company trained in using TNT. But he didn't have the codes for accessing the locked cabinet containing the TNT."

"Who did have those codes, Mr. Klein?"

"Well, George Peterson, my father-in-law who owns the company. And I do."

"You do?" asked Burton.

"Yes, but I certainly wouldn't try to blow up myself. My life isn't that bad," said Klein, with an accent in his voice that Burton thought sounded like Klein was trying to convince himself as much as the police officer.

"What about your father-in law?"

"No," said Klein. He then looked down at the floor and uttered in a barely audible mumble, "He could hardly keep running my life if I were dead."

Burton said nothing. He made a mental note that he'd touched a sore spot.

◆　◆　◆

BEFORE HE COULD CONTINUE, Burton's new partner, Melissa Garth, who had recently joined the department from another suburban police force, poked her head into the kitchen and announced: "ATF's here."

Already! thought Burton. He could hardly be shocked to learn that agents of the federal Bureau of Alcohol, Tobacco, Firearms and Explosives would rush to the scene of a car bombing. ATF agents were no strangers to weapons and weapons violations. Still, Burton supposed, even most ATF agents had never seen an actual car bombing. And ATF did have a field office in St. Paul, just twenty miles away from Eden Prairie.

He supposed it was better coming sooner rather than later, when he would have invested even more time into the investigation. Just as he had predicted, the Eden Prairie police were going to be pushed out of the case. He had thought he might make it until noon, rather than being shut out by mid-morning.

It wasn't that Burton thought poorly of the ATF, that he doubted their greater expertise in dealing with this unique kind of crime, or even that he resented the fact that they would take control of the investigation of a crime taking place in his town. He knew that ATF forensics agents and labs could do a better job evaluating the evidence from an event involving explosives than could the Eden Prairie police department or even the Hennepin County Sheriff's crime lab.

No, what annoyed Burton was thinking about the time that he and his fellow officers had already spent this morning at the scene. Everything they had done would now be second-guessed and repeated. They undoubtedly would be pressed into escorting federal agents around for days without being able to contribute anything meaningful.

Burton was also upset about how the department might look in the eyes of the public, as Eden Prairie police got pushed to the sidelines. Phone calls from local press and concerned citizens still would pour into the Eden Prairie police department, while Burton and his fellow officers either would know nothing or be forbidden from sharing anything they did know.

"Excuse me, Mr. Klein," Burton said turning back to Klein in the kitchen nook. "Please wait here. I may have to move on now, but someone will be back in a few minutes to talk with you."

"LIEUTENANT BURTON," said a slight, short, clean-shaven, gray-haired man waiting for him on the porch, "I'm Alex Kramer, special agent in charge with the ATF's violent crimes bureau at the St. Paul division."

"Pleased to meet you, Agent Kramer," lied Burton.

"Call me 'Alex,'" Kramer replied. "I'm sure you're thinking we're going to sweep in here, take over, and push you aside. Well, not to worry, Lieutenant."

"'Ed' is all right," said Burton.

"Not to worry, Ed. Between you and me, with federal budget cuts, we're short-staffed at ATF, especially here in the St. Paul division. I've got several positions vacant and don't know when, if ever, I'll be able to fill them."

Burton remained dubious. He knew all too well that federal law enforcement tended to guard jealously its jurisdictional priorities. Why would ATF be willing to share any of the glory with a city police department?

Kramer sensed Burton's skepticism. "So now you're thinking," Kramer said, "even if short-staffed, why would any federal law enforcement agency be so eager to partner with a city police department? Or why wouldn't we look for support from the FBI before turning to city law enforcement?"

Burton didn't say anything, but nodded slightly.

Kramer smiled and said, "We really are short-handed at ATF. And the local FBI isn't in much better shape. Oh, yes, federal budgets on law enforcement have gone up—but that money is going mostly to Homeland Security. If a case has a terrorism angle, then the federal resources are nearly unlimited. But you and I know this car bombing isn't going to turn out to have any link to international or even domestic terrorism. It's too targeted. Homeland Security will lose interest very quickly."

Burton nodded again, more vigorously.

Kramer widened his grin and continued in a confiding manner, "Given the sensational nature of a car bombing case, I'm sure the FBI could find agents only too happy to help. The problem is that the FBI wouldn't just help on the case. They'd take the case. I don't want to lose ATF jurisdiction here. This is so clearly an ATF matter—involving explosives, damages to a vehicle, a death—that I don't want to set a precedent by surrendering this matter to the FBI just because ATF doesn't have the manpower to handle it alone right now.

"So I think we've got a win-win situation for both ATF and Eden Prairie police. If you want it, you folks get to be fully involved in the case and get credit as full partners. And ATF gets to keep the matter and maintain jurisdictional authority."

"Won't the FBI or other federal law enforcement agencies constantly try to push their way into the case?" asked Burton.

"Of course, of course," agreed Kramer. "But I've got just the story line to fend them off. Remember that botched ATF raid on that

Laotian drug lord's house here in Eden Prairie, where we expected to find a cache of illegal firearms and came up with diddly-squat?"

Burton nodded again. Every cop in Eden Prairie was familiar with that episode, even though the local police hadn't been invited to the party. Eden Prairie was hardly immune to the ravages of the illegal drug scourge, but the more violent episodes usually occurred in the inner city areas. In this case, an "alleged" Laotian gang leader from St. Paul apparently had thought to find sanctuary away from the rough-and-tumble of the streets by buying a house out in the western suburbs. Burton knew that Eden Prairie police had kept an eye on that house from time to time, particularly after a drive-by shooting a few months earlier in which multiple shots had been fired at the house. No one had been hurt, and no one at the house was talking. Word on the street was that it was part of a drug war between two rival Laotian gangs.

"So here's my line," related Kramer. "I'll say that one of the reasons we came up empty in that firearms raid was that the feds had decided to go it alone and had failed to consult with the Eden Prairie police in advance. I'll say that the local Eden Prairie police could have strengthened intelligence on this gang leader through their greater familiarity with the Eden Prairie situation. Then I'll say that we cannot afford to make that mistake again and thus ATF is taking the lead in effective investigation by fully cooperating with local law enforcement."

Burton smiled appreciatively. "You do know that we in the Eden Prairie police department really didn't know any more about that Laotian drug boss than you guys did. The fact he had a house here in Eden Prairie didn't exactly mean that Eden Prairie cops were on intimate terms with him."

"I know that. You know that," replied Kramer. "But it certainly sounds like it could have been true."

"And in this car bomb case," returned Burton, indulging his fondness for quotations, "as Henry Kissinger once said, it would have 'the added virtue of being true.' From what I've learned thus far, this case has all the trappings of a simple homicide, even if the weapon was most unusual. Basic police work may be the key. And we certainly can do that."

"Now to be sure, I'll have jurisdictional authority over the case and it may result eventually in a federal prosecution," emphasized Kramer. "And we'll want to make sure the wreckage is studied by our forensic experts without any interference. But if you're willing, and your police chief agrees, I'd appreciate your help in conducting interviews with witnesses, doing the leg-work in the investigation, and such things. I promise you'll be kept in the loop and be a real part of the investigation."

"I'd be happy to," said Burton with feeling. "In fact, I was just talking with Bill Klein, the owner of this house and of the car and the father of the child killed here."

"What's he told you so far?"

"Well, the most notable thing he's told me is that he works for a construction company, that the company uses explosives for demolitions, and that they just fired a guy who worked with those explosives."

Kramer's eyebrows raised. "Well now, that's certainly a coincidence," he remarked in a sarcastic tone.

"I don't like coincidences," said Burton.

He really didn't. It wasn't that Burton didn't believe in coincidences. He had spent an entire career delving into people's backgrounds and activities, discovering the surprising ways in which one person's life intersected with a multitude of other people that he or she often didn't even know, and trying to figure out why people had done the stupid (and sometimes criminal) things they had done.

Burton encountered coincidences all the time. Life was messy. Loose ends were common. Unlike the stereotypical mystery or detective novel, in the course of real police work and criminal investigation, lots of loose ends were never tied up.

Whenever he thought of coincidences, Burton was reminded of what Mark Twain once said: "Of course truth is stranger than fiction. Fiction has to make sense."

Real life didn't . . . have to make sense, that is. People did odd things for no apparent reason, often unable to explain even to themselves why they had done them. Other people, affairs, objects, and even weather and animals intervened in most unexpected ways. Random events occurred. Hence coincidences.

But that didn't mean he had to like them. Burton knew that an apparent coincidence would make his work harder. He'd have to follow the conjectural path all the way back as far as he could before giving up on the possibility that it was something much more than a coincidence.

And even when he was left at the end of a case with no alternative but to dismiss some twist of events or peculiar connection as nothing more than a coincidence, it made him uneasy. He remained forever uncomfortable about the resolution of the case, harboring residual doubt about whether he read the evidence correctly and had reached the right conclusion.

"Well," said Kramer, as he turned toward the burned-out car, "as long as you keep me fully informed, please feel free to follow this lead wherever it goes."

"Will do." And Burton went back into the house.

KLEIN STILL SAT SLUMPED in the chair at the breakfast nook, staring down at the floor, when Burton returned to the kitchen.

As he approached, Burton saw movement out of the corner of his eye. He jerked his head to the side, only to see a small orange-and-white cat creeping out from the next room and moving toward a food bowl sitting in a corner in the kitchen. The cat stopped short when he saw Burton, looked him right in the eye, and then slinked away down a stairway leading to the basement of the house.

"Mr. Klein," Burton picked up the conversation. "We were talking about your construction company."

"It's my father-in-law's construction company, Insignia Construction," corrected Klein. "I just work there."

"But you said you have access to explosives?"

"Yes."

"And Mr. Pirkle—the fired employee—worked with explosives as well?"

"On occasion, yes."

"And your father-in-law . . . His name again is?"

"George Peterson."

"Could you please write down his name and home address for me?"

Klein stood up, accepted a sheet of paper from Burton's notebook, borrowed Burton's pen, moved over to a nearby desk in the kitchen, wrote something down on the sheet, and then handed the sheet and pen back to Burton. Klein sat back down. Burton remained standing.

"I don't want to hold you much longer, Mr. Klein. But please tell me a little more about this Olin Pirkle and what happened."

"Well, George—my father-in-law . . . and my boss—was noticing that the construction supplies had been running out a little faster than they should each month. He suspected someone was helping themselves. There's quite an underground market for construction supplies. Theft is a constant irritation for construction companies. George asked all of the supervisors to keep an eye open.

"Just last week, I noticed Pirkle walking out to the parking lot after work with what looked like something rather big stuffed inside his shirt. I thought it was really odd. By the time I caught up to him, he had already thrown open the back of his van, pulled something out of his shirt, and tossed it in."

"So," Klein continued, "I said to Pirkle, 'What's going on here? Would you please open up that van and show me what you just threw in there?' Pirkle got rather testy, told me it was none of my business, and brushed past me to the driver's door and left. I wasn't a cop so I couldn't hold him there or make him open the van door and show me what was in there.

"I told George all about it. Next thing I heard was that Pirkle had been fired."

"Is that all?" asked Burton.

"After everyone in the office had learned that Pirkle had been fired, other employees came up to me and said they'd seen him carrying supplies in his arms at the close of work several times over the past couple of years, but thought nothing of it. Pirkle was one of the more senior employees and was often given considerable responsibility. So I took notes on what they'd told me and put together a list of what they'd seen Olin carrying. It added up to quite a lot. And it didn't seem to connect to any project that Pirkle would have been assigned to, especially not during the evenings.

"So I reported a suspicion of theft by Pirkle to the Golden Valley police. Insignia Construction is headquartered in Golden Valley."

"Okay," said Burton. "I'll follow up on that. The only other thing I want to ask about right now is when you last used explosives at work and whether Pirkle was there."

"Just a couple of days before Pirkle was fired. We were preparing a field between the Twin Cities and St. Cloud for a strip mall. You know, they call St. Cloud the 'Granite City' for good reason. In this particular area nearby, which is called 'Boulderville,' we are preparing the ground for a simple foundation. But with the granite base there, it can be like mining a rock quarry. So we've had to use quite a bit of TNT to break up boulders and blast rock formations into more manageable pieces."

"Was Pirkle involved?"

"Yes, he was the one who directly handled the TNT after I retrieved it from the locked cabinet. I supervised."

"Did anything unusual occur? Did any TNT go missing?"

"It was just routine."

"I'm no expert on this, Mr. Klein, but I assume you all have paperwork for using explosives."

"Oh, yes, there's lots of paperwork, which is what I spend much of my time doing. And I've kept all the records on TNT up to date and complete."

"And where would those be?"

"At the company headquarters. They get filed in the main office, where George runs the show." Klein looked up at Burton, his hands now limp in his lap. He stared blankly, not so much *at* as *through* Burton.

Burton decided to wrap up the questioning. "All right, Mr. Klein. I'll let you go now. Be sure to lock up the house as best you can," instructed Burton. "I'll see that someone comes and boards up the broken windows. You should pack a suitcase because you'll have to stay somewhere else tonight. This house and the yard are now an active crime scene.

"Please wait just a few more minutes so that I can arrange for my partner, Officer Garth, to escort you to the hospital."

~3~

ieutenant Ed Burton asked uniformed officers to drive a squad
car alongside Bill Klein's mini-van to the hospital. He also asked
his partner, Officer Melissa Garth, if she would be willing to
stand guard at the hospital through the day, until the department
could make other arrangements for the evening and night.

Burton then went back to his unmarked police car. He pulled
out the sheet of paper Klein had given him and had just begun to
punch the home address for George Peterson into his GPS, when the
dispatch radio crackled:

"Ed, there's a George Peterson who's been calling the police
department every few minutes, saying he's the father of the woman
who was in the car bombing. He heard about it when someone called
him to say they'd seen it on the news. Peterson said he tried driving
over to the house but couldn't get past the police barricades blocking
the street. He wants to know where his daughter and grandson are.
He's very persistent, Ed."

"Tell Mr. Peterson to meet me at his . . ." Ed paused and
looked again at Klein's handwritten directions to the Peterson house.
He changed his mind. "Tell him to meet me at Insignia Construction
in Golden Valley. Get me the directions there, and tell Mr. Peterson
I'm on my way."

George Peterson was a man of average height—five foot, nine inches—and a slim build. Burton, who struggled to keep his weight under control, even though he was still in his late-forties, couldn't help but admire a man in his sixties who had stayed so trim. Peterson was completely bald, except for a thin and closely-cropped strip of gray hair around the lower back of his head.

Although Burton had seen Candace Klein for only a few moments before she was ushered into the ambulance at the crime scene, and her face had been scratched from hitting the pavement after the explosion, Burton could see the resemblance. Father and daughter both had the same prominent, but not unseemly large, nose. And both had large, intelligent eyes.

Peterson was standing right outside the front door to Insignia Construction, as Burton walked up.

"Mr. Peterson," began Burton, "I'm Lieutenant Ed Burton. I think it would be best if we went inside and you sat down."

Instead, Peterson interposed a series of questions in a rapid-fire stream, "What's going on? No one will tell me anything. Please, please let me know where my daughter is? Is she all right? What about my grandson?"

"Please, Mr. Peterson, I promise to tell you everything I know about them. But first, let's go inside to your office."

Peterson seemed reluctant to move at first. But then he opened the front door, stepped aside to let Burton through, and led the way into the building. Burton saw a large open work area with several desks and a couple of long tables where about half a dozen employees were standing together with curious and anxious looks on their faces. Peterson walked through the group, accepting friendly and sympathetic pats on his back.

Without pausing to say anything to his employees, Peterson escorted Burton to the far back of the building, where he had a spacious office. They both went inside, where Peterson turned away from his desk and instead went over to a small table with two chairs. Burton closed the door behind them. Peterson sat down. Burton remained standing.

Speaking more slowly this time, Peterson said, "I know it's bad. I heard on the news about the car explosion. They say it was a car bomb. They say there were deaths. Are my daughter and grandson both dead?"

Burton couldn't help but notice that Peterson didn't ask about his son-in-law, Bill Klein.

"No, Mr. Peterson. Your daughter's pretty shaken up, but I think she'll be fine. But I'm afraid the boy was in the vehicle when it exploded. I'm very sorry for your loss."

George Peterson's chin dropped to his chest. His hands started up toward his face, but then fell back into his lap.

"Where is she? When can I see my daughter?"

"She's been taken to the hospital and undoubtedly will be kept overnight for observation. I'd like to ask you a few questions and then you can go to the hospital to see her."

"And my grandson?"

"I'm afraid he's presently at the medical examiner's office. It may be a couple of days before we can release the body for burial."

Peterson lifted his head up and looked at Burton. "Please, Lieutenant, leave any arrangements regarding the boy to me. I don't want my daughter to have to see him . . . like that."

"I understand. I'll need to share the death certificate with your daughter and son-in-law. But unless they ask to see the body or object in some way, I'll instruct the medical examiner's office that any identification can be made with you. I know this is delicate and awkward, but I may need you or Mr. Klein to get the boy's dental records for me today."

A pained expression crossed Peterson's face and his chin dropped down again. "We'll take care of it before the day is out," Peterson replied.

Peterson remained silent, looking down at the floor. Burton patiently waited.

After a couple of minutes, Peterson looked up again and focused directly on Burton. With a surprisingly fast recovery of composure and the tone of a man who was accustomed to the lead role, Peterson declared, "Now, then, you said you had questions for me."

"Yes, Mr. Peterson. Your son-in-law, Bill Klein, tells me your company handles explosives."

"That's right. Most every construction company does. We're tightly regulated, everything's on the up-and-up, and I insist that the TNT is kept carefully under lock in the magazine—that's the storage locker—just like the regulations require. And all daily transactions and inventories are kept contemporaneously and up to date."

"That's what Mr. Klein told me too."

"He sure better have said that. Those records are mostly his responsibility."

"Before I leave this office this morning, I'd like to get a full set of those records, especially for any work sites involving Olin Pirkle."

"Pirkle?" asked Peterson as his eyes narrowed. "Does he have something to do with this?"

"I can't say, Mr. Peterson. We're checking into every possibility. Could you tell me about Olin Pirkle? I understand he was fired last week?"

"Yes. Very disappointing. Very disappointing. Olin had been with me for fifteen years. I've had to lay-off many employees, including some who had been with me a long time, with the economy being in the toilet." Peterson then muttered, "Damn politicians and their government spending, taxes, and regulations are going to kill whatever's left of private enterprise in this country."

In a louder voice, Peterson continued, "But I'd never expected to dismiss Olin. I trusted the guy. I was pretty sure someone had been skimming construction supplies. Bill caught Olin carrying something out to his car and told me about it. I couldn't believe it at first.

"I called Olin into my office first thing the next morning, and he blew me off and then blew up. I started by saying he'd been a friend and employee for so long, that if he was having financial problems I wished he'd come to me, that maybe I could forgive him if he'd just made a mistake and was straight with me.

"He got angrier and angrier, said the whole thing was an insult, and stormed out. I didn't have any choice but to dismiss him at that point," concluded Peterson. "I later heard from other employees that

Olin had been seen carrying lots of supplies out over several months. It seems now there's little doubt he was the person stealing from me."

"What have you learned from the Golden Valley police about their investigation into the theft?" asked Burton.

"What police investigation?" asked Peterson. "I had no choice but to fire Olin. But I didn't make a police report."

"Mr. Klein did."

"Well, well, what do you know?" said Peterson with raised eyebrows. "I wouldn't have thought Bill had the initiative to do something like that without running it by me. Still, I can't say he was wrong to report it to the police."

"Last question," said Burton, "before you get me those records on the explosives. I understand that Pirkle was the one who used the TNT at the Boulderville construction site a few days before he was fired. What can you tell me about that?"

"Nothing really," replied Peterson. "I wasn't at the site. That was Bill's watch. I knew TNT was being used there. Bill had the lock codes for the TNT. As far as I know, it was just routine."

AFTER COLLECTING the Insignia Construction records on the explosives, and taking leave of Peterson, Burton placed a cell phone call to Alex Kramer at the ATF. He related what he had learned so far and told Kramer he had the records on explosives from Insignia Construction. Kramer arranged to receive the records from Burton and have them analyzed at the ATF office. He told Burton he'd been able to fast-track the forensics investigation and reserve priority lab time to examine the car bomb debris. If all went well, they should have preliminary results from the lab within a couple of days.

BURTON'S NEXT STOP was at the Golden Valley police department. He came as a courtesy to let the police of this neighboring suburb know

he had been questioning George Peterson in their jurisdiction. He also wanted to find out the status of the theft investigation into Olin Pirkle.

Golden Valley police officers had visited Pirkle's apartment, located nearby in western Minneapolis, right after receiving the theft report from Bill Peterson at Insignia Construction, five days prior.

Pirkle had refused to permit them into the apartment that he shared with a roommate, insisting on talking with the police in the hallway of the apartment building. He adamantly denied he had stolen anything from Insignia Construction. When he was confronted with the accounts of other employees, which the police had learned from Bill Klein, Pirkle had shouted that he didn't know why Klein was trying to ruin his life.

Not convinced they had probable cause quite yet for a search warrant on the apartment, the Golden Valley police left the scene. An officer returned the very next day—that would have been four days ago—only to learn from the roommate that Pirkle had left shortly after the first visit from police and had not come back.

The roommate was willing to let the officers into the apartment. On questioning, the roommate said he thought Pirkle had been acting odd. Pressed further, the roommate said he thought Pirkle kept a lot of his stuff in a storage locker somewhere. But the roommate didn't know where that was.

Officers had gone back to the apartment building a couple more times, as recently as that morning. But Pirkle had not returned.

Burton and the Golden Valley police agreed that the combination of the credible theft accusation and the fact that Pirkle had worked with explosives justified issuing a public advisory that he was a person of interest. After getting the go-ahead as well from Kramer at ATF, the Golden Valley and Eden Prairie Police Departments issued a joint press release complete with a photo taken from his employee records. The report said that Olin Pirkle was being sought by police as a person of interest in the car bombing.

Given that the press almost surely would make Pirkle's absence the top story of the day, they might hope for leads from the public to run Pirkle down, wherever he was.

~4~

[Hours after the Tragedy]

The day of J.D.'s exit from the world had been too much like the day of his entrance.

When her son was born, Candace Klein had been alone in the hospital, without husband or family.

After her son had died, she was again alone in the hospital.

For that solitary hour, attended to by medical strangers, Candace's family had dissolved into a husband who was not there . . . and a son who would never be there again.

TEN YEARS AGO, as she was completing the second of three years at the University of Chicago Law School, Candace had found herself in the fortunate position of achieving grades that ranked her in the top ten percent of her law school class and then being selected as the managing editor on the prestigious *University of Chicago Law Review.*

With those law school credentials, Candace decided to seek a clerkship with a judge for the first year after graduation. Clerking for a judge, especially a federal judge, was a distinctive honor as well as a tremendous opportunity to observe judges at work behind the scenes. Having spoken with many former clerks, including several of her professors, she knew this was the kind of formative experience—and distinctive professional credential—that followed a lawyer throughout her career.

In the early twentieth century, when judges first began hiring clerks to work with them in chambers, these assistants were referred to as "elbow clerks" because they sat within arm's reach of the judge's desk. Today still, judicial clerks work directly with judges, helping with legal research and often preparing the first drafts of written court decisions.

Because her husband Bill's job with an engineering firm was in Chicago, Candace had hoped that she could land a clerkship with one of the judges for the United States Court of Appeals for the Seventh Circuit with chambers in Chicago. But her professors encouraged her to cast her net more widely, in order to increase the chance of getting a federal judicial clerkship somewhere.

After discussing it with Bill, they agreed that she should submit a few applications to judges in the Sixth and Eighth Circuits, both federal appellate courts for the geographical regions to the east and west of Illinois. Candace would put a priority on gaining a clerkship with the Seventh Circuit in Chicago. If the only clerkship offer did emerge somewhere else, the two would give serious consideration to her accepting the precious opportunity, if they could work out an arrangement for a long-distance marriage for a year.

As it happened, her first offer for a clerkship—and it came shockingly fast—was from a judge for the Eighth Circuit with chambers in Iowa City, Iowa. By that point, she had interviewed with three judges, two in the Seventh Circuit in Chicago and Judge Payton Bowers of the Eighth Circuit. And she heard back first from Judge Bowers.

Judge Bowers was a former justice of the Iowa Supreme Court, who had been appointed to the federal appellate bench by President George H.W. Bush. As a graduate of the University of Iowa College of Law, located in Iowa City, and then an attorney in nearby Coralville, Judge Bowers had decided to set up chambers in Iowa City when he was appointed to the Iowa Supreme Court. When he was later confirmed to the United States Court of Appeals for the Eighth Circuit, he had no desire to move elsewhere. Although there was no federal courthouse in Iowa City—the nearest federal courthouse was in Cedar Rapids—there was a federal building and post office, where space was renovated for Judge Bower's chambers.

During Candace's interview in his chambers, Judge Bowers was friendly and informal. By the time he shifted the conversation to her thoughts about certain controversial legal issues pending in various federal courts and then explored her understanding of the federal appellate courts, Candace was very much at ease. She displayed her affinity for legal topics well and even demonstrated her quick wit in response to questions. She left the federal building believing she had made a strong impression.

She had only traveled about half way home on the four-hour drive back to Chicago when her cell phone rang. It was Judge Bowers offering her a clerkship on the spot—if she accepted within the hour. She had been warned by her professors and other former judicial clerks that some judges made "exploding" offers, which had to be accepted almost immediately or the judge would move on to another clerkship candidate. But she'd been given to understand that she'd have at least a day to think about it.

After thanking the judge, explaining that she would call her husband right away, and promising to call the judge back within the hour, Candace pulled over at the nearest rest area off the highway and called Bill. Bill was off on a construction job. His cell phone went right to voice mail. She left a message, telling him to call her back right away. And she sat in her car and waited. As the minutes ticked down, Bill did not call back. She tried to call Bill again, but was forwarded directly to voice mail a second time.

Anxious to talk with someone she knew before making such a potentially life-changing commitment, Candace placed a call to her father, who fortunately was in his construction office in Minnesota. Hearing the pride in her father's voice after she told him she had been offered the chance to work with a federal judge heightened her excitement and dampened her anxiety. Her father told her that, of course, she should accept, that she should rejoice at her good fortune, and that a husband concerned for her success could only concur.

She tried to connect with Bill a third time, but again to no avail. She waited some more.

When the hour was nearly up, Candace returned the call to Judge Bowers and accepted the clerkship.

When she got home that night, Bill assured her that she had made the right decision. He said that, if she had reached him on the phone, he would have told her to take the proverbial bird in the hand and not lose it in the hope for an offer from a Chicago-based judge. He reminded her that they had talked about the possibility that she would have to leave Chicago for a year for a clerkship, so this was not wholly unanticipated. They would work it out.

She did not tell Bill that she had spoken to her father or what he had said.

BILL HAD BEEN so understanding that her initial guilt about accepting a clerkship with Judge Bowers, and thus declaring an effective—if temporary—separation from her husband, faded quickly as her excitement grew about this once-in-a-lifetime opportunity. And they need not be separated for all of the clerkship year, as Chicago was only four hours away. So they planned to trade-off making the trip to see each other every week. One weekend Bill would travel to Iowa City, while the next weekend Candace would drive back to Chicago.

Alas, life got in the way of those plans. They learned in March, during her last semester of law school, that Candace was pregnant. The projected delivery date was November, when she would be less than half-way through her one-year clerkship for Judge Bowers in Iowa City.

Candace thought about withdrawing from the clerkship. But she and Bill agreed that backing out now would be unfair to the judge in having to find a replacement after most other clerk candidates had committed to other judges. And it would deny her a valuable experience that would not come her way again.

James Daniel had come into the world about a month earlier than expected, barely two months into her clerkship during that year she lived in Iowa, while Bill remained in Chicago. On a chilly autumn evening in October, nine-and-a-half-years ago, only about an hour after her water broke and with minimal labor, she gave birth at the hospital of the University of Iowa medical school. Despite being about four weeks earlier than expected, James Daniel arrived into the world in fine health—a little jaundiced, but that faded within a few days.

Candace gave birth alone, without her husband or any member of her family present in the hospital with her. There just hadn't been time. She'd called Bill immediately after her water broke, as she grabbed her already-packed bag to rush to the hospital. He had jumped right in the car to drive from Chicago to Iowa City. But J.D. would not wait. Bill arrived nearly three hours after the birth.

◆　　◆　　◆

AND SO IT HAD HAPPENED again, on the day she lost her boy. Alone in the hospital.

Bill came to the hospital as soon as he could, less than an hour after she was transported by ambulance. Still, the fact that Bill was not at fault for his tardiness on either occasion did not absolve him in her mind. Not today. She knew she was being unfair to him. But she didn't want to be fair . . . not right now.

Bill did not need to tell her that J.D. was gone. She'd known that the moment she had turned her head to see the flaming hell behind her on the drive.

"Hell"? No, no, no! She couldn't permit that word to come anywhere near her or anyone she knew. J.D. was anywhere but in hell. And to conceive of her own miserable situation as sending her to a personal hell was the first step toward despair. Despair, she knew, was a sin.

A police officer, a young and rather short woman who identified herself as Officer Melissa Garth, was waiting outside the hospital room to which Candace was wheeled after being examined by the emergency room physician. Officer Garth was reluctant to tell her anything. After Candace persisted, the petite woman reluctantly confirmed what Candace already knew. Yes, there had been a small body in the burning car. Of course, Candace knew that was coming. She knew what she had seen in her driveway. And from the moment Candace first set eyes on Officer Garth, she could see the sorrow in the officer's eyes.

When Bill later came to Candace's hospital room, after being waylaid to fill out medical forms at the admissions desk, he knew she already had been informed. He knew better than to recapitulate the horror to her.

And by her brusque manner, Bill knew that Candace did not want to talk. She knew she was being unkind to him, that he too was dying inside. But she could not open up to him yet. He could have tried, though, and perhaps that would have broken the ice. But once again Bill simply acquiesced to the preferences of those around him. So Candace maintained a sullen silence, answering his pedestrian questions with monosyllabic responses.

WHEN HER FATHER arrived in her hospital room that afternoon, she didn't speak to him either. There was no need. Her father immediately took her in his big arms, held her tightly yet tenderly, and cried with her. For the first time since she was a child, she rested her head on his big shoulders, held on to him with all her strength, and abandoned herself to her tears.

When her father finally stood up, looked over at Bill, and nodded to him, she looked at the clock. Nearly an hour had passed. Her father told her he would see her tomorrow.

Only after her father had left the hospital room and she realized that Bill was still sitting in the corner did Candace comprehend that she had locked him out again. She had shed no tears with Bill and had only briefly embraced him. By weeping in her father's arms, she had placed Bill in a separate category, without even knowing she was doing it. She had further increased the distance between them and at the very moment that each of them had a desperate need for the other.

◆　◆　◆

WHEN THEY HAD uprooted from Chicago and moved to Minnesota three years ago, a job for Bill in the family business had seemed like a Godsend. Her father, George Peterson, said he could use a part-time engineer at Insignia Construction, filling out the job with Bill working as a construction supervisor as well. It was one more sign that coming to Minnesota was the right call. Or so it had seemed.

Bill was immediately high on the idea, as it would give him a place to land immediately after the move to the Twin Cities. From that comfortable sinecure, Bill could look for a more permanent position that better employed his engineering skills.

Candace should have known better. It was not that her father didn't mean well or that he was given to unpleasant moods or that he exhibited a temper. He was a very stable person, typically in control of himself—and in control of others. To quote Shakespeare, "aye, there's the rub."

George Peterson was a take-charge kind of guy. And he couldn't stop himself from being constantly involved in their lives. With Bill in the office every day, her father had immediate and intimate access to even the most trivial of family events and decisions. And George Peterson always had a word of insistent advice or critical comment—starting with where they should buy a house, how much they should spend on it, what they should repair first, where they should get furniture—and on and on.

In offering unsolicited advice, George probably was no worse than almost any father, father-in-law, and grandfather. It was the constancy of it, more than the content, that set Bill's teeth on edge.

If the three of them had had a chance to set down their own roots in Minnesota, her father's well-intended counsel almost surely would have blended into their family deliberations as helpful advice from a well-meaning, loving, and experienced family man. But because George Peterson had become such a large and dominating figure from the very day the moving truck had pulled up at 3732 Dunnell Drive in Eden Prairie, Minnesota, Bill felt overwhelmed almost immediately. He just couldn't seem to get his bearings. And he was nervous to say anything since George wasn't just his father-in-law; George was also his boss.

To be frank, thought Candace, it was Bill's fault too. If he had asserted himself from the beginning, her father probably would have taken little or no offense and accepted a greater equilibrium in their relationship. By being passive, Bill had allowed a pattern to develop in which George appeared to grow bigger and bigger, while Bill saw himself as getting smaller and smaller. And still Bill wouldn't say anything, other than by offhanded and often snide asides, mostly to Candace.

Still, Candace admitted to herself, she had known what was going on. She had known what Bill was feeling, even if he didn't share those feelings. Why hadn't she said something? Would that have made it better? Or would it have made things worse? Would Bill have felt emasculated by having his own wife speaking up for him to his own boss (who also happened to be her father)?

So Candace too felt stymied and uncertain. The months had passed into years. As she became more apprehensive about the situation, and Bill remained sullenly silent, they became more and more distant. She felt guilty about letting this whole situation fester for so long.

And on top of that, three years after they left Chicago, the economic downturn still lingered. Other engineering jobs were not to be found, at least none attractive in either compensation or work assignments.

Insignia Construction was hardly immune from the financial impact. Candace knew her father had been letting a few long-time workers go as construction work slowed. He was holding on to Bill, undoubtedly because he was family. Bill had to know this too.

She could easily guess how this made Bill feel. Trapped. In more ways than one.

~5~

[TWO DAYS AFTER THE TRAGEDY]

URING THE NEXT couple of days, Burton and his new part-ner, Melissa Garth, continued to do the considerable leg-work involved in such a major investigation. They came up with pre-cious little that advanced the ball.

Every neighbor within two blocks of the Kleins was inter-viewed, being asked what they knew about the Kleins and whether anyone had been observed entering the Klein property. As far as Bur-ton could tell, they learned nothing of value to the investigation.

Every employee at Insignia Construction was questioned as well, with a particular focus on the use of explosives and on the be-havior of Olin Pirkle. Other than concluding it was more and more likely that Pirkle truly had been stealing construction supplies, Burton and Garth didn't learn anything more of value there either.

And Olin Pirkle was still in the wind. But his face now graced the front page of every newspaper in the region and appeared at the top of the television news.

ON WEDNESDAY MORNING, two days after the bombing, Alex Kramer called to arrange a meeting at the St. Paul office of the ATF. Ed Burton quickly arrived, and they sat down together in Kramer's office.

Burton summarized the work he and other officers from the Eden Prairie police department had been doing—the search for Pirkle and his questioning of Klein, Peterson, and various neighbors and In-signia Construction employees.

Burton also shared again what the Eden Prairie police had found at the crime scene before the ATF forensics team had arrived. "The responding officers were careful to steer clear of the front drive and yard where the car had exploded. They did only a quick check of the house and surrounding areas for anything obvious. They found no one other than the Kleins present and no evidence of forced entry anywhere on the premises.

"Of course, any night-time intruder wouldn't have needed to actually break in. Our officers found the side door to the garage had been left unlocked." Burton sighed. "Too many people in Eden Prairie forget to close and lock their garage doors, which accounts for the high rate of bicycle thefts we have. You'd be surprised how often our patrol officers have to knock on some homeowner's door in the middle of the night because they can see the main garage door left up. Of course, when it comes to a small side door to a garage, patrol officers wouldn't be able to tell it had been left unlocked.

"So, that's all we've got. I know it isn't much. But we're still working on it. What do you have?" Burton looked expectantly at Kramer.

"Well, we have preliminary results from the lab. It's not con-clusive, but more 'coincidences' are racking up," said Kramer, in that same sarcastic tone he had used at the crime scene a few days before.

"It was definitely TNT used in the car bomb," Kramer re-vealed, "at least a couple of sticks. A blasting cap was wired through a timer, apparently set for about three minutes, that was triggered by the electrical ignition of the car. But we can't definitively say that the TNT came from Insignia Construction or any other particular place."

"But surely dynamite or TNT or whatever—I'm no explosives expert—is closely monitored," said Burton. "Can't these explosives be easily traced?"

"Well, the short answer is no," responded Kramer. "In theory, explosives are closely monitored. There are pages and pages of regulations about how to store them, how to transport them, how to maintain a daily inventory, how to report losses. Nonetheless, hundreds of pounds of dynamite and TNT are reported lost or stolen each year. Most of it was probably misplaced or was detonated without being properly logged as having been used. But we know some of it was stolen from construction sites.

"And as for tracing, unused explosives are marked with manufacturer information and shift codes, so we can rather easily track those back to the manufacturer and from there to the purchaser. In this case, despite our best efforts, the blast and the ensuing fire in the car made the manufacturer's markings on these sticks unrecoverable. Whoever planted the bomb may also have removed any markings from the fabric sealing on the explosive."

"But can't you identify the source of the explosives by a chemical analysis?" asked Burton.

"By examination of the post-blast residue, including the explosive vapor collecting on nearby surfaces, we can confirm it was TNT used in this bomb. We're still conducting tests, trying to determine the mix of chemical materials in the TNT. By cataloging the impurities and solvents different manufacturers put into the substance in their own manufacturing processes, we can generally identify the manufacturing source of the TNT. So there's a good chance we'll eventually identify the manufacturer. But we're not going to be able to do more than that."

"I thought I'd read something about using chemical markers or microchips or something in explosives so the source could be identified afterward?" asked Burton.

"Congress, back in the 1990s mandated that 'taggants,' such as coded microchips, be added by manufacturers to plastic explosives, which in theory makes it possible to identify the specific batch of plastic explosives from post-blast residue. But the explosives manufacturers and the mining industry strongly opposed requiring taggants for other commercial explosives, arguing that it would be potentially unsafe, very expensive, and largely ineffective.

"They insisted that introducing any foreign materials into the formula may make the explosive unstable and also that distribution of taggant microchips into the environment may be unsafe. And given that criminals almost always build homemade bombs from black powder or from other chemicals, rather than use commercial explosives, the benefit to law enforcement arguably was limited and did not justify the added cost of integrating taggants into the manufacturing process.

"In any event, Congress didn't include TNT in the law requiring taggants."

"But at least you can identify the manufacturer of this TNT, by its chemical composition?" inquired Burton hopefully.

"Probably. But that really gets us next to nowhere. Each manufacturer sells to dozens of commercial buyers here in the Twin Cities, primarily in the construction industry. And most construction companies buy TNT from more than one manufacturer over the years.

"If you're asking whether we'll be able to say that this TNT *might* have come from Insignia Construction, the answer likely will be 'yes.' But then we'll have to also admit that the TNT instead might have come from any company on a long list of other construction companies in the area as well."

"So the car bomb *may* have been built with explosives taken from Insignia Construction," summed up Burton. "But *maybe not.*"

"We do have another interesting bit of forensic evidence," added Kramer, "although I'm not sure that, in the end, it helps very much either. We found shredded bits of duct tape among the residue at the site, some of which had traces of the protective covering for TNT attached to the sticky side of the tape. It looks like the bomb maker used duct tape to attach the bomb to the undercarriage of the car."

"What's the significance of that?"

"Maybe two things. First, it could point to an amateur. A professional—like a professional assassin—with experience in building car bombs would more likely use a magnet to attach the bomb to the car. On the other hand, from what we can tell so far, the way the timer was connected and the way the bomb appears to have been wired into the ignition does suggest a greater level of sophistication."

"Would a civil engineer have the level of sophistication necessary to do this?" interrupted Burton.

"Almost surely. And I don't want to overstate how sophisticated this fellow would have to be. While the average person on the street would not know how to pull this off—and thank God for that—it isn't exactly rocket science either."

"I'm sorry, I interrupted you," apologized Burton. "You said the duct tape being used is significant for two reasons. What's the second reason?"

"After we found the scattered and melted pieces of duct tape in the post-blast debris, one of your fellow Eden Prairie officers went back to the crime scene for us and found a roll of duct tape hanging on a nail in the garage at the Klein house. An analysis of the color, grade, and elemental composition of the duct tape used in the car bomb, when compared to that found in the garage, confirms that both were the same brand from the same manufacturer. But not more than that."

Burton interjected, "I remember that in a kidnapping case in Minneapolis a few years back, one of the key pieces of evidence against the defendant was a comparison by prosecution experts of the duct tape that had been used to tie up and gag the victim with a roll of duct tape found in the defendant's car. Can't you connect the duct tape in the car bomb to the same roll found in the Klein garage?"

"You're referring to a different forensic technique," answered Kramer. "The prosecution experts in the case you describe probably were applying the method of duct tape end matching, trying to find patterns in the tears between the two separated pieces of tape. But in our case, the duct tape is too fragmented and melted even to attempt that kind of tape-end comparison.

"Again, the best we're able to do is confirm that the duct tape used in the car bomb is the same brand of duct tape found in the Klein garage."

"And," laughed Burton, "we Minnesotans are awfully fond of our duct tape. I probably have four rolls of different brands from four different manufacturers, in my garage right now."

Kramer added, "Naturally we've been looking for fingerprints as well on everything we have, especially the duct tape which is a very good surface for prints. Unfortunately, all we've found are some smudges on the few surviving and unmelted scraps of the duct tape. We didn't find any usable prints."

"So the car bomb may have been built with explosives taken from Insignia Construction and may have been attached to the car with duct tape from the Klein garage," summed up Burton. "But maybe not."

"That's right. Maybe. Maybe not. Still, as we discussed previously, it does seem like quite a coincidence that a car driven by the wife of a guy who works with TNT is blown up by a bomb made out of TNT."

"I don't like coincidences," muttered Burton.

~6~

[FOUR DAYS AFTER THE TRAGEDY]

SHE'D HEARD SOMEWHERE that a person's mood truly could color her perception of the world. Not just figuratively, but literally. Emotion, so it was said, could change how the eyes conveyed visual impressions to the brain or how the brain interpreted what the eyes perceived.

When a person flew into a rage, the rush of blood throughout the body, including the eyes, actually could make a person "see red." Likewise, the heights of ecstasy could cause the receptors in the brain to vibrate with every slight change of tint, making colors appear more vivid.

Candace couldn't speak from personal experience to whether these other assertions about mood affecting color perception were true. But she now could attest in all too personal a way that grief did render the world gray and dull.

Yes, the colors were still there. She had not been struck color-blind after all. But the tones looked watered down, as though someone had added a touch of gray pigmentation to every other hue.

The picture in her eyes was like that of early twilight, when the increasing darkness began to drain away the luster of the day. But the pallid shades were not accompanied by a corresponding murkiness of coming nightfall. The room remained bright, painfully bright, even as the colors became drab and pale.

OTHER THAN WHEN she asked for a rest or someone insisted that she lie down for a while in her bedroom, Candace was never left alone that afternoon. She would have preferred to be alone in her sorrow, although she knew that being in the company of loved ones probably was good for her. And she could hardly object to a gathering of family and close friends at their house after the funeral.

Her father was there, of course. And brothers Jeffrey and Byron with their wives. Jeffrey had brought along his two small boys, ages four and six. The little ones were hustled off to another room and constantly watched over by a revolving set of guardians.

Candace had suggested, when her nephews arrived, that they could play with the toys in J.D.'s room. But everyone had silently agreed that J.D.'s room was off-limits today. Despite having made the suggestion, she was glad that no one had invaded his room.

Father Alexander Cleveland, or Father "Cleve" as everyone called him, was present as well. A portly man of fifty-three years, with a full beard that had turned mostly white, Father Cleve was looking more and more like Santa Claus with each passing year.

He had been pastor at St. Gregory's Catholic Church in the southwestern suburbs of Minneapolis for nearly twelve years now. Candace and her family had been parishioners at St. Gregory's since they arrived in the Twin Cities three years ago.

Father Cleve's dark eyes spoke an eloquent homily of grief and love every time he looked her way.

THE TELEVISION WAS turned on for a while, then turned off, and then turned on yet again. When the grim silence and quiet whispers in the room grew too much to bear, the TV would come back on, droning in the background. When the jarring and quickly changing images on the screen became too unsettling, someone would switch it off.

At first, the TV was turned on to one of the cable news stations, probably "Fox News" as that was Bill's favorite. But the news constantly rebroadcast her personal pain. Car bombings were hardly common occurrences anywhere in the United States, and the additional tragedy of the death of a child made this a compelling story nationwide. The helicopter footage of a burning car being extinguished below sickened her stomach every time she saw it. Quick shots of her family arriving at the church for the funeral and then the cemetery for the burial were hard to watch.

Even more disturbing to her than seeing her tragedy as the fodder for a news story was how quickly it was followed by a lighthearted story about the rescue of a beached whale in North Carolina or by an advertisement for the Valley Fair amusement park south of Eden Prairie. How could there be any other story worthy of attention today? How could anyone think about a day at an amusement park when her boy was gone?

Her family quickly decided they should tune the television to something else, such as one of the cartoon networks. Watching a rerun of "SpongeBob SquarePants" actually helped for a moment, as she briefly became lost in its trademark "nautical nonsense." The fact that it bore no relationship to reality was all the better . . . for a time. But the fact that this was a show designed primarily for a youthful audience soon brought her mind back to the boy who would never see another cartoon program. And so she asked that the television be switched off yet again.

POOR LITTLE TUCKER the cat wandered through the rooms without ceasing, never stopping to curl up or accept a petting from anyone who reached down to him. Candace knew it was foolish to attribute human characteristics to an animal. Still, she felt in her heart Tucker's incessant movements meant he was looking anxiously for J.D. No, it wasn't a foolish thought. A cat does know how to give and accept love.

No one could have doubted the possibility of genuine affection between a human being and an animal after watching Tucker and J.D. together after school each day. She remembered how Tucker would meow with delight when J.D. came home. He would rub against J.D.'s legs as he took off his back-pack. When J.D. sat down in the living room, Tucker would climb up on to J.D.'s shoulders and push his feline head against J.D.'s face.

To be sure, Tucker also may have been restless after spending three nights lodged at a pet kennel while the house was off-limits during the police investigation. The poor little guy had not been out of the house at all in the three years they'd had him, other than a short trip to a vet for an annual check-up. Candace had even arranged for a cat-watcher to visit their house each day and play with the cat whenever the family went on a trip for more than a single night. So three nights in a strange place without anyone he knew would have been stressful for Tucker.

At one point, Candace reached down and picked up the cat. Tucker tolerated it for a moment, but then started to struggle, so she let him leap back down to the floor. The cat returned to his persistent circumlocution of the house.

TONIGHT WOULD BE Candace's first night back in the house. It had now been four days. For the past two nights, the police had insisted that she and Bill stay at a downtown Minneapolis hotel, with a police guard outside the room. She had simply acceded to that request, not really able to think very clearly in the first day or two. She did realize that the police were worried that whoever had targeted them with the car bomb might try again.

She and Bill mercifully had not been asked to identify the body. They were told the matter already had been handled. She suspected her father had played some role in making that decision and sparing her from that encounter, but she knew she would never ask him.

They were asked, however, to review the death certificate, which Lieutenant Ed Burton had brought to them in the hotel room. When she saw the "Cause of Death" stated as "Homicide," she was startled. And then she was surprised it had surprised her. She had been so adrift in her bereavement that she had given little thought to who had done this terrible thing.

Someone had attacked her family. Someone had hated them so viciously that they had placed a bomb in Bill's car.

But before her thoughts had advanced very far down that dark and frightening trail into the woods of speculation about people of malice and hate, the face of J.D. would bring her back again. The loss of J.D. consumed every cogitation and occupied her entire mental world.

The funeral and burial had been that morning. No one ever tells you about all the mundane and morbid details that follow a premature death. Seeing the death certificate. Selecting a funeral home. Choosing cremation or burial. Finding and purchasing a cemetery plot. Arranging for inscription of a headstone. *For a child.*

Candace had insisted on saying something at the burial, but she didn't trust her voice. So she decided she would be well advised to read something . . . something short. She borrowed one of her favorite passages from one of her favorite Shakespearean plays, appropriately a tragedy.

She began to recite the words from Hamlet: "Good night, sweet prince." Then, to her dismay, she began to sob. Father Cleve, God bless him, had stepped over immediately and finished: "And flights of angels sing thee to thy rest."

NOW AS SHE STOOD in the kitchen of her home, she found every item on which her eyes rested reminded her of J.D. Pulling some more coffee cups out of the cabinet, for example, regressed her back to the day that J.D. had expressed his undying "love" for kitchen cabinets. This had been part of his awkward juvenile campaign to prevent the family from moving from Chicago.

Like any young child, he had been afraid of change at first. At the local café in their Chicago neighborhood on that morning some four years ago when the decision to move to Minnesota had suddenly come together over breakfast, J.D. had listened quietly with increasingly wider eyes. But he had said nothing.

When they got back to their apartment, he had suddenly turned to his parents and announced, "I don't want to move. I really, really love our sofa." Candace smiled and told him, "that's okay, honey, we'll take the sofa with us when we move."

J.D. then switched gears and said, "But I really, really love the kitchen table." Candace gave the same reply, that they would take the kitchen table with them.

The little boy paused for a moment and then tried again, "But I really, really love my bed." Candace assured him that they would move his bed too.

J.D. hesitated a little longer this time, got a thoughtful look on his face, and then asked in a calm voice: "Are we taking the kitchen cabinets with us?" "No," Candace had said, "those are attached to the apartment."

"But I really, really LOVE the kitchen cabinets," he pleaded.

Candace had to admire the little guy's clever efforts to find some fixed object to love that would conflict with any plan to move.

But as months passed and plans for the move to Minnesota became concrete, J.D. had become increasingly comfortable, as children ordinarily will. When moving day came, he had fully reconciled himself.

A few days before the move, as they had been talking about a new neighborhood in Minnesota, J.D. confidently asserted, "I'm good at making friends." Candace thought to herself this was truly an example of belief confirming reality. If a person thinks he is good at making friends, well, then he probably is.

On the day they moved into the new house, J.D. ran off playing with kids in the neighborhood before the moving truck had even arrived. He indeed had proven he was good at making friends.

There was no doubt that Minnesota had been good to J.D.

Minnesota had not been so good to Bill.

◆　◆　◆

CANDACE HAD BARELY SPOKEN to Bill in the past four days, al-though they had almost never been apart. That is, they had never been apart after he finally arrived at the hospital.

She understood the police had insisted Bill remain behind to an-swer questions. She understood Bill then had to wait for a police escort to the hospital, because they were worried about the family's safety.

Still, she resented the fact that she had gone to the hospital alone.

Other than the most basic of exchanges—was she in any pain, could he bring her anything to the hospital, what clothes should he have the police retrieve from the house—Candace and Bill had not spoken to each other in the eighty-some hours since the . . . the . . . the explosion.

She didn't even know how to label what had happened in the narrative in her own head. The "explosion"? Not descriptive enough. The "episode"? Too casual, like an "episode" of a television show. The "event"? Sounds like a code word or euphemism.

Should she call it the "murder of her son"? It was that, wasn't it?

Was it also the "end of her family"? She didn't want to think about it like that, but she found her stricken mind meandering toward that devastating summation.

In fact, Candace was struggling not to think about anything at all, other than to keep the face of J.D. always before her. Just get through the morning. Now just get through the afternoon. And later just get through the evening. Then just get through another night with-out sleep.

It was now Thursday afternoon, four days later. After his late arrival at the hospital, Bill had not left her side for more than a mo-ment. He sat in the hospital room with her all night, as the doctors kept her overnight for observation. He drove her to the hotel, in her mini-van of course, which only served to remind her why he was not driving his treasured red coupe. And all through the following day, as they sat in the hotel room, fielded the constant stream of calls to their cell phones, and eventually fell asleep on the hotel room bed, Bill was always there.

And still they had not said anything of substance.

Now, as the house filled with people coming by to offer their condolences, she could sense that the interruptions of others and the return to their own home would prompt Bill to break the impasse.

When she excused herself from friends and neighbors in the living room to go out to the kitchen, she anticipated Bill would follow her and say something.

She could never have anticipated what he then *did* say.

"We have been so lucky," Bill said to her.

In an instant, fury leaped within her. Her body became rigid. Her eyes flashed. Lucky? How could he be so heartless as to call this cruelty, this obscenity, fortunate?

Before she could utter hot words of reproach, Bill continued: "Having J.D. come into our lives is the luckiest thing that could ever have happened. Even had I known he would be taken from us so soon, I would have regarded myself as the most blessed of fathers and would have treasured every minute with him without regret."

The flame of anger inside her died down as rapidly as it had risen.

By the time she opened her mouth to respond, she could agree quietly: "Yes, we were lucky."

She leaned over and kissed Bill on the cheek. She smiled at him briefly before returning to the living room.

EVEN THOUGH SHE was not in a social mood, she could not help but be moved by the number of people who had come to the house. She'd known her father and her brothers and their families would be there.

Many of her father's long-time employees had dropped by as well.

The few high school friends still living in the Twin Cities made an appearance.

That police lieutenant, Ed Burton, who had come to see her in the hotel room over the past couple of days, and his partner,

Melissa Garth, who had been outside her hospital room that first night, both stopped in to express their sorrow. They stayed only a few minutes.

And many of her law professor colleagues and staff from the University of St. Thomas paid respects, along with more than a dozen of her students.

It suddenly occurred to Candace she should be keeping track of who had come so she could send each person a handwritten thank-you note afterward. When the law school dean, Colleen Ordway, stepped over to greet her, Candace remarked that she was going to find a pen and paper to write down who had come so she would never forget their kindness. Dean Ordway told her she had already anticipated that need and had taken the initiative to put a pad of paper next to the front door as a memory book to be signed by each person as they came in the house.

Colleen Ordway had been raised Irish Catholic in Boston, but people often assumed she was a native to Minnesota, frequently asking whether she was connected to the family that founded the Ordway Theater in Minneapolis. (Actually, the Ordway Musical Theater took its title from the middle-name of heiress Sally Irvine, its pioneering financier.) But Dean Ordway shared nothing with the theater other than the happenstance of the same name. As a woman who had reached a leadership pinnacle in the legal academy, Dean Ordway had been a mentor to Candace since she had arrived back in the Twin Cities. And she had become a great friend.

When she later left the house with a group of other professors and staff members from the law school, Dean Ordway said nothing other than, "We're all here for you. Not just today. All the way through." It was enough.

The last person to leave the house was Father Cleve. He sat down on the couch beside Candace, touched her hand, and said, "It will be all right. Not today. But it will be all right."

"No," she responded, not in hard words of resentment, but in hollow tones of sorrow. "It will not be all right. It will never be the same again." She looked down at her hands folded in her lap.

"It won't ever be the same," Father Cleve agreed. "But it will be all right."

He paused and waited for her to look back up at him. "The fracture in your heart will never fully heal, not until we all are joined together again at the Feast of the Lamb. We live in a broken world. And we all are wounded by that brokenness. But God gives us the grace to overcome those wounds.

"As you know, Candace, every priest who has pastored a parish for more than a few years sees the loss of parents and the loss of children. The latter is always the hardest. But having seen parents grieve and being with them in their time of need, I can say this with confidence. As hard as it is to believe today," he assured her, as he continued to touch her hand, "you will smile again. You will laugh again. You will always hold J.D. in your heart, and that part of your heart will always hurt a little. But you will also find joy in his memory. And you will again find joy in this life."

"Why, Father Cleve? Why?" asked Candace.

"Ah," Father Cleve answered. "That is the question all parents ask when a child is taken too soon. And I have to answer honestly by saying that I don't know. I do know this," he finished in a gentle voice. "Even before you shed your first tear of grief as as mother, He already had poured forth tears for you as your Father in Heaven. His heart was broken first. He knows who you are and where you are. He knows what it is to lose a Son."

~7~

AS HE WALKED THROUGH the door of the Eden Prairie Police Department at 8:30 a.m., Ed Burton glanced at the *Minneapolis Star Tribune* lying on a table. It had now been six days since the car bombing. The front page of the paper bore a large photo of Olin Pirkle pasted beneath yet another banner headline about the bombing.

From this head-shot of Pirkle taken from his employee identification card at Insignia Construction, you'd think he was a morbidly obese man. His face was broad, his nose wide, his neck thick, and his jowls hung low. From talking with other Insignia Construction employees, Burton knew Pirkle was lean from the neck down. In fact, behind his back, other employees at Insignia had called Pirkle the "Living Bobblehead," because his head appeared disproportionately large for his body. Burton hoped the mismatch between head and body was not preventing members of the public from identifying Pirkle as the man shown on the widely-circulated photo.

Burton's partner, Melissa Garth, was already at her desk.

Ed called over and inquired, "So any public sightings of Pirkle today?"

"Oh, yes," she replied in a weary voice. "Dozens. Pirkle's been seen everywhere from San Diego, California, to Portland, Maine—there's even one reported sighting in London. And a surprising number of sightings of Pirkle in Las Vegas, Nevada."

"Accompanied by Elvis, no doubt. Anything credible?"

"One recent sighting appears particularly credible. A ticket window worker at a bus terminal in Denver, Colorado, claims to have sold him a ticket. Denver police are checking it out to see if the ticket guy can remember where Pirkle was going . . . if it was Pirkle.

"And, there is one old sighting that is extremely credible."

"Why would I care about an old sighting of Pirkle?" queried Burton.

"Because the guy who sighted him was the manager of the U-Store-It down in Burnsville."

"Ah, that storage locker Pirkle's roommate mentioned," realized Burton.

"Yes," Garth replied. "The manager is there now. I've just typed up an application for a search warrant—we've certainly got enough from the other employees at Insignia to get a warrant to search for stolen goods. I've got a judge waiting in his chambers, and we can pick up the warrant on the way down to Burnsville."

As Garth and Burton started toward the door, Chief Anders Colter came out of his office, motioned toward them, and said, "You'd better come in and see this." Colter pointed back to the television in his office.

On the screen were several men standing behind a podium, one of whom was speaking into a microphone. The caption running at the bottom of the television screen identified the man speaking as Minnesota United States Attorney Robby Sherburne.

Sherburne was in mid-sentence as the three went into Chief Anders's office to watch: ". . . no different than the Oklahoma City truck bombing a quarter-century ago, and I promise you the end result here will be the same: the death penalty for whoever committed this heinous act and stole the life of that young boy."

The men standing behind Sherburne didn't applaud but most appeared to nod in agreement. Burton recognized Alex Kramer of the ATF among them. Kramer wasn't nodding. Burton thought he looked irritated.

A puzzled look came over Garth's face as she turned to Colter and Burton, "I thought Minnesota didn't have the death penalty."

Colter replied, "Minnesota doesn't. But this is a federal case, since it involved explosives, and some federal criminal statutes do have a death penalty. It just isn't used very often. And especially not in Minnesota. There hasn't been an execution in Minnesota, under either state or federal law, in more than a century.

"My bet is Sherburne is trying to make a name for himself, set the stage to run for governor next year," offered Chief Colter. "If a Democrat like Sherburne gets credit for the execution of a child-killer, it'll cut the knees out from under any Republican opponent on the crime issue."

"What bothers me," said Burton, "is that Sherburne's calling for the death penalty when we haven't arrested anyone, haven't even clearly identified a suspect. I wish the political prosecutors would give us in law enforcement a little more time to do real police work before deciding to hang someone for this."

Colter chuckled and remarked, "Sherburne reminds me of the Queen of Hearts demanding the head of the Knave of Hearts before the end of his trial for stealing the queen's tarts. Remember the queen's line in Lewis Carroll's *Alice in Wonderland*: 'Sentence first—verdict afterwards.'"

"Sherburne's worse than the Queen of Hearts," drolled Burton. "He's not just putting the sentence before the trial. He's pronouncing sentence before an arrest. We've only started on this investigation. The Queen of Hearts at least had a clear suspect in the Knave of Hearts. Sherburne doesn't even know who he is trying to have executed!"

Shaking his head, Burton walked with Garth out to their police car. After stopping by a local magistrate's office to get the search warrant, they proceeded to Burnsville, about twenty miles south of Eden Prairie.

As they drove the short distance, Burton placed a call to Alex Kramer. When Kramer picked up, Burton bypassed any formalities to say: "What the hell was that?"

"You were watching?" asked Kramer, sounding chagrined. "I promise you I had no idea Sherburne was going to say something like that. I had briefed him on the progress of the investigation and expected him to give the typical non-responses to the press about how we were doing everything possible, we appreciate help from the public, etc. I never imagined he'd put the death penalty on the table before we've even arrested anyone.

"In any event, he would still need sign off from Main Justice in Washington, D.C., to do that." Kramer sighed and added, "But Sherburne can probably get that D.C. approval in a case like this. And now that he's announced it, the Attorney General would look weak if he tried to pull Sherburne back. That was probably part of Sherburne's calculation in speaking to the press today."

"Well, I'm glad to know you weren't a part of that, as I don't want to be a part of it either," interjected Bill.

"Sherburne is a consummate politico," Kramer acknowledged. "We all know that. But usually he has the sense to stay out of the way and let those who know what they're doing do the actual work. He then takes the public credit. But he sees this episode as his shining moment in the sun, his way to make a name for himself. And he doesn't want to waste any time. I guess this confirms the rumors he's planning to run for governor next year.

"Anyway," Kramer finished. "Let me worry about that for now. Just keep doing your job. I'll try to keep Sherburne from making that job any harder."

BURTON AND GARTH arrived at the U-Store-It on the outskirts of Burnsville, where they met the manager in the office at the front of the facility.

Satisfied by the warrant, the manager led them to a large garage-style storage unit the paperwork said belonged to Olin Pirkle. The manager brought a set of bolt cutters he kept in the office to cut off locks when clients failed to pay rent on their storage units. After removing the lock and rolling up the metal door on the storage unit, the manager stepped back.

Most of the storage unit was filled with old furniture and what looked to be boxes of books and papers. But in one back corner, stacked from floor to ceiling, were crates of floor tiles, copper plumbing pipes, bundles of electrical wire, and roofing materials.

"Well, it sure looks like Pirkle is guilty," remarked Garth.

"Yes," agreed Burton. "Guilty of theft. I don't see anything that suggests he is guilty of murder."

Burton and Garth sorted briefly through the storage locker, finding no evidence of any explosives.

"Maybe he stole only two sticks of TNT—the very two sticks he used to make the bomb he attached to Klein's car," suggested Garth.

"Maybe," acknowledged Burton. "Maybe. But we need a lot more than this to lock down a case against him. It's a pretty big step from theft to murder."

Garth called police dispatch to arrange for another officer to bring a couple of Insignia Construction employees to the Burnsville storage site and do a thorough inventory of the construction supplies found in Pirkle's storage. There was a chance they'd find something linking Pirkle to explosives or the bombing. Somehow Burton doubted it. At least they had solved one crime.

Garth called Burton back to the car. "Just heard from dispatch. The ticket seller at the bus terminal in Denver's pretty sure he sold a ticket to Pirkle. Denver police think he's a credible witness and the lead's solid."

"Does he happen to remember what bus Pirkle bought a ticket for?"

"Not for certain, but he thinks he remembers it was for a bus going to the upper Midwest, like Des Moines or Chicago or maybe even Minneapolis."

"So," pondered Burton, "maybe Pirkle's coming home. Maybe we'll get lucky."

CANDACE KLEIN LOOKED again at the large image of Olin Pirkle on the front page of the *Minneapolis Star Tribune*. The paper was lying in front of Bill on the table in the breakfast nook of their house. Bill seemed always to be right there in the kitchen whenever she had looked for him in the two days since their return to the house.

Bill's eyes were red and puffy. Well, she probably looked about the same, worried Candace. Neither of them had gotten much sleep over the past few nights.

They had talked a little—more than a little—in the days since the funeral. They didn't converse for hours. And the words didn't flow easily. Their tentative interchanges these days were nothing like their animated convocations during those long-past days in Chicago when they had enthusiastically joined with renewed purpose in planning for the family transition to the Twin Cities. Nonetheless, Candace discovered that even the limited and episodic communication she had restored with Bill was more comforting than she would have expected.

The ice had been broken when Bill finally spoke to her during the gathering at their house after the funeral and burial. Their exchanges remained brief, but were becoming regular. And they were slowly becoming less awkward. Most importantly, they were talking again. They were in it together again. She could feel it.

In these early attempts to re-connect as husband and wife after the tragedy, they mostly shared memories about J.D. Yesterday evening, they had recalled the family vacation to Key West in Florida just last year. J.D. had never been to the ocean. And once he saw the expanses of water and felt the surprisingly warm waves, he resisted any attempts to get him to come out. In the words of the cliché, J.D. took to water like a fish. The little boy was overjoyed to be swimming in the ocean along the sandy Florida beach. Candace and Bill hardly had the heart to drag him out, if only for a moment so as to be slathered in another layer of sun-tan lotion.

Each recollection of J.D., so vibrant in his young life, made Candace's heart ache. But she knew it was an ache she needed to feel, that she wanted to feel. She couldn't move on before she had moved through it.

Turning from the front page photo of Olin Pirkle and the accompanying story, Candace said to Bill, "The reporters are hinting the dynamite might have come from my father's company. And that you're the one who was in charge of all the dynamite for construction demolition."

"If the news reports are right, ATF apparently found that the explosives used in the . . ." Bill was unable to continue for a moment. "That the explosive materials were consistent with TNT manufactured by one of the companies that supplies Insignia. But lots of other companies receive TNT from that manufacturer as well. The ATF can't say for sure where it actually came from."

"It sounds like the police think it might have come from Insignia," persisted Candace. "And they say you were the one with the code to the lock on the explosives."

For the first time in several days, an edge crept back into Bill's voice when he replied, "I think you knew I supervised construction work. That required getting down and dirty, including using explosives. It's not like your dad has me designing buildings or using my construction engineering degree."

At first Candace was put off by his tone and considered stepping away. But then, she thought, at least he's starting to talk about what's been bothering him for the last three years. To think it took something like this for a husband to tell his wife how he really feels.

"In any event," continued Bill, "it almost certainly wasn't our TNT. And I certainly had nothing to do with, with . . . this."

"I know, I know. Please, please know I never—never—have thought even for a second that you had anything to do with this. Bill, I love you. I know you. You would never try to hurt me, to hurt . . . J.D."

Bill's face softened. He smiled sadly at her. He reached over and took her hand.

Candace then asked, "Is there any possibility that someone else got some of your dynamite?"

Bill switched to technical terminology, which Candace saw as an encouraging return to some semblance of normalcy for her husband.

At the same time, she was a little resentful for being patronized. Her father had raised her alone, while building his construction business, after Candace's mother had died of cancer when she was in elementary school. As a necessary consequence, Candace had spent many an afternoon (and even some evenings) with her father around construction sites when she was a child and then a teenager. As Bill well knew, Candace had at least passing fluency in construction geekspeak.

"First of all, to be technical," lectured Bill, "we use TNT or Trinitrotoluene, not dynamite. TNT's more stable and thus more effective for construction purposes.

"As for whether someone could have taken some of our TNT, I just don't see how it could have happened. We store it in regulation magazines—that's like a big storage cabinet or locker—and we limit who has access to it. We keep careful track of it, even when on a construction site. Still, I suppose anything is possible . . . ."

"Has any dynamite . . . I mean, TNT ever gone missing?"

"Well." Bill looked disconcerted. "I don't think so."

"That isn't exactly a definite and confident no," interceded Candace. "You don't sound sure about it."

"I pretty much am."

"That's not quite the same as saying that you're absolutely sure that none of the company's TNT might have been taken."

"All right," said Bill after hesitating and looking even more abashed. "I'm going to tell you something, but you've got to promise you'll keep it between us. With the ATF involved in this case, they'd jump all over this. I'd get in trouble. The company would be in trouble. And I'm sure that it doesn't mean anything."

"You know I'm on your side, Bill. However hard it has been, however hard it will be, I made a commitment to you for life. We still can get through this together. You have to trust me. It's when you start leaving me out and keeping secrets . . . that's when keeping faith becomes difficult."

"Well, about two weeks ago, when I was last out at the Boulderville strip mall construction site, I did think for a moment that I had misplaced a couple of sticks of TNT. Things were kind of hectic, and there were problems at the site. I got distracted. I'm sure those two sticks were set off, and I'd just forgotten to keep the checklist straight."

"What do you mean?"

"Well, whenever I take TNT out of the locked cabinet in the van in which we transport it to a construction site, I log off the manufacturer's markings and shift code against a checklist. That checklist identifies by shift code every stick of TNT taken out of the locked magazine at our main warehouse. Well, at one point during the day, I couldn't quite make those numbers line up."

"What happened?"

"Well, when I took another couple of sticks out of the van and started to check off the shift codes from the list, the next two numbers on the checklist didn't line up with the sticks I had taken out of the cabinet."

"You mean you were missing two sticks of TNT?"

"No, no. Probably not. Almost certainly not. And that's why you've got to keep this quiet. Someone else might see it that way. Like I said, I was distracted. I'd obviously forgotten to log two already detonated sticks. It was just a mistake in checking things off. It doesn't mean those two sticks were really missing."

"What did you do about it?"

"Nothing right then, other than admittedly uttering a few foul words to the air—no one else was around at the moment. Later on, during the ride back to the office, I just went ahead and checked off those two sticks as well, so that the paperwork would come out right."

"Is that proper?"

"It's a gray area. It's the daily inventory that really matters, which is the inventory at the central magazine back at the warehouse. Since I was pretty sure that we had detonated those two sticks, I'd just record that in the daily inventory. I suppose one could argue that, since I couldn't line up the shift codes perfectly, we should have reported two sticks of TNT missing to the ATF. But that's just bureaucratic stuff.

"Writing up a report form and getting the company listed with the ATF as having lost some TNT would have been overkill for what was a perfectly innocent mistake."

"How could you not know whether you had lost two sticks of explosives?"

"You have to understand just how solid the granite composition is at this construction site. On that day alone, we probably detonated thirty sticks of TNT. Forgetting to log a couple of sticks isn't all that surprising."

"Have you ever lost explosives before?"

"I told you," Bill's voice became sharper, "I didn't lose it. I just forgot to check it off, is all."

"Has that ever happened before?"

"I'm very meticulous, Candy. I do my job well."

"That's not an answer."

"Yes, it's happened another time or two," Bill admitted reluctantly. "I remember all too well the first time I made that kind of mistake. It was during my first months on the job for your dad. I checked TNT out of the office locker, went out to the site, used some of it, then brought the rest back. The checklist showed one stick missing. Your dad insisted we file a report with ATF for that one stick. And he was really steamed.

"Within a few days, we found the missing stick, which was still in the warehouse locker and had fallen behind another stack. But the ATF won't remove the lost or missing report when you find the explosive. They just add a subsequent notation that the TNT was found. The company is still listed as having filed a report of missing explosives.

"So, yes, on one or two other occasions, like that time a couple weeks ago at the Boulderville site, I lost track for a moment. It isn't exactly scintillating work supervising guys breaking up rock. I'm sure I just wasn't paying attention and thus missed checking sticks off when we used them. I didn't see the point of going through all that again when I know it almost certainly is only a paperwork mistake.

"And it isn't as bad as it sounds. Based on what I hear from folks at other construction companies, I'm hardly alone in reconstructing the records from time to time, rather than making something out of nothing and ending up for no good reason on the ATF missing explosives list."

"Could Pirkle be responsible for the missing two sticks of TNT?"

Bill paused, creased his forehead, and looked thoughtful. "Yeah, I guess that could account for it. And it's certainly starting to look like he had something to do with this. I was pretty sure the two sticks had been used but not logged. And maybe I'm still having a hard time getting my head around the idea Pirkle could have stolen TNT, then tried to kill me. You know, now that I think about it, maybe that's what happened."

"Does anyone else know you just checked off the TNT sticks later?"

"Well, I suppose if Pirkle stole the TNT, he obviously would know I'd failed to make a report of missing TNT. Even if he didn't take any TNT, Pirkle might know I filled in the records afterward . . . if someone reminded him. I'm sure he saw the checklist at some point that afternoon, and if he had looked closely, he would've seen a couple of numbers hadn't been checked off in order. Pirkle was driving the truck and sitting right next to me on the ride back to the office when I pulled out the checklist and marked off those two sticks. I don't know if he was really clued in to what I was doing, and I certainly wasn't highlighting it for him. But if someone prodded his memory, that is, asked him the right questions, he might put two-and-two together and realize he'd seen something not quite right on the checklist and then had seen me marking things off after we'd left the site."

"Pirkle isn't exactly a friend of yours now, even if he didn't steal the TNT."

"No," Bill emphasized. "Which is another reason we need to keep this quiet. Either Pirkle's the one responsible for taking the TNT, or he might be prompted to remember that I 'corrected' the TNT use records."

"Either way," sighed Candace, "there's no love lost between the two of you."

"So let's let sleeping dogs lie," agreed Bill. "If Pirkle's guilty of stealing the TNT and of the . . . bombing . . . then questions may eventually be asked about the errors in the records. There could be some regulatory problems later, but my guess is it'll slide by in the aftermath of ATF's celebration that they solved a big crime. But if we let the cops know about what I did with the records now, they may start to look in the wrong direction. An innocent mistake could start to look like something nefarious."

◆　　◆　　◆

ED BURTON WAS feeling restless. He was not about to spend the rest of the afternoon and evening waiting around on the hope that Olin Pirkle would be so nice and cooperative as to come home to Minnesota on the bus.

Around 4:00 p.m., Burton told Garth he was going to take a drive up to that construction site near St. Cloud where Pirkle and Bill Klein had been using explosives to prepare the ground for the strip mall foundation.

If he left right now, he might get ahead of most of the rush hour traffic from Minneapolis to the northwest suburbs and beyond. And even if the drive took a couple of hours, he'd have a chance to sit alone, quietly behind the wheel . . . and think.

When Burton reached the "Boulderville" construction site, after about an hour and a half on the road, he hadn't come up with any new ideas. Maybe solitary contemplation is overrated, he thought. Still, the time on the highway had settled him down. He felt more rested, more alert, even though he had been driving in heavy traffic some of the way northwest from the Twin Cities.

He got out of his car and looked around the construction site. It looked unremarkable to him, although he knew he was no expert in construction and hadn't spent much time on construction sites. Even standing outside the chain-link fence surrounding the site for the strip mall, he could see the blasted holes in the granite and broken rock, undoubtedly resulting from the use of the explosives. It all looked just as Bill Klein and George Peterson had explained.

Spending a few more minutes gazing at the site—at least the portions he could see from outside the fence—produced nothing pertinent to his investigation. Nothing provoked a new line of thought. Nothing moved things forward.

Disappointed, he turned and looked in the opposite direction, away from the construction site. A clump of bushes and trees somehow had found root in the stony ground about fifty feet away to the southwest. The paved road on which Burton had driven ran past the construction site in a southeast to northwest direction.

To the southeast, alongside the road, the vista was barren grasslands, without any trees, bushes, or buildings. His view was unimpeded, all the way to a fast-food restaurant about half a mile away. Even as Burton watched, a pickup truck rolled up to the drive-through window of the burger place.

The burger joint and what looked to be a low-rise office park neighboring it were the first encroachments of civilization into this desolate stretch of land. The Insignia Construction site marked the next human incursion into this previously undisturbed quarter. Eventually this entire area would be developed, with a housing subdivision planned nearby. In a decade or two, as newly-planted trees reached upward, sod lawns were laid down on the fallow ground, and sprinkler systems were installed to water the previously arid fields, this landscape would be transformed.

Burton's ruminations then jumped back a step. *Hey, wait a minute,* he thought. *If there's a drive-through window at the restaurant, there might also be a security camera. Nah,* he corrected himself, *that's probably a dead-end.* Even if they did have a camera, the footage from a couple of weeks ago surely had been erased. And the burger place was half a mile away. Any security camera probably didn't even cover this area. Still, he supposed, it was worth checking out since he was already out there.

GEORGE PETERSON WAS ushered by Ed Burton into a slightly darkened room inside the ATF division headquarters in St. Paul. As he came into the room, Peterson's man-in-charge composure had slipped a little. Peterson was accustomed to summoning others to his office, not being summoned himself. And no one had told him why he was being asked to come to a federal law enforcement office.

"Mr. Peterson," said Burton, "this is Alex Kramer of the ATF." Peterson and Kramer shook hands. "We need your help. We've got something we want to show you."

Another man in the room was attaching a projector to a computer. Then a grainy video was projected on to a large screen in the room.

Burton explained, "This is a security video from a burger place down the road from your Insignia Construction site in Boulderville. We got very lucky with this. Security video typically is on a continuous loop and thus is overwritten with new video when the hard-drive fills up with video data. But the restaurant was new and the hard-drive pretty large, so the video recording was not yet full and starting to overwrite. As a consequence, we were able to get video going back more than three weeks. To add to that luck, the video camera at the drive-through window of the burger place is pointed directly to the northwest with a largely unobstructed view of the construction site.

"Now here's where our luck runs out. As you can see in the video, we have only a partial view of the site, and it is at a great distance, so we can't see people very well and certainly can't tell exactly what they're doing. And the video runs for days, so we've had to try to narrow our observations down to what seem more likely to be significant moments. We've focused it on the two days in which you've told us explosives we're being used at the site. We hope you might guide us through what we're seeing."

The video was fast-forwarded, and then stopped at a point where a van pulled up on the road alongside the construction site.

"Mr. Peterson," asked Burton, "can you identify the van?"

"Yes, that's the van in which we transport the explosives."

"That's what we thought," said Burton. "Now we've put bookmarks on this video at every point during those two days in which a lone person is in the vicinity of the van. When there's a group of people near the van, we assume no one would be up to 'no good,' because others would be watching. But when someone appears alone next to the van, that might be significant. Or it might not. It turns out that happened only four times. Given the half-mile distance, and the fact that the rear of the van is pointed away from the camera, we can't actually see if anyone is opening the back door to the van. But at least we can narrow things down by seeing who would have been alone near the van and thus have had the opportunity to do something improper."

"By 'something improper,'" Peterson said, "I assume you mean stealing TNT from the van."

"That's a possible theory, yes," replied Burton.

The computer technician forwarded the video to the first bookmark. A figure entered the camera's range and moved behind the van and then came back out again. The technician froze the image and zoomed in on it, which did little to clarify the image.

"Even at this distance," said Peterson, "I can see some of his face and tell by the way he walks that he's my son-in-law, Bill Klein. But there's nothing surprising about him being alone near the van. He was in charge after all."

"We understand that, Mr. Peterson, keep watching."

The video leapt forward to the next bookmark. Again, a lone figure could be seen walking toward and going behind the van. Again, the video was stopped, and the technician magnified the figure.

"That's Olin Pirkle," said Peterson confidently. "No doubt about it. You can see how the head is pretty big and the body's quite slim. He's a pretty distinctive figure."

"One more, Mr. Peterson." And again the video fast-forwarded to a bookmark, then froze, and the image once again was enlarged.

Peterson stared intently at the screen, squinting as though he could adjust for the poor quality of the video. Eventually he said, "I just can't tell who that is. I'm ninety-five percent sure it isn't Bill or Olin. Remember there were about a dozen workers at the site. I don't know all of them well."

"That's okay," said Burton.

The video was restarted and that figure moved out from behind the van and then quickly out of the camera's range.

The video kept rolling, not fast-forwarding to another scene. Within a couple of minutes after the person Peterson couldn't identify had exited from the frame, another figure moved toward the van.

"That's Bill again, I'm pretty sure," said Peterson.

"You've been a big help," Burton told Peterson. He and Kramer stood up, shook hands with Peterson again, and saw him out the door.

After Peterson left, Burton and Kramer walked down the hall and sat down in Kramer's office.

"Good work, Burton!" said Kramer.

"Just luck," said Burton. "The burger place happened to have security video, the video hadn't been overwritten, and the camera happened to be pointing in the right direction. And, anyway, it is hardly definitive evidence of anything."

"No, but it is another piece to add to the puzzle. We now know both Bill Klein and Olin Pirkle had access to the van when no one else was around. Given that Klein seems unlikely to have been trying to kill himself or his wife, Pirkle is starting to look like a real suspect."

"But," Burton said. "We can't see whether Pirkle took something from the van. And there's that third person Peterson couldn't identify."

"Yeah, but that probably means nothing. As Peterson said, it could be one of the other dozen workers. Or for that matter, it could be a random passerby."

"A passerby? Out in an undeveloped area? Next to a construction site where they were setting off explosives?"

"Does seem unlikely. Still, it could just be a coincidence."

I don't like coincidences, thought Burton. But he kept his feelings to himself.

~8~

FOR CENTURIES, GOOD and wise people have known that nothing soothes the troubled soul more than devoting oneself as a servant to other people who are also in trouble. One of those good and wise people was Sharon Tipplett.

Sharon Tipplett was an exceptionally tall, lean, and physically fit black woman in her mid-forties. She looked like a basketball player—and indeed she had been a star basketball player at her Chicago high school and had been recruited to play basketball for Northwestern University.

Being a star in high school, however, proved not to be a predictor of athletic prowess in the highly charged and hyper-competitive world of NCAA Division I sports. After a disappointing performance and progressively less playing time during her freshman and sophomore years, Tipplett surrendered her athletic scholarship. She left the basketball court to focus all her energies on the classroom.

She was committed to completing her studies at Northwestern, which meant finding financial support to replace her athletic scholarship. Coming from a line of military service members going back to her grandfather, Tipplett joined the Reserve Officers Training Corps. Located on the shores of Lake Michigan, the Navy ROTC program at Northwestern had a long and distinguished tradition.

After graduating from Northwestern, Tipplett served her country in the Navy for more than a decade, including service on a noncombat supply ship in the Persian Gulf during the first Gulf War. When the Navy began to assign women to combat vessels in the years immediately following the Gulf War, Tipplett was among the first so commissioned. She served as an officer on an aircraft carrier, the USS *Dwight D. Eisenhower*, while it was deployed in the Mediterranean to enforce the United Nations no-fly-zone over Bosnia and Herzegovina against aggressive incursions by Serbian aircraft.

Tipplett left active service with the Navy at the rank of lieutenant. She decided to return to Northwestern University—this time for a law degree.

After a few years in practice with a small firm in the suburbs of Chicago, she heard an increasingly louder call to help her fellow veterans. As servicemen and women returned from the wars in Afghanistan and Iraq, many of them were suffering injuries both visible and invisible. Tipplett saw first-hand the growing need to provide legal representation for those seeking veterans disability benefits, struggling with mortgage and debt problems (especially for those who had been in the National Guard or Reserves and thus had to leave ongoing civilian jobs when called up for active duty), and encountering marital and family difficulties.

Her small law practice was devoting more and more time to representing vets. Because many of these vets and their families could afford to pay little or nothing in legal fees, Tipplett found it difficult to sustain a for-profit law firm.

The University of St. Thomas in Minneapolis happened to be looking for a new faculty member for its clinical programs, when Tipplett happened to be looking for a place to establish a pro bono law practice serving veterans. The faculty at St. Thomas was attracted to Tipplett's mission, and she was hired to direct a new Veterans Clinic.

With law students working under Tipplett for class credit, the Veterans Clinic at St. Thomas had become a beacon of hope for financially strapped veterans and their families. The clinic charged no legal fees and covered most court and related expenses from the law school budget, which occasionally was augmented when the clinic could recover legal fees from the government in successful veterans disability cases.

About three weeks after Candace had lost J.D., Tipplett gently encouraged her to assist in the clinic for a few hours each week, if she was looking for something to occupy her attention. Tipplett reminded Candace of the words of St. Francis of Assisi that "it is in giving that we receive." By giving comfort to those in need, Tipplett told her, we receive comfort ourselves.

During the summer when there were no law students working for class credit, Tipplett had to carry the full load herself on those cases not yet concluded. Tipplett was delighted to have the help—and she knew that it would be therapeutic for Candace.

Tipplett invited Candace to work on a case involving an Iraq War vet who had suffered a back injury when the vehicle he was riding in was damaged by one of the improvised explosive devices that were a constant hazard for American military transports in Iraq. Although his most immediate and obvious injuries had healed, and x-rays indicated no abnormalities in his spine, he still experienced severe back pain, which made it impossible for him to hold on to a job and support his family. His physicians explained that back pain often is difficult to diagnose by objective medical tests and frequently cannot be connected to anything that would show up on x-rays or even a CT scan. Nonetheless, the Board of Veterans' Appeals at the Department of Veterans Affairs had denied the man's request for disability benefits, ruling there was not sufficient medical evidence of his claimed back pain.

To add to his troubles, the man's youngest child, a boy about J.D.'s age, had been diagnosed with acute childhood leukemia, which Candace learned was one of the most common childhood cancers. While his wife did have health insurance for the family from her job, the amount of the deductible, uncovered charges, and various other non-medical expenses were more than the family could handle.

In an effort to overturn the negative decision of the Department of Veterans Affairs, Tipplett was working on an appeal of the denial of disability benefits to the United States Court of Appeals for Veterans Claims, a special federal court created by Congress for these kinds of cases. Tipplett had prepared a draft of an appellate brief, which she knew was decent. But, she candidly had to admit, the brief was not yet great. Given that Tipplett had to devote time simultaneously to working with the vet's creditors to negotiate more reasonable payment schedules, she had feared she would not be able to further polish the brief before the filing date.

Enter Candace.

Just as Tipplett had sagely predicted, Candace found that working on the legal problems of other people in a miserable situation made her feel less miserable herself—at least for a while. She spent several hours with this vet and his family as she worked on the appeal, including taking a trip with the family to the hospital to visit the boy. Candace came to see not only a family in trouble, but a family with hope. And she realized she and Tipplett were bolstering that hope. As she had seen the family's faith grow over the past several days, she found her own faith being renewed as well.

Candace had been working diligently on the brief for two weeks now. The overarching theme to the brief was drawn from a 1946 Supreme Court decision in *Fishgold v. Sullivan Drydock & Repair Corporation*, which held that veterans benefits are "to be liberally construed for the benefit of those who left private life to serve their country in its hour of great need." Relying on the "veterans friendly" interpretive approach directed by the United States Court of Appeals for the Federal Circuit, Candace had strengthened the argument made by Tipplett that the Department of Veterans Affairs had the duty to assist the veteran in substantiating his claim, not to reject it because precise medical evidence could not be found.

Today was the day before the brief was due to be filed in the Court of Appeals for Veterans Claims. Crunch time was here. So on this day, Candace had planned to work late into the evening to make sure the brief was perfect—or as perfect as she could humanly make it—so that it could be printed and filed the next day.

On other days, Candace had been careful not to work late into the evening, so as not to leave Bill alone in that house. They were talking again, a little more each day. And she seemed to be the only one who could get through to him, as he otherwise moped around the house by himself. But she could not avoid a late night session today, on the eve of the due date of the brief.

Since she'd be away until late that evening, she'd encouraged Bill to do something outside the house as well. A neighbor family had invited them over for dinner and a movie. She urged him to go, even without her. Bill was reticent, but said he'd think about it.

As she left for the law school that morning, Bill told her he was planning to go. She hoped he would. She didn't want him to spend another evening in his chair at the breakfast nook watching television.

AT 10:30 P.M., she decided the brief was as good as it was going to be. She printed off a final copy to leave for the clinic support staff. They would arrange for it to be printed into a bound booklet and filed with the court. At last, the brief was finished and would be filed tomorrow.

She arrived back at the house in Eden Prairie at about 11:00 p.m. It was raining. Water ran down the driveway of the house and into the street.

Both the driveway and the front windows to the house were brand new. Her father, George Peterson, had insisted on taking care of all repairs. After all, he'd said reasonably, he did run a construction company. The least he could do was have his crew make simple repairs.

Still, as Candace drove the mini-van over the place in the driveway where the car had exploded, the now unblemished condition of the blacktop looked wrong to her. Somehow, she thought, there should still be some sign, some marking, that this was the place where her baby, her J.D., had died. It shouldn't be so easy to sweep away the debris and replace the blacktop. Things should not return to normal.

She pulled the mini-van into the garage. She noticed that the other car stall was empty and, for a moment, thought, oh, good, Bill must not have come home yet. Then she remembered that the stall was unoccupied because they now had only the one vehicle.

The empty car stall in the garage did strike her as right and appropriate. The vacancy bore silent vigilance that something . . . someone . . . was missing.

Then she shook her head and said out loud, "Come on, Candace, you're becoming maudlin."

She opened the door from the garage to the house, hoping Bill would not be there, that he would have gone to the neighbors' place as he said he would, that he would still be there watching a movie.

But no.

Bill was sitting in his favorite place at the breakfast nook in the kitchen, with all the lights off. He was settled there in the shadows, not even watching TV.

Candace sighed. "Bill," she said, in a tone she hoped sounded sympathetic rather than frustrated, "it's really not good to sit alone in the dark."

He looked up at her. Diffuse moonlight permeating the window at the back of the house illuminated part of his face.

It wasn't Bill.

"Why can't you all leave me alone?" the man in the kitchen said, softly at first. Then in a loud voice, he insisted: "LEAVE ME ALONE!"

With that exclamation, he stood up. The moon beams shining through the window flashed on metal.

He had a gun in his hand. It was a small gun. But to Candace, it looked so big, it could have been a bazooka.

As he shouted again, "LEAVE ME ALONE," he gestured wildly with his right hand, which held the gun.

Candace found her eyes following the gun, seeing only the gun. Her head was turning back and forth as the gun moved back and forth, almost hypnotically.

Then, abruptly, she ordered herself: *snap out of it, girl. If you're going to survive this, you have to keep a clear head.*

She knew who it was immediately, although she had never met him. She'd seen the picture in the *Minneapolis Star Tribune*. And her husband had described him.

There he was in their kitchen—Olin Pirkle—with his large head teetering on top of his skinny body.

Pirkle became aware he was waving the gun around and dropped the hand holding the gun down next to his right leg. "I don't want to hurt you," he said in a quiet, morose voice. "I don't want to hurt anyone. I've never wanted to hurt anyone. Everything's such a mess now."

The anger in his voice and manner had melted away. He sounded tired. He looked tired. In fact, he looked like he could barely stay on his feet. His eyes were bloodshot. He swayed as he stood. Then he fell back into the chair.

Candace began to back away toward the hallway that led to the front door of the house.

"Oh, no," said Pirkle, twitching to alertness and leaping to his feet. "We're going to have a talk. You're not going anywhere. We're going to wait right here until your husband comes home. Yes, and then we're going to have a talk. Just the three of us."

Candace stopped moving and stood still in the kitchen.

"I don't think Bill's coming home tonight," she lied. "He thought I was going to be working all night, so he's staying at a neighbor's house."

Pirkle looked at her skeptically. "I don't think I believe you. Why would he stay at a neighbor's house? Why wouldn't he sleep in his own house? That doesn't make sense."

It doesn't make sense, does it, thought Candace. *Why would Bill stay overnight with neighbors? You'd think I could come up with a better fib than that.* She realized she was under great stress. But she couldn't afford not to think straight. *Calm down,* she told herself. *Slow down that heartbeat. You've got to be very careful here.*

"I think we'll sit right down here in the kitchen and wait for your husband. I think he'll be home soon. And if he really is staying somewhere else, then we'll just have to wait until morning."

"I could call him," volunteered Candace, pulling out her cell phone from her pocket.

"Nice try, nice try," responded Pirkle, now harsh again in inflection. "You're not calling anyone. Now throw that cell phone over into the sink. We wouldn't want to spoil the surprise for your husband."

Candace obeyed and threw the phone. It landed in the sink with a clunk, rattling a couple of dishes left unwashed in the basin.

Pirkle then appeared to regret what he'd said, or at least how he'd said it. "I'm sorry, I'm sorry. I know I'm scaring you. I won't hurt you. I wouldn't hurt anyone. I just need to talk to you and Bill.

"Everywhere I go, there's pictures of me on the television, in the newspaper. I've been hiding as best as I can. You can't imagine how hard it was just to come home on the bus without being recognized. I'm so tired. And the police keep coming to my apartment building. I can't even go home. You've got to get the police to leave me alone."

As if on cue, a siren sounded nearby and drew closer. Other sirens joined the first, moving toward the house.

"How . . . what . . . how did the police know I was here? How could they know already?" asked Pirkle frantically, as his eyes darted from side to side. As he said this, he began waving the gun around again.

Candace heard vehicles pulling up outside the house and out in the street. She could hear car doors opening and then slamming. People talking. After several minutes, a voice boomed through a bullhorn: "Pirkle. We know you're in there. Come out now with your hands up and no one will get hurt."

Pirkle dropped down low, as though someone might see him from the back yard through the kitchen window. "You too," he ordered. "Get down."

Candace lowered herself to the floor on her knees.

"I've got to think, got to think," said Pirkle in a plaintive voice. "What do I do now?"

"You haven't hurt anyone," counseled Candace. "If you would just walk out the front . . ."

"No, no, no," intruded Pirkle. "Stop talking. I need to think. I need you to stay quiet while I think this out."

Pirkle moved up into a crouch and started crawling on his hands and knees into the hallway. But to keep Candace in his sights, he couldn't move very far down the hallway, not far enough to be able to see the whole front yard through the windows at the front of the house.

The telephone rang, startling both of them. It undoubtedly was the police, trying to reach Pirkle and talk with him. The phone rang about a dozen times and then fell silent.

"All right," Pirkle said, "I've got to tie you up now so I can move around and see what's going on outside without worrying about you slipping away."

Candace's body stiffened. She was certain she would scream if Pirkle touched her.

"Please, please, please," she said in a deliberately pleading voice. "Please don't tie me up."

Pirkle looked at her again, appearing to be chagrined. "I honestly don't want to scare you," he said. "I'm not a bad person. I just wanted to talk with you and Bill. I just need you two to tell the police to leave me alone."

"You *are* scaring me. Please, please," Candace repeated, "don't tie me up."

Pirkle paused and seemed to be thinking. "All right. I won't tie you up. But I've got to keep you secure somehow, while I think. Maybe I could just lock you in a closet . . . or the basement."

The door to the basement was adjacent to the kitchen. Pirkle scrambled over, opened the door, and looked down. He flicked on the light and looked down again. He jiggled the door knob.

"This door doesn't lock," he said.

Candace thought, all right, now she had a chance. Stay calm. Don't sound too eager.

"The door opens out into the kitchen," she observed. "You could move a piece of furniture in front of it and then I couldn't get out of the basement."

Pirkle peered intently at her, as though he was trying to read her mind. Candace worried, oh, no, he's getting suspicious. He'll think she wants to be sent down to the basement. She had to be crafty.

"Please," she said, trying to sound even more desperate than she felt. "Anything other than tying me up."

Pirkle was still dubious. "But what if you've got a gun or something down in the basement?"

"We don't have any guns in the house," she said truthfully. "And if we did, we certainly wouldn't store them in the basement. And, even if there were something down there, once you've pushed a desk or table in front of the door, I couldn't get through to you."

A spotlight pierced through the dark, coming in the kitchen window from the backyard. Pirkle fell flat down on the floor, but kept the gun pointed in her general direction.

"All right, all right," said Pirkle in a frightened voice. "All right, all right. I've got to be alone for a while to think. Get down in the basement."

Pirkle motioned with the gun toward the basement door. Candace quickly moved through the door and on to the stairs leading down.

Behind her, Pirkle closed the door. She quickly climbed down to the bottom of the stairs. She waited until she heard him moving something large, probably the desk from the kitchen, in front of the door.

As she stood at the foot of the basement stairs, she heard a soft "meow." Tucker walked out from under one of the storage cabinets in the basement. Not surprisingly, the skittish cat had run down into the basement to hide when a stranger had broken into the house.

"Well, little buddy," she whispered to Tucker, as she leaned down and picked him up. She quietly mouthed to the cat, as if he could understand: "It's a good thing my father's construction company does only commercial work. If Pirkle had done residential construction, he would immediately recall that building codes require new houses with basements to have an egress window in case there's a fire. Even so, I suspect he's going to figure out pretty soon that letting me go into the basement wasn't a good idea. We'd better move quickly."

She ran behind the stairs to the other side of the basement. She jerked aside a curtain. There was the oversize egress window, which could be pushed out into a window well next to the foundation, allowing a person to crawl out of the basement.

Candace paused, listening carefully and hoping Pirkle wasn't near the basement door.

Now, she thought, it would just be her luck if the window stuck or made so much noise that Pirkle heard it before she could get away.

◆　◆　◆

LIEUTENANT ED BURTON stood in the steady downpour near the driveway, carefully keeping his car between him and the house as a screen. Even though water streamed down his face, because he wasn't wearing a hat, it never occurred to him to duck into the car to keep dry. All of his attention was focused on the Klein house. He still held the bullhorn in his hand. So far there had been no response from anyone in the house.

Down the street, sitting in the back of a squad car with a patrol officer in the front seat, was Bill Klein. He'd been at a neighbor's house and had seen his wife's mini-van pass by on the street toward their house.

When he arrived home and walked up toward the front door, he'd heard someone—someone definitely not his wife—shouting. Peeking through the windows beside the front door, Klein had seen that Pirkle was inside with his wife. And that Pirkle had a gun.

When Burton arrived on the scene, Klein was agitated and kept insisting he should have gone in and tried to negotiate with Pirkle or attempted to rush him and seize the gun. Instead, Klein had returned to the neighbor's house to call the police. Now he was torn with regret and guilt.

"What kind of a husband doesn't run in to protect his wife?" asked Klein.

"The kind of husband who's still alive," responded Burton.

Burton had assured Klein he'd done the right thing by retreating and calling the police. The police were trained for this kind of situation.

But Burton felt for the guy. To have lost his child and now to have his wife being held hostage in his own home. It couldn't get any worse for him.

Well, Burton corrected himself ruefully, it could get worse. Pray to God it doesn't.

It had been about fifteen minutes since his initial attempt to contact someone in the house, long enough for the other officers to work themselves into place at the back of the house.

Burton was about ready to try again on the bullhorn, when he heard a voice behind him, saying his name.

He turned to see a very wet Candace Klein holding a very wet— and very unhappy—cat.

He was so startled that he couldn't speak.

Candace said again, "Lieutenant Burton?"

"Thank God!" he finally exclaimed. "Where did you come from?"

Candace explained how Pirkle had decided to lock her in the basement, giving her the opportunity to escape through the fire egress window. The window was set inside bushes along the side of the house and she'd run from there into the neighboring yard and then worked her way back to the front where she saw Burton next to his car.

Burton walked Candace Klein back to the squad car where Bill Klein was waiting. He didn't think he'd ever seen a man so relieved.

Burton returned to the group of police officers at the front of the house and spoke to the other officers by radio. He explained there was no longer a hostage situation and directed the officers to slowly approach the house from all sides.

"Let's be careful," Burton said. "There's no reason to risk any of us now that Mrs. Klein is safe. But let's be sure Pirkle doesn't get away either. Mrs. Klein was able to run away from the house without any of you noticing," he added accusingly. "Let's tighten up the net so Pirkle can't do the same."

◆　◆　◆

BILL AND CANDACE sat together in back of the police car, with the cat on Candace's lap. The patrol officer in the front seat told them the police were now moving closer to the house, in both front and back.

A few minutes later they heard a gunshot. It sounded like it came from the back yard.

90

After several more minutes, they saw Burton walking back down the street toward the squad car.

"We got him," said Burton. "Pirkle must have realized pretty quickly you'd escaped. He tried to slip away out the back of the house. The idiot pointed a gun at us, and one of my officers fired. He was hit in the abdomen. He was in a lot of pain, but has now lost consciousness. My guess is he'll pull through, but he's seriously injured. An ambulance has already been called. Just wait right here in the squad car for a few more minutes, please."

Burton walked back along the street, into the driveway of their house, and then out of view behind the bushes and trees lining the road.

Within a few minutes, an ambulance pulled into the drive of their house. Shortly thereafter, the ambulance rocketed away with lights flashing and sirens blaring.

Burton returned to the squad car, opened the door to the back seat, and leaned in. He touched Candace's arm lightly, unobtrusively. "Mrs. Klein," he said, "let's get you back inside. It's safe now."

"No," Candace said quietly but firmly. "No. I'm never going back inside that house."

Bill looked over at his wife. Then he spoke up. "We're going to find a hotel for tonight. I think it's time for us to find a new home. I'll come back in the morning to pack up some stuff."

Bill climbed out of the squad car and went to the garage, where he backed out the mini-van into the street. He came back to the squad car, opened the door, and walked with Candace to the mini-van. Candace was still carrying Tucker the cat.

As he drove the mini-van away from the house for what Candace hoped would be the last time, Bill said, "It's all over, honey. They got him."

He looked over at her and repeated, "It's all over."

Springing unbidden to Candace's mind was that childhood taunt by the winner to the loser of a playground contest: "It's all over . . . but the crying."

~9~

[SEVEN WEEKS AFTER THE TRAGEDY]

CANDACE STOOD ON the enclosed balcony of a two-bedroom condominium unit on the twelfth floor of a high-rise building on the west side of downtown Minneapolis. It was a sunny day in late June, with no clouds in the sky.

The Basilica of St. Mary—"America's First Basilica" completed in 1915—stood in granite majesty in the center of her view, topped by double spires at the front and a large dome at the center. Turning left to the southwest, she could see the glistening blue water of the lake in the middle of Loring Park. Although the lake had been renamed (along with the park) in honor of civic leader Charles Loring, it remained Johnson's Lake in the hearts of many. What was now an urban park between downtown Minneapolis and the Lowry Hill district had once been the Minnesota farm of Joseph and Nellie Johnson.

While Candace could not see it from this vantage point, the University of St. Thomas law school building—with its distinctive gothic style built of Mankato limestone—was just across the street to the immediate north. And the skyscrapers of downtown Minneapolis lay behind her to the east, the closest being the thirty-two-story international headquarters of Target Corporation on Nicollet Mall two blocks from the condominium building.

In the first week after her home—what had been her home—had been invaded, Candace and Bill had found themselves once again

92

living the lives of vagabonds, moving from one hotel room to another, with all their immediate necessities packed into a couple of suitcases.

She had resolutely refused to return to the house. Bill kindly accommodated by retrieving the things they would need for a few days in one local hotel or another, until they could find a more permanent place to live.

Candace then received a phone call from Dean Colleen Ordway, saying a recently retired colleague, Feliciano Zuazo, had learned through the law school grapevine about what had happened and how Candace had been rendered homeless by circumstances. Zuazo had an offer that, after initial hesitation, Candace realized she could not refuse. Indeed, it was a gift, a blessing, a reminder she was not alone. She had a larger community of friends and colleagues who would sustain her during this time of difficulty and who needed but to be asked to offer succor.

This emeritus law professor and his wife had moved to the San Diego area to spend their retirement years closer to their son stationed in the Navy there. After their children had left home, Zuazo and his wife had moved from their house in the Lake of Isles neighborhood of Minneapolis and into a condominium unit in a high-rise building directly across the street from the law school in downtown Minneapolis. Now that the Zuazos had retired and moved to California, the condo had been on the market, but, in this difficult economy, the Zuazos had received no offers even close to the asking price.

So Feliciano Zuazo had the following proposition. If Candace would agree to pay the nominal rental price of $100 a month, the condominium was hers for the next twelve months. And, he insisted, Candace would be doing him a favor. He could remove the unit from the market until real estate prices in the Twin Cities stabilized. And he could rest assured the property was not being left unattended. Or to think of it in another way, Zuazo said, Candace would be house-sitting for him.

At first, Candace was reticent. For more than three years, she had loved working downtown, while living in a suburb. She could savor the offerings of the big city, being close to courts and major law firms, lots of restaurants, and theaters (the Twin Cities having more theater seats per capita for plays and concerts than any city in the country other than New York). Then she could also enjoy the benefits of a smaller city setting, larger yards, calmer neighborhoods, and the more responsive city government and services that came with a suburban community. When last year she'd been troubled by an episode of minor vandalism in her Eden Prairie neighborhood, the chief of police had been the one to return her call and explain how the matter was being addressed. That would never happen in the big city of Minneapolis.

Moreover, during the past few weeks she had taken to going to morning Mass each day at St. Gregory's in the southwest suburbs. Without that anchor in her life, without being able to spend half an hour each morning with God and then talk briefly with Father Cleve, she didn't know how she could go on. And the 8:00-a.m.-sharp time for morning Mass ensured that she would resist the temptation to remain in bed and wallow in her grief.

After some thought, though, she realized she and Bill really needed more geographical distance from her family tragedy. Neither of them was wealthy, so they could hardly ignore the gift of a nearly rent-free condo for a year in a luxury high-rise. Since she'd been commuting from Eden Prairie to Minneapolis for work each day, she could just as easily commute from Minneapolis to the southwest suburbs for morning Mass— and be going in the opposite direction of the rush hour traffic.

So Candace and Bill decided to try condominium living in downtown Minneapolis. The unit was empty—truly empty. Not a single stick of furniture remained inside the two-bedroom apartment, and every wall was bare (other than the mirrors in the bathrooms). When they had moved to San Diego, Professor Zuazo and his wife naturally had taken all their possessions. In any event, Candace and Bill would want to furnish and decorate their new home with their own furniture, knickknacks, home items, and books.

That meant that someone had to go back inside that house, to pack things up and move them to their new home. Bill told Candace to leave the logistics to him. She needed only to be in the condominium unit on moving day to direct the movers where to place the furniture and into which rooms to put the boxes as their household possessions were transported from Eden Prairie to Minneapolis.

Bill had been oddly vague, even evasive, about the moving arrangements. Candace was so relieved not to have been asked to help gather things inside that house—and was so tired in general—that she simply acquiesced and didn't ask questions.

Today was moving day. Candace had opened up the unit and made arrangements with the building management for access to the loading dock area and to the freight elevator for moving things into the unit. Earlier that morning, she and Bill had driven the mini-van over to the condominium building and carried in those few possessions they had with them in the hotel.

And Candace had brought Tucker the cat to his new home. She had taken Tucker out of the house that night of the home invasion and carried him into their hotel room so that the little guy wouldn't have to spend another night alone in the house. At this moment, Tucker was walking slowly through the two-bedroom unit, sniffing at everything and then rubbing against walls to leave his scent. When the movers arrived, she'd close him inside the laundry room to keep him out the way.

Now Candace stood on the balcony, relaxing while she waited to hear from Bill, who had promised to call when the movers were on the way.

Her cell phone rang. She was surprised because it was too soon for the movers to have completed loading a van back at the house.

It was Bill. "Candy, you need to come over to the house."

Her heart hammered hard inside her chest and she could only stammer: "Bill, I . . . I . . . can't. I really meant it. I'll never go inside that house again."

"I know, I know, honey," Bill replied. "I promise you, you don't have to put one foot inside the house. But you really, really do need to come over here."

Hearing the trepidation in her voice, Bill hastened to add: "Don't worry. It's a good thing."

"But how would I even get there?" asked Candace. "You know we have only one vehicle now, the mini-van."

"The mini-van is still in the parking space in the underground parking at the condominium building, right where you are. I got a ride to the house with someone else." Once again, Bill was being mysterious.

Because it now was mid-morning, and long past rush-hour, the drive from Minneapolis to Eden Prairie took Candace only about twenty minutes.

As she turned onto Dunnell Drive, she began to see cars and trucks parked tightly along the street, as occasionally happened when one of their neighbors was hosting a large party on the block. The number of parked vehicles increased as she drew closer to the house at 3732 Dunnell Drive. She slowly pulled into the drive.

Before her vision blurred with tears, she was stunned by what she saw. At least fifty people filled the large front yard. Dean Colleen Ordway. Other law professors. Staff from the law school. Dozens of law students she had taught over the past three years. They were all wearing work or casual clothes.

More colleagues and students were coming out of the house carrying furniture and boxes toward pickup trucks and vans that had been backed in close to the front door and garage. Even through her tear-filled eyes, there was no mistaking the towering Sharon Tipplett as she came out of the house carrying two boxes toward a pick-up truck.

Bill came over to the mini-van and helped her out, as tears streamed down Candace's face. Dean Ordway was the first to come over and hug Candace, saying, "I made a couple of phone calls, and others made more calls. Everyone who heard wanted to help. We've got this, Candace. We've got this for you."

Able only to repeat "thank you," Candace embraced each of the many people who made up the moving crew as they took a break from their work to greet her.

At the end of the line was her friend and law school clinic colleague Sharon Tipplett, who hugged her, and said, "Oh, no, we've got you crying again."

"These aren't tears of sadness," Candace assured her. "Thank you, thank you."

After a set of boxes had been loaded into the Klein mini-van, Bill got into the driver's seat, while Candace climbed into the passenger seat. Bill said, "I think Dean Ordway and the law school crew can get the rest packed and moved. Let's go home."

Candace slid over to the left on the seat and hugged Bill tightly. The only words she gave Bill were the same she had been repeating to everyone else: "Thank you." But a deeper meaning, a stronger feeling lay behind those same words when she shared them with her husband.

As Bill backed the mini-van out of the driveway, she thought: *Going home. I hope so. I need a home.*

ROBERT (ROBBY) SHERBURNE wasn't a bad lawyer. But he wasn't a good one either. Or, to be fair, it was hard to judge whether he might have become a good lawyer because he'd never really practiced law. He might have a law degree. He might be the United States Attorney for the District of Minnesota. But Sherburne saw his job as a political one. And he practiced politics pretty darn well, or at least he thought so.

Sherburne's father, Wilburn, had been elected to two terms as Minnesota Secretary of State in the 1970s. Affectionately known as Burney Sherburne, he then became the nominee for governor of the Democratic-Farmer-Labor Party (which is Minnesota-speak for the Democratic Party). That was back when getting the party nod was almost always the equivalent of being elected to state office in Minnesota. Not that year; not for Burney. So Burney never again ran for political office. In those halcyon days of DFL domination in Minnesota state politics, there would be no second chance for a DFLer who couldn't even beat a Republican.

It was a different time now, as Robby Sherburne knew all too well. Republicans did win statewide office in Minnesota, more than once in a blue moon. To be sure, the DFL nominee for governor or attorney general or senator won more often than not. Republicans hadn't reached parity in state bids for elective office—but they were getting there. So if Robby Sherburne wanted to take the advantage in a race for state office, he could hardly do better than to run from a platform as a criminal prosecutor and thereby seize for himself the traditional Republican theme of being tough on crime.

After losing the gubernatorial election in the 1970s, his father, Burney Sherburne had become a mover-and-shaker behind the scenes as a partner in one of the major Minneapolis law firms. He organized fundraising events for DFL politicians and party campaigns, diplomatically dealt with insiders, helped quietly resolve scandals, and offered legal counsel to a new generation of politicians. Wilburn Sherburne would never be remembered in political history among such giants of the Minnesota DFL Party as Hubert Humphrey or Walter Mondale. But, even decades later, Burney's name meant something to many of those active in DFL politics.

After Robby Sherburne got his law degree—quite appropriately in the then-recently named Walter F. Mondale Hall, which houses the University of Minnesota Law School—he joined his aging father's law firm. Other new associates were relegated to the grunt work of drafting commercial instruments or reading through thousands of pages of electronic documents to respond to discovery requests in a big lawsuit. Robby Sherburne instead followed in his father's footsteps and chatted up clients and potential clients.

With his political connections, cultivated charm (for those he liked or wanted to like him), and boyish good looks, Sherburne was a natural "rain maker." He didn't do the legal work; he managed it for the client.

When the time came to start his own political career as he neared the end of his thirties, he didn't think small but lobbied to be nominated as the United States Attorney for the District of Minnesota. With his last name and the endorsement of his now-late father's friends, the incumbent DFL United States Senator for

Minnesota agreed to put forward only Sherburne's name to the new Democratic presidential administration.

Robby Sherburne had never practiced criminal law, and, in fact, had never tried a case. But he was sold to the new Democratic presidential administration as a strong manager, with good political instincts.

Sherburne was resentfully aware that some inside the Justice Department in Washington, D.C., had resisted his nomination. He had not been helped by the timing of a story in *Twin Cities* magazine on the most eligible bachelors in the metropolitan area, which featured a picture of him with a loosened tie and jacket thrown over his shoulder, in which he had been described as Kennedy-esque in appearance. The story had reinforced the widespread perception in Washington, D.C., that Sherburne was nothing more than an ingratiating pretty boy with a great haircut. But in the end, he got what he wanted, as he expected he would.

Nearly every prosecutor in the country aspires to higher office. Many of those who became United States Attorney hoped to be named a federal judge. Not Robby Sherburne. He was a thoroughly political man. He hoped to make the office a stepping stone to the United States Senate or the governorship.

Another DFL politician had recently been elected to one of the state's two United States Senate seats. The other seat was held by a Republican who would not be up for re-election for four more years.

So, with the next gubernatorial election only eighteen months away, Sherburne had set his sights on the governor's residence at 1006 Summit Avenue in St. Paul.

The political attractiveness that the United States Attorney position held for Sherburne had proven to be a decidedly mixed blessing, given the office's primary responsibility for federal criminal prosecution. Because it was such a demanding position with considerable public responsibilities, Sherburne had to be at least minimally competent in the job, if only as a manager of other people. But he knew better than to expose himself in court with any regularity, carefully reserving his court appearances to those occasions when he was most likely to shine. Fortunately, the office attracted many of the best and brightest in the legal community, so a good political manager—and Robby Sherburne prided himself on that—could float along on the superior quality legal briefing and trial court skills of the real prosecutors who went into court every day and put the criminals in jail.

To this point, Sherburne had been very careful not to be overtly political in his superintendence of the United States Attorney's Office, although no one in the office, the legal community, or the media had any doubt as to his political motivations. Still, the accomplished career lawyers in the United States Attorney's office could be guided only to a degree before they would complain that their professional integrity was being compromised.

For that reason, Sherburne had adopted a strategy that he called (if only to himself) "political percolation." And "percolation" was a good description of how he had exercised political influence. Politics had not dominated the day-to-day life of the office. Instead, he allowed his political motivations to slowly permeate the office, filtered always by the appearance of legal merit and just results.

Which cases got the best prosecutors assigned and which cases were pushed to trial rather than accepting a plea bargain were determined, only in part but definitely in part, by the political impact perceived by Robby Sherburne. Because the most spectacular cases often were also the ones deserving of the greatest attention by the prosecutor's office, political advantage and prosecutorial merit usually came together. And, on Sherburne's watch, no criminal case for which the evidence was weak had yet to be pursued for political motives. Not yet.

But Sherburne had begun to worry that time was running out if he was to secure the state-wide visibility and crime-fighter reputation necessary to make a strong run for governor in the next year. He feared his light and incremental political touch—his strategy of "political percolation"—was failing to pay sufficient dividends for him. The political progress was too slow.

Then into Sherburne's lap fell a car-bombing case—with a child victim, no less. It was the kind of sensational case every politically ambitious prosecutor dreams about. The case screamed melodrama. Getting attention from the media and public was easy. And Sherburne had made sure he was out there early, implanting into the public mind his prominent role as the tough-minded prosecutor. He had held a press conference just a few days after the bombing, in which he announced that his office would seek the federal death penalty for the perpetrator.

Even weeks afterward, the car bombing and speculation about the continuing investigation remained front-page news. There, however, lay the problem. It now *was* weeks afterward.

One of the local television stations recently had begun the evening news by declaring that "today is Day 45 of the Minnesota car bombing case . . . and still no arrest." It wouldn't be long before other news outlets followed the trend. No one with any sense of political history could fail to remember how the nightly news reports that it was "Day 100" or "Day 350" of the Iranian hostage crisis, with no resolution in sight, had played a major role in turning the public against President Jimmy Carter, leading to his landslide loss to Ronald Reagan in 1980.

Sherburne was determined not to let that happen to him. He was no Jimmy Carter. It was time to get results.

So it was a very unhappy Sherburne who fidgeted in his office chair and endured a most disappointing update by the ATF and local law enforcement on the continuing investigation into the car bombing.

Sherburne interrupted ATF special agent Alex Kramer, "Are you absolutely certain it can't have been Pirkle? Everything was pointing so nicely in his direction."

"No doubt," said Kramer.

To Sherburne's annoyance, as he still couldn't understand why an Eden Prairie police officer was part of this federal investigation, Lieutenant Ed Burton interjected, "Pirkle's guilty as sin. But of theft, not murder."

"Hell," Burton followed up without waiting for Sherburne to acknowledge him, "Pirkle wasn't really a danger to Mrs. Klein. Turns out that the gun he took with him when he broke into the Klein house was one of those replicas that get mounted on walls. It didn't even have a firing pin. He only meant to scare the Kleins and make them listen to his woes. He isn't the sharpest tool in the shed. By waving that toy gun around, he got himself shot."

Sherburne pointedly ignored Burton and continued to stare coldly at Kramer. "I thought Pirkle was in bad shape. Are you sure his answers to your questions in the hospital are reliable?"

"Yes," Kramer answered. "Pirkle remains in serious, but not critical, condition. He's lost a kidney and may have some permanent paralysis. He'll be in the hospital for months. But he has been conscious long enough to share his travel itinerary with us for that week when we were looking for him."

Again without invitation Burton took up the story from Kramer, as Sherburne finally deigned to turn and glare at him. "And it's much more than Pirkle's word, sir," said Burton. "We've been able to back-track along his path across the country and confirm his story.

"After he was fired from Insignia Construction by George Peterson, Pirkle fenced some more of the construction supplies he had stolen, pocketed the money, and took the bus to Las Vegas. The guy had a real gambling problem, which is what prompted him to start stealing from the construction company. He was in Las Vegas losing the rest of his money when the car was bombed. He can't have been the culprit."

Sherburne reluctantly favored Burton with a question, "How can you be so sure? Just because Pirkle was in Las Vegas at some point—or says that he was there—isn't proof of anything. And how do we know the exact time-line for the placing of the car bomb in the Klein car?"

Kramer answered first, "With respect to the time-line, we know the car bomb had to have been duct-taped to the bottom of the car within a few hours before it exploded. Forensics confirms that, having been wired into the ignition the way it was, the bomb would have exploded just a couple of minutes after the car was started. Since we have multiple eyewitnesses in the Eden Prairie neighborhood that Bill Klein had been driving the Honda coupe the day before, the bomb had to have been installed sometime between the evening before and the morning of the explosion. That's a window of about twelve to fifteen hours."

"At that very time," Burton again picked up the thread, "we know for certain Pirkle was more than 1,600 miles away in Las Vegas."

"But couldn't he have flown back on a late-night flight, just in time to plant the bomb?" asked Sherburne hopefully.

"No," replied Burton. "We have video surveillance from the Las Vegas casino, along with multiple eyewitnesses. Pirkle was there all night long. In fact, he had a couple of short winning streaks during which he cashed in chips, for which he had to show I.D. and sign paperwork with the casino. Everything confirms it was indeed him and he was there all night long—and all the next day for that matter."

"Bottom-line," finished Kramer. "Pirkle's not our guy."

"Then," declared Sherburne firmly, "it has to be Klein. We can tie the TNT to his company, he had access to the TNT and obviously had easy access to the car, and he conveniently arranged for his wife to drive the car that morning. He's our man, then."

"I'm not so sure," said Burton. "First, we can't really tie the TNT to his company. We know only that it *may* have come from there, among many other possible sources. Second, I've got to tell you, I was there when Candace Klein escaped from Pirkle at the house and was reunited with her husband in the back seat of the squad car. Bill Klein was genuinely relieved."

"Or he was putting on an act for you, officer," retorted Sherburne. He had come to a decision. "If you're not sure it was Klein, then I think it's time to make sure. Pull out all the stops. We've got more than enough on Klein to get any search warrants we need, to subpoena financial records, to turn his life inside-out. He's your target. I want this tied-up, gentlemen."

After Sherburne dismissed them from his office, Burton talked with Kramer as they walked out of the building. "I may be wrong, and I have been wrong before," said Burton. "It just doesn't feel to me like it would be Bill Klein."

"You've admitted yourself, Ed, that there are some strange co-incidences that link Klein to explosives, to the car, and on and on," observed Kramer. "I don't like how Sherburne is fast-tracking this either. But looking more closely at Klein now is the logical next step."

"Yeah, I suppose you're right," agreed Burton. "And I don't think Klein has been entirely forthcoming. I don't have the sense he has lied to me, but I'm not sure he's telling me everything. And, for that matter, Candace Klein may know more than she's saying as well."

◆　◆　◆

MOVING BOXES—SOME still taped shut and others ripped open but not fully unpacked—littered the main living area of the condominium unit. While the furniture was mostly in place, other belongings were strewn throughout the rooms—on tables, on beds, on the floor. The place had yet to feel like home to Candace. *That'll come*, she said to herself. *It'll take time.* She couldn't fairly judge the place until they'd fully unpacked and put everything in its proper place.

Now the unpacking would have to wait. Lieutenant Ed Burton had called to ask if he and his partner, Melissa Garth, could come over to ask some more questions. And they'd revealed to Candace and Bill that Olin Pirkle had a solid alibi for the night in question.

"So it isn't over . . . as if it ever can be," sighed Candace.

"You know what this means, Candy," said Bill. "It means they're thinking it was me."

"Then you've got to tell them everything, Bill. This is a murder investigation. The fact you could get into trouble with the ATF for not reporting the missing dynamite hardly compares with being suspected of murder. You've got to be forthright with them or it could get worse."

Bill's voice became tense, a modulation that Candace hadn't heard in several days. "I told you, it's not really missing. And, it's not dynamite, but TNT. I was pretty sure it was detonated at the site, and I just forgot to check it off on the log. We have to keep this between us. No good will come from sharing this . . . this paperwork mistake with Burton."

"What about Pirkle?" asked Candace. "You said he would remember you didn't check off the TNT on the log until long after you had left the construction site and while you were in the truck riding back to the warehouse."

"What I said was that he *might* be prompted to remember something, that he might recall something hadn't looked quite right, if someone knew what questions to ask," responded Bill. "From what I can gather, Pirkle remains in pretty bad shape. He's not going to be questioned in any detail, now that he's no longer a suspect. And I doubt he'll be putting two and two together any time soon, if ever."

LIEUTENANT ED BURTON and officer Melissa Garth knocked on the door to the condominium unit. Candace Klein opened the door, invited them in, apologized for the mess, and suggested they sit down at the kitchen table. Bill Klein was already seated there. Garth and Candace took seats as well. Burton remained on his feet.

"As part of our investigation, we have to look at all possibilities, please understand," said Burton. Candace nodded. Bill sat stony-faced. "In our search, we discovered there is a million dollar life insurance policy on your life, Mrs. Klein. And Mr. Klein is the named beneficiary."

Bill revolved in his chair and shot an odd look at Candace.

"That's right," answered Candace. "But I'm the one who took out the policy, and Bill knows nothing about it. You see, I'm a good mark for any insurance salesman. I'm the classic risk-averse person. It drives Bill nuts how I'm always suggesting getting this or that type of insurance policy for this or that kind of risk. At one point, I even had an earthquake rider on our homeowners policy."

"But we don't get earthquakes in Minnesota," submitted Garth.

"Not yet. But there's always a first time!" responded Candace. "Oh, I know I'm being a little silly. But the earthquake insurance rider didn't cost that much at first, so I thought, why not. Then the price went up, and Bill talked me out of continuing it.

"Anyway, I've made sure that we have homeowner's and car insurance of course. But we also have a long-term disability policy, a personal liability umbrella, and accidental death and dismemberment coverage. I have my own malpractice insurance policy for any pro bono legal work or consulting I do. And both Bill and I have some minimal life insurance coverage through our jobs.

"Then, a couple of years ago, my father suggested . . ." Candace hesitated, glanced nervously over at Bill, and then returned her eyes to Burton. "My father suggested that, since I was earning a significant income that . . ."

Bill interrupted, "You mean your father thought you were the primary bread-winner for the family, now, with me collecting only the few dollars he doles out for me as a favor at the construction company."

Candace began to twist her necklace in her right hand. "He just thought it was a good idea to provide for the worst case scenario, for J.D.'s future, if something should happen to me. That's all. And he even paid for it."

"That figures," whined Bill.

"Well, as you can see," Candace said with a chuckle, trying to lighten the mood, "Bill would never have gone along. So I did it on my own. The policy is a term life policy through my membership as a lawyer in the American Bar Association. For a million dollars in coverage, it does cost about fifteen-hundred dollars a year, which is a little steep for us at this point in our lives. Since it was my father's idea, I pay the premium from our checking account, and my father reimburses me."

"So you see," Candace concluded, "there's nothing suspicious about this policy. It was my policy. Bill knew nothing at all about it." Turning toward her husband, she said, "Sorry, Bill. But you know me."

◆　◆　◆

"WHAT DO YOU THINK, boss?" asked Garth as they walked out of the condominium building.

"I believe her," said Burton. "The life insurance policy is in her name, and it was purchased through her membership as a lawyer in the American Bar Association. Bill Klein couldn't have obtained a policy through that organization. So I guess that eliminates one possible motive."

"Yes," agreed Garth, "he couldn't have killed her for the life insurance proceeds if he didn't even know about the policy on her life."

"I doubt everyone will see it that way, though. The only thing that Sherburne is likely to hear is that there is a million dollar policy on the life of the woman nearly killed in the car bombing," predicted Burton. "I'm guessing he won't give any benefit of the doubt to Klein.

"If I were Bill Klein, I think I'd get myself a lawyer."

BACK IN THE CONDO, Bill turned to Candace and said, "Well, I'd better get a lawyer. They aren't just looking at all possibilities, like Burton pretended. If they're going through our financial records in that detail and spinning theories of why I would . . . why I would do something so horrible, so unthinkable . . . that means they're focusing the investigation on me now."

Candace agreed but tried to frame the directive more inclusively for both of them, "Yes, *we'd* better get a lawyer."

~10~

THE PEACE OF HER family's suburban home had been twice shattered, first by a bomb that stole the life of her child and then by an invader who destroyed any lingering semblance of residential security. Abandoning that defiled domicile, she had retreated to a condominium apartment in downtown Minneapolis. And the tribulation had followed her there, not only because there could be no sequestering of a mother from her bereavement, but also because police investigators had interrupted their temporary repose to cast suspicion on her husband.

Her remaining place of refuge—not from grief but from interlopers—had been her office at the University of St. Thomas. Without so intending, because the room had been decorated long before that awful day in May, Candace's work space now served as a schizophrenic shrine to both her professional triumphs and her personal tragedies.

Attached to the walls of the office were frames exhibiting her law school diploma, law school awards, and state and federal bar admission certificates, along with portraits from her clerkship with Judge Payton Bowers and her days in law practice. Her bookshelves contained dozens of legal texts, including prominent displays of her own published journal articles.

On the deep wooden desk and attached credenza that encircled her office chair, she had distributed various family knickknacks. A central place at the front of the desk had been reserved for school art projects created by James Daniel.

108

Arrayed along the window shelf beneath the office's large windows were a series of framed photo montages Candace had created each year to send with Christmas cards. The annual compilations illustrated the family's activities during the year, including such events as the first day of school, birthday parties, and family vacations.

Last year's medley of images depicted J.D. in his Catholic school uniform, a dinosaur-shaped cake at his ninth birthday party, and Bill, Candace, and J.D. smiling as they posed outside the Split Rock Lighthouse on the North Shore of Lake Superior near Duluth. This had become the final episode in the series. The family chronicle in pictures had come to a premature end.

Now Candace's last sanctuary had been breached by the trespassing heralds of calamity.

Earlier this morning, as she sat before her computer screen reading yet another set of sympathetic emails from friends and colleagues, past and present, a knock had come at her office door. When she opened it, she had encountered a young man who identified himself as a process-server and handed her an envelope.

Inside had been a subpoena issued by the United States Attorney's Office, which invoked the authority of the United States District Court and ordered her to appear and testify before the grand jury empaneled to investigate the car bombing. While the specific subject on which she would be questioned before the grand jury was not revealed in the subpoena, she had little doubt that federal prosecutors planned to intrude into the most intimate corners of her life. Given that Bill plainly had become a target of the investigation, prosecutors presumably would ask her about confidential marital conversations and then seek to turn her answers against her husband.

On the recommendation of Dean Colleen Ordway, a well-regarded criminal defense attorney had been contacted. He had kindly agreed to meet with Candace and Bill in her law school office that afternoon.

Now, in preparation for the meeting, she decided to refresh her own understanding of the legal issues raised by the subpoena. As it happened, a couple of years previously, she had been one of a group of young law professors who had co-authored a text book for law students to provide an overview of critical concepts in the law of evidence. Fortu-itously—or fatefully in retrospect—she had been assigned to write a chapter summarizing several of the evidentiary privileges that offered a protection to those being asked to testify or provide evidence in court.

Candace pulled down the law book from her shelf and skimmed through the pages of text she had written on the topic of the "marital privilege":

"MARITAL PRIVILEGE" has an august sound, a distinctly legalistic flavor. And, indeed, the marital privilege is a venerable legal doctrine, dating back hundreds of years in Anglo-American legal history. But the basic nature of the marital privilege is easily understood and remains grounded in common societal conventions. As with other evidentiary privileges recognized in American courts, the marital privilege reflects our society's considered judgment that certain relationships serve espe-cially valuable purposes in human affairs so that we should foster trust within those relationships by ensuring confidentiality.

We encourage people to seek counsel from a lawyer and be secure in the knowledge that their confidences will be safeguarded. We do this not only because the lawyer must be well-informed to represent the client effectively and fairly, but also so that the lawyer may help the client follow the law, which benefits the public as well. If the lawyer is to be able to counsel the client to do the right thing, legally and morally, the lawyer must have full access to information from the client—and the free flow of information depends on the assurance of confidentiality. Thus, the "attorney-client privilege" prevents intrusion upon those con-fidences by holding that confidential communications are immune from legal process.

We encourage people to seek medical care and to fully inform med-ical practitioners about their symptoms and injuries, along with how the condition arose or the injuries were contracted, so that the most accurate diagnoses can be reached and the most effective remedies can be prescribed. If the patient feared that sensitive or embarrassing revelations would be betrayed to others, the patient might withhold crucial information, leaving the physician unable to competently perform the healing arts. Thus, the "physician-patient privilege," today extends to other licensed medical professionals as well.

We admire those who admit their transgressions, desire reconciliation from wrongdoing, and seek to reform their lives by sharing their innermost thoughts with a spiritual leader. We respect the right of privacy in such religious exchanges and the therapeutic value of spiritual counseling. We also recognize that to permit lawyers and judges to invade the sanctity of the confessional would be a most egregious violation of the freedom of religion. So the "clergy-penitent privilege," expanding beyond its origin with the rite of confession in the Roman Catholic Church, now precludes examination in court of any member of the clergy or other minister of religion about communications made by a person seeking religious advice or comfort.

So too, society has long valued marriage and protected the intimacy of spousal partners. The law of evidentiary privilege has formed to secure the harmony of the marital partners and to preclude undue invasions into marital privacy. Nearly three quarters of a century ago, the Minnesota Supreme Court said: "The family is the basic unit of society as the cell is of the body. To cause strife between the parties to a marriage contract is to undermine this institution and thus to weaken the entire social structure. Courts and legislatures have recognized the burden which antagonistic interests impose upon the intimate relations of husband and wife and the harm to the public which results from marital discord and have, as a general rule, refused for this reason to permit one spouse to testify against the other without the latter's consent."

Over time, what was called the "marital privilege" has become two overlapping but different evidentiary rules.

The first is now called the "adverse testimonial privilege," which permits one spouse to decline to be called to testify in court against the other spouse. This privilege extends beyond statements made by one spouse to the other to include things that the spouse saw or learned from other sources.

Nineteenth-century jurist John Henry Wigmore wrote that "there is a natural repugnance in every fair-minded person to compelling a wife or husband to be the means of the other's condemnation," although he warned that an overly broad privilege was an obstruction to finding the truth in court. In the classic 1980 decision of *Trammel v. United States*, the United States Supreme Court stated the "modern justification" for the testimonial privilege may be found in "its perceived role in fostering the harmony and sanctity of the marriage relationship."

The Supreme Court has held that this particular privilege belongs to the spouse called to testify. The spouse may choose to waive the privilege and testify in court, even over the objection of the other spouse. As the Court explained, "when one spouse is willing to testify against the other in a criminal proceeding—whatever the motivation—their relationship is almost certainly in disrepair; there is probably little in the way of marital harmony for the privilege to preserve."

The second is the "marital communications privilege," which may be raised by either spouse to prevent the other from disclosing confidential statements made during the marriage. In the 1839 decision of *Stein v. Bowman*, the United States Supreme Court described this rule "as essential to the enjoyment of that confidence which should subsist between those who are connected by the nearest and dearest relations of life. To break down or impair the great principles which protect the sanctities of husband and wife, would be to destroy the best solace of human existence."

Legal scholars Charles Alan Wright and Kenneth Graham identified the central question at the core of all privileges, including the marital communications privilege, as asking "what kind of people are we who empower courts in our name to compel parents, friends, and lovers to become informants on those who have trusted in them?"

For decades, legal commentators have severely criticized the marital privilege rules, especially that strain of it that goes beyond protecting intimate spousal communications to allow one spouse to refuse to testify against another. Legal scholar and Texas law school Dean Charles Tilford McCormick, writing in the 1950s, characterized the broader adverse testimonial privilege as an "archaic survival of a mystical religious dogma." More recently, others have argued that granting evidentiary protections unfairly elevates married couples to a special status, discriminates against family arrangements not recognized by the state, and imposes burdens on others who are unable to secure the same evidence from a married witness as from an unmarried witness.

Nonetheless, the federal courts and many state courts continue to recognize the adverse testimonial privilege, and every jurisdiction continues to afford substantial protection to confidential spousal communications.

For every evidentiary privilege, there are exceptions. From the time of its inception with the English common-law courts many centuries ago, the marital privilege has not prevented a wife from being a witness against a husband for a wrong committed by the husband against the wife.

As Wigmore wrote 150 years ago in his characteristically colorful terms, "if the promotion of marital peace, and the apprehension of marital dissension, are the ultimate ground of the privilege, it is an overgenerous assumption that the wife who has been beaten, poisoned, or deserted, is still on such terms of delicate good feeling with her spouse that her testimony must not be enforced lest the iridescent halo of peace be dispelled by the breath of disparaging testimony."

ONLY A FEW MINUTES after Bill joined her at her law school office, the lawyer, Andrew Dietrich, arrived. They explained that they wanted him not only to represent Bill to defend against any criminal investigation or charge but also to represent Candace in resisting the subpoena to testify. They insisted that they were undivided partners and wanted to present themselves to the world in that way. Selecting a single lawyer to provide joint representation would further that purpose and bearing of alliance.

"Well," responded Dietrich with slow deliberation, "I have to advise against this course of action. I do understand that you two see yourselves as in this predicament together and for that reason want to have the same legal counsel. But others might perceive a conflict of interest here. And, by others, I have to include the judge who will hear this matter and who could refuse to allow me to proceed as counsel for both of you."

"There are at least two reasons we want to have the same lawyer," interjected Candace, taking charge of the conversation. "First, yes, we do want to maintain a united front, but not only as a message to the rest of the world that we unequivocally reject any suggestion that Bill had anything to do with this event. We also want joint legal representation so we can work through this together, fully participating as a married couple to defend against these outrageous accusations.

"And, second, we are not a wealthy couple. Mr. Dietrich, you come very well recommended by Dean Ordway, and we know that your legal services will not come cheaply. We've already taken out an equity loan on our house in Eden Prairie, which we are prepared to pay into your trust fund to cover your fees. But we cannot afford to hire a second attorney to help me resist the United States Attorney's effort to force me to testify."

Andrew Dietrich was a man in his mid-fifties. He was average in almost every way. He was of average height and average weight (for a man in middle age). He looked so average that, if he were a criminal instead of a criminal lawyer, witnesses would have great difficulty picking him out of a lineup. He wore his suits off the rack, purchased whenever there was a two-for-one sale at the Men's Wearhouse in the U.S. Bancorp Center on Nicollet Avenue in downtown Minneapolis.

But when it came to criminal procedure, Andrew Dietrich was anything but average. No criminal defense lawyer in the state could match Dietrich in his mastery of the sometimes Byzantine amalgamation of federal and state rules governing the procedures of a criminal investigation and prosecution. No one possessed a finer map for successful travel through the confusing maze of federal and state criminal procedures. As Dietrich often would say to young lawyers who asked for the key to his success as a criminal defense lawyer: "Read the court rules. If I know the rules of the game, and you don't, I'm going to beat you every time."

"I do hear what you are saying," Dietrich responded to Candace, "and I might be willing to go along, with some precautions and qualifications. But I am ethically obliged, as you well know Professor Klein, to make sure you do understand there is a potential conflict of interest between the two of you, if not now then at some point in the future.

"Right now your interest, Professor Klein, is to avoid testifying. That does fit neatly with Mr. Klein's interests as well in preventing intrusion by the prosecutors and grand jury into his life. But if you should change your mind and wish to testify—or if a judge should order you to testify on penalty of being held in contempt—then your personal interests may diverge from Mr. Klein. And even the mere possibility that this could occur might cause a judge to rule that this joint arrangement may not continue."

Dietrich paused and looked again through the grand jury subpoena that Candace had handed to him when he arrived for the meeting in her law school office.

"If I agree to be retained by you, Professor Klein, as well as by Mr. Klein, my first step will be to file a motion to quash the subpoena to testify to the grand jury on the grounds of marital privilege. There is a legitimate basis for a joint legal representation on this particular matter. Each of you does possess one or another aspect of the marital privilege.

"Professor Klein, as you well know, the adverse testimonial privilege belongs to you. You are entitled to raise the privilege to refuse to testify against your husband.

"Mr. Klein, both you and your wife own the marital communication privilege and are entitled to object to the other being asked to testify as to what you said in the privacy of the marital relationship."

Candace nodded. "That's my thinking as well. I've written about the marital privilege in my scholarly work." She handed a copy of the evidence book she had co-authored to Dietrich. He looked through it briefly and then set it next to his brief-case to take with him.

"Now once the United States Attorney learns I've filed a motion on behalf of both of you objecting to the grand jury subpoena to Professor Klein," warned Dietrich, "I would anticipate an immediate response—not only to oppose the motion to quash the subpoena but to disqualify me from representing more than one of you."

Dietrich paused. "But that's probably a good thing . . . indeed, now that I think about it, it's almost perfect. After all, at some point in this matter, if Mr. Klein is charged with a federal explosives crime, the judge assigned to the case would be obliged under federal criminal procedure rules to investigate whether there is a conflict of interest. So there's no avoiding the conflict issue. The issue of my joint representation of both of you will inevitably demand an evaluation by the judge.

"But by provoking the U.S. Attorney to seek immediate disqualification in direct response to our motion to quash the grand jury subpoena to Professor Klein, we'll get a ruling from the judge earlier rather than later. And that's good, because it then will let us know whether we can proceed this way before we're too far down the line.

"Moreover, even as early as a ruling by the judge could come, it won't be rendered until after we've already made the case for the marital privilege applying here to protect Professor Klein from being forced to testify against her own husband. So even should I then be disqualified from representing you, Professor Klein, the lion's share of the legal work on your behalf will already have been accomplished."

Candace and Bill looked at each other and both nodded to Dietrich. "That sounds ingenious, Mr. Dietrich," said Candace.

Dietrich smiled. "Thank you. And if we're going to go forward, I must insist that you call me 'Andy.'"

"Very well, Andy," agreed Candace. "And we go by Candace and Bill. So, it sounds almost like we can't lose then."

Dietrich immediately tamped down overly high expectations. "Well, if I don't say so myself, it is a pretty good plan. But it doesn't guarantee a positive result. The U.S. Attorney almost certainly will argue that the marital privilege is overcome here by the spousal crime exception. And the law is probably on the government's side."

Candace broke in: "In my chapter in that book I handed to you, I briefly touched on the exceptions to the marital privilege. And since this morning, I've conducted a little more research myself into the case-law. I know it's far from a sure thing that I'll be able to use the privilege to avoid testifying here. But in recent years, few courts have applied that exception to a spouse not volunteering to testify. And I've found only a couple of reported court decisions in which a wife has been held in contempt of court for refusing to testify against her husband in a domestic violence case. And this is no domestic violence case."

"I'm sure that I'll benefit from your help on the legal briefing, given your own expertise on the law of evidence," said Dietrich. "But I still think it's an uphill climb to convince a court that the spousal crime exception doesn't cover a situation in which the prosecution theory is going to be that the husband tried to kill his wife. And, courts or state legislatures increasingly impose a child abuse exception to marital privilege as well."

Candace's voice trembled, "But this isn't a child abuse case. No one is even suggesting that what happened . . . to J.D. was anything other than an accident."

"I understand that, Candace," said Dietrich reassuringly. "But we have to assume the U.S. Attorney will make every plausible argument —and perhaps some that are not so plausible.

"And, of course, there is also the risk, the considerable risk, that I will be disqualified from being a lawyer for both of you. So the remaining question I must raise now with you is also important. If I am disqualified, will I be disqualified from representing either of you and be out of the case altogether? Or would I be able to continue representing you, Bill, even if I am prevented from continuing to represent you, Candace?"

"Isn't there something we could do, some way of managing things so that if the worst happens, and you are disqualified, you would only be prevented from continuing as my lawyer but could still be Bill's lawyer?" asked Candace.

"I think so. We should anticipate this problem in our response to the motion for disqualification that almost surely will come from the United States Attorney. My suggestion is this: I will represent to the court that we have carefully restricted my representation of Bill to this point so as not to inquire about any matters known only to the two of you. As would be my initial step in a client interview anyway, I will ask you two only what you understand law enforcement to know about this case, that is, what evidence do they have. I'll ask you both to refrain from sharing any confidences with me for now, either about what you have discussed in the privacy of the marital relationship or what either of you knows individually.

"Then if I am disqualified from representing Candace, I should be able to continue representing Bill. I'll have learned nothing from Candace—and Bill will have shared nothing in Candace's presence when meeting with me—that could be adverse in any later proceeding."

Before departing from Candace's office, Dietrich made arrangements with Bill and Candace to sign a retention agreement hiring him as their lawyer and to accept an advance payment for his expected legal fees. Dietrich shook hands with both, said he would begin work on the court papers objecting to the subpoena immediately (with Candace's valuable assistance), and returned to his office.

Candace gave Bill an encouraging kiss on the cheek and sent him back to the condominium. Long days of work lay ahead for her, but at least she was able to bring to bear her expertise and experience to fight this next battle.

ONE OF ED BURTON's fellow officers at the Eden Prairie police department was a daily communicant at St. Gregory's Catholic Church. He'd often told Burton that, especially for a cop, there was no better way to start the day than with prayer. He had mentioned to Burton that Candace Klein had begun coming to morning Mass at St. Gregory's a few weeks ago after her son had been killed.

Burton knew it was a sketchy thing to do, waiting for her just outside the door at St. Gregory's this morning. He felt uncomfortable ambushing her like this, especially at a holy place of worship. But he wanted to catch her away from her new home in that condominium in Minneapolis. And he wanted to talk with her privately.

The door opened and several people, including the priest, came out on to the steps. The priest spoke briefly with each one as they passed out into the world. The last person in line was Candace Klein. Burton heard the priest tell her to remember that Easter always comes after Good Friday. Burton wasn't sure what that meant, but she seemed to take some comfort in those words.

"Mrs. Klein," said Burton as he stepped forward.

"Lieutenant Burton," she replied coldly. "You shouldn't be here. You shouldn't be talking to me."

"I'm sorry, but I really do think I should speak with you."

"Actually, you really must not. I hired a lawyer a few days ago, Lieutenant. You undoubtedly know that."

Candace unconsciously shifted into law professor mode. "It is highly inappropriate for you to be contacting me outside the presence of my lawyer. Under the ethics rules for lawyers, there is a 'no-contact' rule that prohibits one lawyer from interfering with another person's relationship with her lawyer by contacting that person directly. That 'no-contact' rule guards against inadvertent disclosure of confidential information or a damaging admission being taken from a client whose lawyer is not present. In fact, under the Minnesota Rules of Professional Conduct, your approach to me counts as serious professional misconduct."

"Well, I'm not a lawyer," said Burton. "I'm just a lowly cop. And you're a lawyer anyway, so what's the harm?"

"The fact I happen to be a lawyer doesn't change the fact that I am represented by a lawyer, so the 'no-contact' rule clearly applies. And the fact that you are not a lawyer is also no excuse. You're acting under the supervision of a lawyer, so you're bound by the same ethical responsibility. United States Attorney Sherburne should know that."

"He's not my boss, Mrs. Klein."

"And you're not under federal supervision in this investigation?"

"Well . . ." wavered Burton.

"I thought so. Whether or not Mr. Sherburne is your immediate superior, this is a federal investigation, and thus you are acting as an agent of the United States Attorney's office today."

Candace paused for a moment, looked carefully at Burton, and then continued more sympathetically, "I suppose it's understandable you would make this mistake. As I explain to law students when teaching professional responsibility, federal law enforcement and state law enforcement are often in different positions with respect to the 'no-contact' rule."

She continued to speak as though she were back at the podium in front of a law school classroom: "At the federal level, investigation of crime generally occurs under the auspices of the Department of Justice, meaning federal law enforcement personnel ordinarily are subject to direct control and supervision by lawyers. Thus, FBI agents—and even ATF agents although part of the Treasury Department—tend to be directly subject to lawyer professional standards. By contrast, state and county prosecutors usually have little or no supervisory control over the police who investigate crimes. That doesn't mean local police can do anything, of course, but they are not directly subject to professional ethics rules. But that's not true in your case, as you're acting on behalf of a federal investigation."

Hoping to alleviate the tense atmosphere, Burton affected a jocular tone as he said, "Thank you for enlightening me, professor!"

Candace did not accept the invitation, said nothing in reply, and remained formal in her demeanor.

Burton then tried a different tack. "Sorry, then," he said. "The truth is that I think I'm doing you a favor this morning."

"Oh," said Candace skeptically. "And how is getting me alone to talk without my lawyer present doing me any favor?"

"I came to tell you your husband is about to be arrested."

"And how is arresting my husband doing me a favor?" she said, plainly now annoyed.

"No, no, you're misunderstanding me," insisted Burton. "Your husband being arrested . . . that's going to happen. I'm under orders to bring him into custody by the end of the day. The favor that I'm trying to extend is to give you advance notice and then to arrange with you and your husband for me to come to your condominium apartment this morning so that we can do this quietly.

"Not only am I not Sherburne's puppet, Mrs. Klein, he has no idea I'm approaching you in this way."

For the first time since Burton had stepped in front of her, Candace's face softened. "I guess that is a kindness, Lieutenant. Giving us a head's up, that is. Not arresting him of course."

She added, "I expect my assuring you that you have the wrong man won't make any difference?"

"It makes some difference to me, Mrs. Klein," said Burton graciously. "I'm not saying you're right, of course, but I know you genuinely believe what you're saying. No, I can't countermand my orders to arrest your husband. And the evidence certainly is piling up against him. But I don't see any reason to make life more difficult for you . . . or him . . . by scheduling the arrest so that the local news media gets to broadcast the 'perp walk' into the jail."

"So will you be taking Bill to the federal lock-up on federal explosives charges? Our lawyer tells me that the United States Marshal has a contract with the county jail in Elk River to detain federal prisoners. Isn't that about a forty-five-minute drive from here?"

"No," replied Burton, thinking he had been rather startled by the directions given to him as well. In fact, he had been surprised that he was asked to make the arrest at all, rather than someone from ATF. "I've been directed to arrest Mr. Klein on a state charge of homicide and transport him to the Hennepin County jail here in Minneapolis."

Candace looked quizzical, but said nothing.

"So, Mrs. Klein, let me escort you back to your condominium building in Minneapolis. My partner, Melissa Garth, is already waiting in the lobby in your building. I'll let you and your husband have a few minutes, under our supervision of course, to gather yourselves and contact your lawyer. From there we'll go over to the Hennepin County jail for booking, with an initial appearance in county district court scheduled for tomorrow.

"I won't pretend this is going to be enjoyable for either of you. But I do promise that, if you'll cooperate with me in taking him into custody this morning, there will be no media circus to navigate outside the jail."

Lieutenant Burton was true to his word.

There was no news reporter or photographer.

There was no crowd of gawkers.

There was no public embarrassment (until Bill's mug shot was published a few days later in the *Minneapolis Star Tribune*).

And now there was no Bill.

He remained in custody in the Hennepin County jail.

Candace was alone, again.

~11~

DURING HER YEARS in law school in the 1980s and then practicing law in the 1990s, Judge Sally Williamson heard frequently about the struggles women in the prior generation had faced to be recognized as full-fledged partners in the legal profession. To shield against the condescending attitudes they had encountered and to exhibit the seriousness of purpose necessary to secure their rightful position at the bar, women lawyers of that feminist era sometimes developed a sharper edge in personality. While respectful and appreciative of her predecessors' trailblazing battle for equality, Williamson nonetheless was glad she had come of age in a later period. Sober formality or a pugnacious manner simply wasn't her style.

It wasn't that Judge Williamson was soft. Any lawyer who entered her courtroom and tried to roll over her would quickly learn as much. When merited, Williamson could be pointed and direct in courtroom demeanor. Rather, Williamson was comfortable in her own skin, happy to be alive, energized by the people around her, and reluctant to put up a guard that kept people at arm's length.

When a white male prosecutor came into her courtroom for the first time, she sometimes could sense a discomfort and observe a stiffness in bearing as that lawyer looked around to see that nearly everyone else in the courtroom—from the judge on the bench to the law clerk at her side and not infrequently on through to the defense attorney and the defendant at the other counsel table—was dark of complexion. She well knew what it was like to be the only person of a different color invited to the party.

But far from believing that turn-about was fair play, Judge Williamson insisted on making everyone in the courtroom feel that they belonged there, including a white male prosecutor unaccustomed to being in an environment in which African-Americans preponderated. Indeed, she insisted on making the courtroom a place, if not of welcome at least not of intimidation, for the criminal defendant as well, who too often was also a person of color and who belonged in that courtroom in a sadly different way than the other courtroom personnel.

Williamson couldn't claim—and never did claim—to fit some too-simple racial narrative of the black girl who rose from poverty in the inner city to the heights of success as a black-robed jurist. Her father had been a middle-rank executive at a suburban bank, and her mother had been a public elementary school teacher, both having graduated from college. She did grow up in a largely black and middle-class neighborhood, being raised in Brooklyn Center, a first-ring suburb just north of Minneapolis.

All of this was hardly to say that she lacked a balanced sense of racial identity. To be sure, she shrugged away the politically correct assumption by some that she had an obligation to fall in line behind certain self-appointed black leaders on the issues of the day. At the same time, she would acknowledge, she remained most at home in that black Brooklyn Center neighborhood, where she had been raised, where she still lived, and where she shared a kinship of common values, cultural background, and many life experiences with her predominantly African-American neighbors.

Williamson had been appointed to the United States District Court for the District of Minnesota after serving as a federal public defender and bar leader for many years. She well understood that her selection from the ranks of many other well-qualified applicants was accountable in part to the desire of a Republican President to tout the diversity of his judicial appointments. So what? She was as qualified as any of the other potential picks.

Other judges on the federal bench had garnered their current posts by virtue of some other "plus factor" that went beyond merits, such as their political activities, social or professional networking, where they'd gone to school, who their parents had been, or how close a friendship they had been able to strike with a United States senator who was in the prime position to make a recommendation to a presidential administration. That one of Williamson's "plus factors" was the justly perceived need to increase racial diversity on the federal bench was not different in kind and, in fact, a much better reason than many for being plucked from the crowd of eligible candidates. And she was proud as well of her prior career defending those accused of crimes, a perspective not often seen in the courts, where prosecutors were much more likely to secure judicial nominations.

In any event, Judge Williamson had always believed, the real question wasn't how you got the opportunity. It was what you did with it once you had it.

One of the men who would appear before her on this day in early August was the living embodiment of another customary way to rise to high government office. Robby Sherburne was United States Attorney only because of his daddy. He had turned out to be a reasonably competent manager of the office. But he also had carried a stronger whiff of partisan politics into the federal prosecutor's office than Judge Williamson thought appropriate. That made her frown slightly, an expression not familiar on her face. Her longtime law clerk saw the slight downturn of the judge's lips, but nobody else in the courtroom was likely to notice.

From the side door leading into her chambers, Williamson looked out at the courtroom. As everyone waited for the court session to begin, Sherburne was affecting confidence in front of a courtroom gallery full of spectators and news reporters. Most of them had undoubtedly come after being notified by Sherburne's media operation that he would be appearing in court.

Still, looking past his swagger, Williamson thought Sherburne looked a little nervous. That wasn't surprising, she thought. As far as she could recall, this was the very first time that the United States Attorney himself had bothered to darken the door of her courtroom on the tenth floor of the federal courthouse. Sherburne usually sent others into the United States Courthouse in downtown Minneapolis, staying behind in his paneled and well-appointed office to call the shots, like some general sitting in a war room far behind the front lines.

Yes, Williamson usually went out of her way to make everyone feel they belonged in her courtroom. But she couldn't drum up her usual enthusiasm to include Robby Sherburne within that embrace.

Williamson's law clerk gaveled the courtroom to order. As everyone in the courtroom stood, Judge Williamson entered, sat down behind the bench, and began. "Everyone may be seated. Counsel, would you please stand up and make an appearance today for the court reporter?"

Sherburne leapt first to his feet, announcing, "I am Robert Sherburne." Now experienced federal government counsel generally declare themselves simply as "appearing for the United States." But Sherburne continued with a pompous flourish, in which he slowly emphasized every vowel of the last four words. "I'm appearing this morning on behalf of the United States of America."

Looking over her glasses at Sherburne, Williamson said wryly, "And what a fine client you have, Mr. Sherburne."

A lower murmur of chuckles, including a couple of louder guffaws, emanated from the courtroom gallery. Sherburne's face turned red, and he sat back down.

As the amused twitter died down, the other lawyer stood as well. "Andrew Dietrich, your honor, appearing on behalf of William and Candace Klein. Mrs. Klein is seated here with me at table."

"Where is Mr. Klein this morning?" asked Williamson.

Not waiting for Dietrich to reply or to be recognized, Sherburne stood again and said, "I believe Mr. Klein is in state custody. He is not presently a party to any federal case, your honor."

"He is quite definitely a party to this set of motions, your honor," retorted Dietrich, "as much as is Mrs. Klein. I will have something more to say later on about Mr. Klein's incarceration. But he is well-informed of this matter, your honor, and I am ready to proceed, even in his absence."

For the next hour, Williamson heard argument on the motion by the United States Attorney to disqualify Dietrich from representing both—or for that matter either—Bill and Candace Klein. The parties then presented opposing arguments on the joint motion by the Kleins to quash the grand jury subpoena to Candace. Williamson occasionally interjected a question to the lawyers, but other than asking each lawyer to stay roughly within time limits of thirty minutes, generally permitted the advocates to make their arguments without substantial interruption.

Having heard from Robby Sherburne for the United States and Andrew Dietrich for the Kleins, Judge Williamson then ruled directly from the bench:

"Counsel, I've now heard arguments from both sides. I have carefully read the briefs presented by each of you in support and opposition to these motions. And I have devoted considerable time over the past few days in researching and considering these difficult questions. While I plan to issue a written decision in the next few days, I want to announce my rulings immediately for the benefit of the parties in planning their future actions.

"I will take up the question of disqualification first, as it goes to the threshold question of whether Mr. Dietrich may represent both or either of the Kleins.

"Because of the substantial liberty interests at stake in a criminal proceeding, and my own painful experiences in the past with criminal defendants being deprived of zealous advocacy because their lawyers were divided in loyalties, I am obliged to satisfy myself that there is no such conflict. Even when, as here, two interested persons claim they are fully in accord and want to be represented by the same lawyer, I must consider the possibility that their interests may eventually diverge. If the lawyer then finds it impossible to juggle responsibilities to both persons, a fair and effective process may be upset. The loser then is not only the clients, but the public interest in fair process.

"I do understand there is no federal criminal case as yet and, even if one does arise, only one of the Kleins would be a defendant in such a criminal proceeding. Nonetheless, both in anticipation of possible criminal proceedings in federal court and to preserve the integrity and fairness of the present proceedings before me, I must consider the risks of conflict of interest presented here.

"As a judge, I am no stranger to the awkward problem of a lawyer who is presently or has previously represented an individual who then becomes a witness in the same criminal case in which that lawyer also represents the defendant. When the lawyer represents a person who may become a prosecution witness, the lawyer cannot provide the same zealous representation to a criminal defendant. The lawyer's duty of loyalty to the criminal defendant demands that he subject an adverse witness to a thorough cross-examination and attempt to undermine the witness's credibility. But the lawyer's duty of loyalty to the witness prevents him from attacking or damaging that witness while on the stand. In such a case, the lawyer cannot offer undivided loyalty to both.

"Moreover, when a criminal proceeding is infected by a defense lawyer's conflict of interest, there is a strong likelihood that any conviction will be overturned on the ground that the conflict of interest deprived the defendant of the constitutionally protected right to effective assistance of counsel. In such an instance, the case must then be retried with new counsel, thereby delaying justice, wasting the time of the court and the members of jury, and forcing other parties in other cases to wait while a new trial is held. We must guard against such a scenario."

Realizing that the judge appeared to be moving against their position, Candace glanced over at Dietrich. Dietrich remained focused on the judge, although the grim look on his face confirmed for Candace that things were not going well.

Judge Williamson continued: "I have carefully balanced Mrs. Klein's interest in selecting counsel of her own choosing, Mr. Klein's interest in the full and undivided loyalty of his legal counsel, and the court's public interest in protecting the integrity of proceedings and avoiding a complicated problem should a full-blown conflict arise at a later date.

"Given that the government is aggressively pursuing the prerogative to call Mrs. Klein as a witness in the grand jury investigation of her husband, a matter I will address next, I have no choice but to conclude that Mr. Dietrich must be disqualified from further representation of Mrs. Klein."

"Your honor," interjected Candace Klein, no longer able to sit still and taking to her feet, "since I am about to be deprived of counsel and will have to speak for myself anyway, may I be heard for a moment and ask you to reconsider?"

"Under the circumstances," Williamson allowed, "I'll hear from you for a moment, but remember that I've already read the briefing, heard argument on your behalf from Mr. Dietrich, and carefully analyzed the question through my own research and deliberation."

"There's no conflict at all here," insisted Candace. "My husband is innocent. I believe it. I know it. We're both on the same page. The United States Attorney is trying to foist a conflict on us that isn't there and trying to divide us."

"I understand your position, Mrs. Klein," responded Williamson. "But I have a responsibility to protect the rights of the person who is or may soon be accused of a crime, sometimes even if that person doesn't himself understand his rights to be in danger. Mr. Klein's entitlement to zealous advocacy by a lawyer who has no conflicting obligations to anyone else is in grave danger here."

"But there's no danger at all. Bill and I are a team," said Candace.

"That's what you think today," said the judge patiently. "But I have to consider the potential for a damaging conflict to arise later. If you should agree to testify for the—"

"That's not going to happen," interrupted Candace. "I will not be a party to the United States Attorney's attempt to destroy my husband for his political gain."

"That's enough, Mrs. Klein." Judge Williamson said firmly. "Mr. Dietrich has made the argument, you have added your views, and now I've made my decision. Under the circumstances, I've been casual about courtroom protocols and allowed you to speak out of turn, but now I need to bring this to a close."

"I do understand," the judge then continued in a more sympathetic vein, "that you feel passionately about your husband's innocence and that you are resisting any effort by the United States Attorney to obtain your testimony. But I need to take a more dispassionate view and appraise the situation in terms of the possibilities that lie before us.

"If you should change your mind and agree to testify, either voluntarily or after being held in contempt for a refusal to testify—and yes, contempt is a penalty that the court can impose—then your husband's rights may be dramatically affected by the fact that you and he have had the same attorney.

"Moreover, should you be held in contempt, and maybe even put in jail, for your refusal to testify, you are entitled to a lawyer who would advise you about all of your options. Mr. Dietrich obviously could not advise you to testify against his own client, so he could not be an independent counselor, serving only you. Whether you think you want that or not, you are entitled to it."

Turning then to Dietrich, Williamson said, "While I am granting the government's motion to disqualify you, Mr. Dietrich, as attorney for Mrs. Klein, I am denying the motion as to Mr. Klein. I accept your explanation that the potential conflict in representing both has not caused harm to Mr. Klein, at least as of this point. And Mrs. Klein's participation thus far will not be held to have voided the protection of the attorney-client privilege. Moreover, I am reluctant to disturb the relationship that Mr. Klein has developed with Mr. Dietrich at this point."

"However," she warned Dietrich, "if you wish to protect the confidentiality of your discussions about this case with Mr. Klein, those communications need to be held outside of the presence of Mrs. Klein in the future. Matters related to this criminal case are not to be shared with her, if you intend to keep those matters confidential.

"Given that she may become a witness in a criminal proceeding against her husband, anything you say to her or anything that Mr. Klein tells her about the conversations between you as lawyer and client would fall outside of the attorney-client privilege and could be used against Mr. Klein.

"So given these unusual circumstances, and given the reasonable expectations of Mr. Klein to this point, I am ruling that all discussions to date remain within the privilege, whether or not Mrs. Klein was present. Even if she later does testify in a federal criminal case, I'll limit the testimony only to things she knows about her husband or that her husband told her directly. I will exclude any testimony about previous discussions held with Mr. Dietrich.

"But that ends today."

Dietrich turned and looked at Candace with his head tilted to one side. She responded with a slight shake of her head. She was disappointed that she would no longer be part of the legal team jointly with her husband. No, she was much more than disappointed; she was very worried about now being excluded from direct participation in what was to come, or even being allowed to share in the conversation. But, Candace had to admit, Dietrich had warned them that this was a very likely outcome. And, at least, she had had the benefit of Dietrich's representation in objecting to the grand jury subpoena—a valuable benefit, even though now proved temporary.

Judge Williamson continued: "My next ruling concerns the motion to quash the subpoena to Mrs. Klein to testify before the grand jury. Now, to begin with, we have an awkward situation here, as I have just ruled that Mr. Dietrich is disqualified on conflict of interest grounds from representing both Mr. and Mrs. Klein. And yet the briefing and argument before me on Mrs. Klein's behalf were made by Mr. Dietrich.

"I am inclined to think that is more a problem of formality than substance, however. While there is a potential conflict of interest—the risk that the interests of the Kleins may become adverse in the future—the situation has not yet hardened into adversity. Thus, the briefing presented by Mr. Dietrich well presents the legal positions of Mrs. Klein as well as Mr. Klein.

"And, Mrs. Klein, knowing of your profession as a legal academic and indeed as a professor on the law of evidence, I suspect that some of the legal arguments I have read in Mr. Dietrich's briefs reflect your own research and contributions as well."

Candace rose again and said, "Yes, your honor, I did work on these legal briefs with Mr. Dietrich. If necessary to say so, I hereby adopt them as my own and ask the court to rule based on the briefing and arguments made."

Judge Williamson nodded. "I thought as much. And I appreciate your willingness to go forward immediately.

"As a general matter, the law has said for centuries that 'the public has a right to every man's evidence' . . . or, in this case, every woman's evidence as well. One of our basic obligations as citizens in a free society is to testify in court to what we have heard and what we have witnessed. Without the court's ability to require every person to be a witness, the search for the truth is undermined, the integrity of the judicial process is compromised, and the just resolution of disputes is impaired.

"Both Mr. Klein and Mrs. Klein have raised objections of marital privilege. Mrs. Klein is raising the adverse testimonial privilege, which permits one spouse to refuse to testify against another spouse. In addition, both Mr. Klein and Mrs. Klein are asserting the marital communications privilege that protects statements made in the privacy of the marital relationship.

"Under the governing precedents from the United States Supreme Court, the contours of these two marital privileges are not perfectly drawn. The Supreme Court has instructed us that the law of privilege is a matter of common law and thus should continue to evolve with changes in society.

"Minnesota and most states—and the federal courts—have held that the marital privilege does not apply in the case of a charge that one spouse committed a crime, especially a violent crime, against the other spouse. This is referred to as the 'spousal crime exception' or simply the 'crime exception.'

"Indeed, the strong societal interest in taking aggressive action against domestic violence has led many states to preclude the invocation of the privilege, even if the spouse who is the alleged victim does not wish to testify. In cases of domestic violence, the deteriorating and dysfunctional relationship between the spouses generally overcomes any concerns about damaging the marriage by requiring the spouse to testify. And to discourage an abusive husband from intimidating his wife into asserting the marital privilege, the law withdraws the privilege and makes the wife subject to the same duty to testify that applies to any witness."

When the judge mentioned "domestic violence," Candace bristled inside and out. Especially having been admonished by the judge for her prior interruption, she wanted to respect the decorum of the courtroom, which also had been instilled into her as part of her professional identity. So, she remained silent and held to her seat.

Nonetheless, despite her intent to be discrete, Candace's distress was apparent to onlookers in the courtroom, as she suddenly uncrossed her legs and sat up straight and rigid in her chair, grimaced with a frown, and gathered her eyebrows tightly above eyes that flashed with indignation.

Whether or not Judge Williamson noticed Candace's discomfort, her next words sounded directly responsive. "To be sure, this case does not appear to present the typical domestic violence scenario. There is no evidence of any prior violence of any kind in this marital relationship. I have no reason to believe Mrs. Klein's action in asserting the marital privilege is based on anything other than a sincere belief in her husband's innocence. I have no evidence before me that Mrs. Klein has been subject to intimidation by her husband or psychological trauma stemming from an ongoing abusive relationship.

"However, I must also acknowledge I do not have the expertise to evaluate the domestic situation nor has there been any social services investigation. And applying the marital privilege based on the judge's own evaluation of the likely guilt or innocence of the defendant in a charge that he harmed or attempted to harm his wife would be putting the cart before the horse.

"Looking to federal cases, the spousal crime exception to marital privilege has been applied in several cases when a spouse is willing to testify against the other spouse. But in each of those recent federal case precedents, the question has been application of the marital privilege to the voluntary testimony of a spouse.

"In addition, while the Supreme Court has not ruled expressly on the constitutional implications of the marital privilege, the Court has defined a zone of privacy that plainly encompasses the intimate marital relationship. Thus, when the government seeks to intrude into the marital relationship by requiring one spouse to share the confidences made by another spouse, the government is intruding into a private relationship that has some constitutional dimension."

Although she remained firmly fixed in her sitting posture, and the scowl on her face softened only slightly, Candace could not help but feel professional pride in hearing these words. She had crafted the section of the written memorandum filed with the court that had raised the constitutional privacy objection to the government's invasion into her conversations with her husband. She was pleased that Judge Williamson at least had acknowledged the relevance of this legal point.

"In most cases," Judge Williamson continued, "a judge can navigate easily between the shoals of not improperly invading marital privacy and of properly applying the spousal crime exception to the marital privilege. By the very fact that a criminal charge has been made against one spouse, based on probable cause that he has abused the other spouse, the government has established a compelling interest that justifies demanding testimony from the spouse who was the alleged target of the violence.

"In this case, that determination of probable cause of guilt is made more difficult by the absence of a pending federal charge, although the existence of a state homicide charge certainly weighs heavily here. We have not yet had a preliminary hearing to determine whether there is probable cause supporting any federal charge against Mr. Klein. The United States Attorney has laid out the evidentiary chain in the government's motion response. But that evidence has not been tested in open court.

"Moreover, as outlined by the United States Attorney, the evidence primarily shows that Mr. Klein had the opportunity to commit the crime, not that he did commit it. There is no direct evidence in the form of an eyewitness or fingerprints on the explosive device. Nor is there strong circumstantial evidence that connects Mr. Klein to the car bomb. The TNT may have come from Mr. Klein's construction company. Mr. Klein may have had an opportunity to secretly access those explosives. And naturally Mr. Klein had access to the car in his own garage. This may well satisfy the minimal level of probable cause, but it is far from a compelling case, based on the evidence presented thus far anyway. Of course, I do understand that the federal grand jury investigation is still ongoing."

Hoping fervently that the tide might finally be turning in her favor, Candace felt some of the tension in her body begin to release. She was beginning to feel optimistic again.

Then the direction of the judge's ruling changed course: "Nonetheless, I am reminded by the Supreme Court and the court of appeals that, especially in criminal proceedings, a privilege should be construed narrowly because it obstructs the search for the truth. As Justice Stewart well said, 'Any rule that impedes the discovery of truth in a court of law impedes as well the doing of justice.'

"Moreover, while the federal marital privilege precedents typically involved the voluntary testimony of a spouse, those rulings—including the Eighth Circuit ruling that binds this court—have adopted an exception to the marital privilege for spousal crimes without suggesting it was limited only to voluntary testimony.

"Indeed, compelling a spouse to testify under this exception for wrongs against a spouse is hardly unprecedented in the federal courts. Fifty years ago, in *Wyatt v. United States*, the Supreme Court held that it was 'not an allowable choice' for a victim witness-wife to 'voluntarily' decide to protect her husband by declining to testify against him.

"In addition, I observe that our own Eighth Circuit, other federal courts, and the state of Minnesota have recognized an exception to the marital privilege to protect the children of either spouse from abuse. Whether this exception truly applies in this case—given that the government's theory is that the child victim here was not the intended target of violence—it still bolsters my conclusion that an exception to the marital privilege does attach here. The fact is that a child died and that the government is investigating whether he died by the hand of his own father, whether intended or not."

Candace dropped her head forward and stared fixedly at the table in front of her. Her hands were clenched in her lap, as she struggled to retain her composure.

"Accordingly," Judge Williamson announced, "I conclude that the exception to the marital privilege in cases involving a charge of criminal violence by one spouse against the other cannot be avoided here. As a matter of law, the marital privilege is not available here. Thus, I am denying Mrs. Klein's motion to quash the subpoena to testify before the grand jury."

Robby Sherburne grinned, looking over his shoulder to smile at the news media in the audience. Candace was stricken, as her downturned face turned pale.

Judge Williamson was not finished. "However, as a matter of my judicial discretion, I am notifying the United States Attorney's office that I will not exercise my inherent powers of contempt to enforce that subpoena.

"Speaking directly to the United States Attorney's office, let me explain what this means. The subpoena is valid, and the marital privilege is not an acceptable objection in this case. But I do not believe the circumstances of this case justify imposing punishment on the recalcitrant witness by holding her in contempt . . . at least under present circumstances.

"First, the government has yet to press any federal charge by way of complaint, much less an indictment. Second, as demonstrated by the government's response to the motion to quash, the government does not clearly indicate what evidence would be extracted from Mrs. Klein if she were to testify. Other than vague generalities, the United States Attorney has not even indicated what specific questions would be asked of Mrs. Klein were she to appear before the grand jury. And, third, while Mrs. Klein's authenticity in believing her husband to be innocent and refusing to act against him does not mean the marital privilege applies, her motivation does play some limited role in deciding what is the appropriate remedy here.

"As matters now stand, we have a rather weak evidentiary case, a sincere and well-meaning spouse refusing to cooperate, and a fishing expedition by the United States Attorney into the communications made in the marriage relationship. I simply am not willing to send Mrs. Klein to jail for refusing to testify.

"Mr. Sherburne, you are free to issue the subpoena. But Mrs. Klein will not be held in contempt if she does not respond."

Turning to Candace, who slowly looked up as her name was said, the judge continued, "Mrs. Klein, let me be clear with you as well. If you refuse to testify to the grand jury and at any trial that follows, you will be in violation of the law. I am not granting you permission to violate the law and ignore the subpoena, even though I am not responding to your illegal conduct with punishment by contempt.

"As a lawyer and a law professor, and especially a professor who teaches lawyer ethics, you have a duty as an officer of the court to follow the law. If you place your loyalty to your husband and your commitment to his innocence above your legal duty, I am not prepared to impose the penalty of contempt and send you to jail until you cooperate. But you will be in contempt of the law and of this court, in substance if not in formal ruling.

"In sum, Mrs. Klein, at least under present circumstances, this is an act of mercy on my part, not of absolution.

"I will allow you to make the decision as to the right course of action. And, having disqualified Mr. Dietrich from representing you and precluding the defense from allowing your continued participation in attorney-client communications, this is a burden that you must carry alone.

"And I do not promise that I will extend that grace to you forever, if circumstances were to change."

~12~

[TEN WEEKS AFTER THE TRAGEDY]

HAVING RULED on the competing motions to disqualify and to quash the grand jury subpoena, Judge Sally Williamson looked to Andrew Dietrich and Robby Sherburne. "Is there anything else today, counsel?"

"Yes, your honor," said Dietrich, as he stood up behind the counsel table. "We wish to bring to the court's attention an egregious violation of the Speedy Trial Act, while William Klein continues to languish in jail. We ask for immediate relief for Mr. Klein, who now is being unlawfully detained because he has not been afforded his right to a preliminary hearing in this court.

"The United States Supreme Court has described the preliminary hearing as a 'critical stage' of the criminal process. In the federal system of criminal procedure, the accused is entitled to challenge the sufficiency of the evidence after his arrest and to ensure that he does not continue to be held in jail. He may not be detained when the United States has failed to establish probable cause for the charges at a preliminary hearing.

"As your honor well knows, under both the Speedy Trial Act and under the Federal Rules of Criminal Procedure, unless there has been an indictment by the grand jury, a person who remains in custody must be afforded a preliminary hearing no later than fourteen days after an initial appearance in court.

"I must now report to the court that it has been sixteen days since Mr. Klein was arrested and fifteen days since his initial appearance. Throughout this period, he has remained in custody. And the United States Attorney has failed to schedule a preliminary hearing, thereby violating Mr. Klein's rights."

Sherburne rose quickly to his feet and said, "Your honor, Mr. Dietrich is mistaken. The federal Speedy Trial Act applies only to a person arrested on federal charges and being held in federal custody. Mr. Klein was arrested by a city police officer, was charged with homicide under Minnesota state law, and is being held in the Hennepin County jail. Thus, the fourteen-day clock for a preliminary hearing has not been triggered under the federal Speedy Trial Act."

Sherburne turned toward Dietrich and smiled smugly.

Lieutenant Ed Burton was sitting in the last row of the gallery in the courtroom, next to Alex Kramer of the ATF. *That sneaky bastard,* thought Burton. *So that's the reason why Sherburne wanted me to arrest Klein and then to take him to the county jail.*

Burton had considered it odd that Sherburne, who had always resented his involvement as a city cop in this federal matter, had suddenly decided to delegate the task of arresting Klein to him. Now Burton understood that Sherburne had been using him to get around federal criminal procedure. Sherburne wanted to preserve the luxury of all the time he could want to marshal the federal case against Klein, while still getting the credit in the news for making an early arrest in this sensational case.

Dietrich was unperturbed. "Your honor, Mr. Sherburne is playing fast-and-loose with defendant's rights under federal law. Mr. Klein may have been arrested by a city cop, but the strings were being pulled by the feds. One need look no further than Mr. Sherburne's press conference that joyfully announced the arrest to the news media.

"The state murder charge is simply for show. This is really about a federal explosives charge. Otherwise, why are we here today talking about the federal grand jury investigation?"

Judge Williamson scanned the audience in the courtroom. "Is the arresting officer present today?" she asked.

Oh, sh–, thought Burton, as he rose reluctantly from his seat at the back of the courtroom. He lifted his right hand up half-heartedly and said, "Yes, I'm here."

"Very good," said Williamson. "Officer, please come forward to the witness stand and be sworn."

"Wait a minute, your honor," interjected Sherburne, no longer looking so satisfied. "Calling a police officer as a witness from the gallery without any advance notice, with no prior preparation, this . . . this is highly irregular."

"That's what we're trying to explore here, Mr. Sherburne," said the judge in a stern voice, "whether things have been, as you say, 'highly irregular.'"

Burton shuffled up to the front of the courtroom, where the bailiff directed him to the witness stand and swore him in as a witness.

"Now, officer, please state your full name and position," directed Judge Williamson.

"Edward Renault Burton. I'm a lieutenant with the City of Eden Prairie Police Department."

"Lieutenant Burton, please tell the court how you first came to be involved in the investigation of the incident at the Klein house."

"I was the lead police investigator called to the scene that morning. The Klein house is located in Eden Prairie, and police dispatch had received a call of an explosion and injuries at that residence."

"Was there any federal law enforcement presence at the scene?"

"Not at first. A patrol car from the Eden Prairie police department responded first, along with an ambulance, and my partner and I came within a few minutes thereafter."

"When did federal law enforcement first arrive?"

"I'd say about sixty minutes after I had arrived."

"Pretty quickly then."

"Yes."

"And who was that?"

"Alex Kramer, special agent in charge with the violent crimes bureau at the St. Paul division of ATF."

"How is it that you have continued to be involved in this matter, after federal law enforcement arrived on the scene?"

"Mr. Kramer asked me to continue to work on the case, to do the police legwork on the investigation. Eden Prairie had a strong interest in this case of course, so my police chief was happy the department would be kept in the loop."

"And who would be in charge?"

"Mr. Kramer said it would fall under federal jurisdiction, that I would report to him and keep him informed."

"And have you done that?"

"Without exception. I have reported at least every other day to Mr. Kramer since the incident in May."

"Did you personally arrest Mr. Klein?"

"Yes, I did."

"When was that?"

"Sixteen days ago, as Mr. Dietrich said."

"Did you act on your own initiative when you arrested Mr. Klein?"

"No."

"Did the Eden Prairie police chief order you to arrest Mr. Klein?"

"No."

"Were you asked to make the arrest by the Hennepin County Attorney?"

"No."

"So who did tell you to arrest Mr. Klein?"

"Mr. Kramer of the ATF."

"And what did Mr. Kramer tell you?"

"He said that Mr. Sherburne had instructed him to have me arrest Mr. Klein by the end of that day and to arrest him for murder."

"And where did you take Mr. Klein after the arrest?"

"To Hennepin County jail for booking."

"Why did you take him there?"

"Because Mr. Kramer told me to do so and said everything had been arranged by the United States Attorney's office and through the Hennepin County Attorney's office so the county jail personnel would know that I was coming in with Mr. Klein."

"When did Mr. Klein make an initial appearance?"

"The next day, in Hennepin County District Court."

"Was someone there for the county attorney's office?"

"Yes."

"What did the county prosecutor tell you?"

"I asked the assistant county prosecutor afterward when he would next need me in court. He told me I needn't worry about that, that the county was just going to hold Mr. Klein until the feds got around to getting a grand jury indictment on the federal charges."

"Thank you, Lieutenant Burton."

Judge Williamson peered over her glasses at Sherburne. "Does the United States Attorney wish to cross-examine Lieutenant Burton?"

"No," said a red-faced Sherburne in a low tone.

"You may step down, Lieutenant Burton," said Williamson. "Mr. Sherburne, do you wish to call any other witness to challenge the accuracy of any of the factual statements made by Lieutenant Burton?"

"No," croaked Sherburne.

"Very well, then," said the judge. "Based on the facts presented to me, and not disputed by the United States Attorney, Mr. Klein may have been arrested by a city police officer but that officer was acting entirely as an agent of the federal government and under direct orders from federal law enforcement officials. Mr. Klein has since been held in state custody with the knowledge of federal authorities and for the sole purpose of later being subjected to federal criminal charges.

"Accordingly, Mr. Klein has effectively been under federal restraint since his arrest. The federal Speedy Trial Act was triggered by his initial appearance. Because more than fourteen days have passed without the United States Attorney scheduling a preliminary hearing, the Speedy Trial Act has been violated."

Dietrich, who had remained standing at the counsel table, nodded vigorously. Sherburne was slumped in his chair.

"Now," Judge Williamson explained, "the remedy for such a violation is not a dismissal of any federal charge. Nor does this violation preclude a later indictment."

Opening up a statute book, she continued: "Instead, Section 3060 of Title 18 of the United States Code states, quote, 'an arrested person who has not been accorded the preliminary examination required by' the statute and within the required period of time, quote 'shall be discharged from custody or from the requirement of bail or any other condition of release.'

"Accordingly, under the law, I must and do hereby order the immediate release of Mr. Klein from detention."

Sherburne shot to his feet: "You can't be serious. You can't be granting release to a defendant in a capital case."

Sherburne was surprised to find himself standing, startled by his own vehement objection. He braced himself, expecting a sharp reprimand by the judge for his outburst.

Judge Williamson was silent for a moment and then spoke directly to Sherburne in a calm and matter-of-fact fashion. "By 'capital case,' Mr. Sherburne," she said as she retrieved a bound law book from the side of the bench and leafed through to a particular page, "I assume you are referring to Title 18 of the United States Code, Section 844 and subparagraph (i)."

Sherburne answered in an unsure voice, "That sounds right. But I don't have the statute book right in front of me, your honor."

"That's all right, Mr. Sherburne," said the judge with modulated reasonableness. "I do have it in front of me. Let me read the pertinent text and you can tell me if this is what you mean: 'Whoever maliciously damages or destroys . . . by means of fire or an explosive, any . . . vehicle . . . used in interstate or foreign commerce or in any activity affecting interstate or foreign commerce . . . and if death results to any person . . . as a direct or proximate result . . . shall also be subject to imprisonment for any term of years, or to the death penalty or to life imprisonment.' Is that what you mean?"

"Yes," said Sherburne gratefully. "That's exactly what I mean. The statute expressly authorizes the death penalty when someone has been killed as a proximate result of use of explosives to blow up a vehicle."

Sherburne had set the trap for himself. Judge Williamson was only too willing to spring it on him.

"Yes," returned Williamson. "Yes, it does. It does indeed, Mr. Sherburne. Minnesota state law of course does not provide for the death penalty. But this federal statute expressly authorizes a death sentence.

"By saying this matter involving Mr. Klein is a 'capital case' and then invoking before me the pertinent federal criminal statute, you have now confirmed by your own words, Mr. Sherburne, that this is indeed a federal case involving a federal charge. If it hadn't been clear already, the pre-textual nature of the state arrest and the state murder charge is now proven out of your own mouth."

Sherburne's face had deepened to dark scarlet.

"So, Mr. Sherburne, to now answer your question about whether I am ordering Mr. Klein's release," Williamson continued. "Yes, I am. Your own conduct has ensured that Mr. Klein must be released. The Speedy Trial Act mandates release from detention when a preliminary hearing is not held within fourteen days of the initial appearance of someone being held in custody.

"Mr. Klein's release is not because of any exercise of judicial discretion in his favor. The court's hands are tied. Mr. Klein is being released because of the actions of the United States Attorney's office in failing to conduct a preliminary hearing within the time period required by the law of criminal procedure."

Judge Williamson had not finished delivering the bad news to the United States Attorney. "The Speedy Trial Act clock is indeed running, counsel. And it doesn't just mean that a preliminary hearing should have been held already. Under that statute, a grand jury indictment must issue within thirty days of the defendant's arrest. So, Mr. Sherburne, that means you've now got about two weeks to complete your investigation and secure an indictment from the grand jury.

"And the Speedy Trial Act also provides that a case must be set for trial within seventy days from the filing of any indictment. So if the United States Attorney does have an indictment within the next two weeks, I'll be seeing both of you, Mr. Sherburne and Mr. Dietrich, for trial in about two months."

After she had collected the papers and books around her and looked over to her law clerk to signal that the court session was about to be completed, Williamson paused and looked reproachfully at Sherburne.

"You will be well-advised, Mr. Sherburne, to follow the law of criminal procedure in this case from here on out. And I will be happy to help ensure that you do."

After the clerk had gaveled the court session to adjournment and the judge had left the bench, Alex Kramer who had also been watching from the gallery came up to Sherburne's side at counsel table.

"You wanted the investigation to go faster, sir," Kramer said. "You should be careful what you wish for."

~13~

THEY HAD BOTH been raised in the Twin Cities of Minneapolis-St. Paul, but they didn't meet until they were students at the University of Wisconsin. The states of Minnesota and Wisconsin had an exchange arrangement allowing college students from one state to attend the public universities in the other state and pay lower in-state tuition. For no better reason than that most of her high school friends had chosen to go to there, Candace Peterson tagged along to Madison, Wisconsin. And there she met Bill Klein.

Well, actually, she didn't meet Bill at the University of Wisconsin either. Even though both came from the Twin Cities and both were studying at the UW in Madison, it took a summer college program in Rome to bring them together. The University of Wisconsin's own international studies program didn't include study in Rome. But John Cabot University—an American institution located in the heart of Rome's Trastevere district—offered summer programs for students at other colleges and universities.

With her Catholic upbringing, Candace had always believed Rome would be the perfect place to "study abroad." The four basilicas: St. Peter's, St. Mary Major, St. John Lateran, and St. Paul Outside the Walls. The Vatican Museum. The Palatine Hill. The Piazza Navona. The Trevi Fountain. The Pantheon.

She'd learned about these treasures of the Eternal City in Catholic grade school. But she'd never had the opportunity to visit.

146

So, for the summer after her freshman year, she signed up with John Cabot University.

For much the same reason, but quite independently, Bill Klein had found himself in the John Cabot summer program as well.

Bill then was a young man of average height with butterscotch hair, which he wore halfway over his ears. He had graduated from another Catholic high school on the St. Paul side of the Twin Cities, where he had been salutatorian of his class, won the graduating class award for promise in engineering, and lettered in track running the 400-meter, although he had never qualified to run at the state tournament.

One night that summer, the group of students in the program decided to go see the opening of a new American movie at the only theater in Rome that played English-language films (with Italian subtitles). As they walked toward the theater as a group, Bill ended up walking next to Candace and then suddenly said, rather forwardly, "Why don't you be my date for tonight?" When she asked why he had said that, he replied in a jocular tone, "Well, I'm a good Catholic boy, and you seem to be a good Catholic girl . . . and very pretty."

As they got in line at the theater, she said slyly, "So I assume you're going to buy my ticket then?" And he did.

After passing through the doors into the lobby, she continued to play the role of the demanding date, ordering, "Now I'd like a popcorn, a chocolate bar, and a soda."

And then she sauntered right past him and into the theater, leaving him alone to go to the snack counter. Several minutes later, Bill staggered into the theater loaded down with snacks and sodas. Candace had held a seat open next to her.

As he sat down, she leaned over, grinned, and said, "I really did take advantage of you, didn't I?" He smiled back and said, "Yes, but it was a fair advantage."

In the days to come, they both laughed about that "first date" and didn't take it seriously . . . or at least they didn't admit to the other that they had taken it seriously. Still, Candace found herself more and more often talking with Bill during breaks between classes and walking alongside him on the various group tours of sites in Rome.

About two weeks later, Bill and another group of students, not including Candace, went on a weekend trip to Bologna by train. When Bill came back late on Sunday evening, Candace was at the main train station in Rome, called Termini, waiting for him. When he saw her standing in the station, he said, "Well, I'm glad to see that I'm not in this relationship all alone." She smiled broadly and said coyly, "So this is a relationship, huh?"

And then she leaned toward him and gave him a peck on the cheek. As she started to move back, he gently pulled her in closer and kissed her on the mouth. She kissed back.

Their first kiss. Such a simple thing. But she could still remember how she felt, those butterflies in her stomach, the worry about whether her nose would bump into his, and, especially, the way the world fell away.

For everyone else that night, the bus trip from Termini to Trastevere (where the student apartments in Rome were located) must have been an ordeal. But, despite everything that went wrong on that sunset bus ride, she treasured those hours as one of the best nights of her life. For all of the other passengers, the mishaps that followed made what would ordinarily be a short cross-town trip seem interminable. For her, it ended all too soon.

To begin with, the bus on the route from Termini to Trastevere was not on time, so they waited nearly an hour for a bus that was supposed to come every twenty minutes. That delay was to be expected. Public buses in Rome were never on schedule. It was not unusual to wait an hour and then see two buses on the same route arriving within a few minutes of each other.

A few minutes before the bus finally arrived, an unseasonable rain began to fall, leaving them both soaked to the skin, as neither had thought to bring an umbrella. Candace was glad she had worn a light jacket, which she didn't often do in the Rome summer heat. At least, then, she wasn't wearing a blouse stuck tight to her skin.

After they finally boarded the tardy bus and it pulled away from the station, the bus driver found himself stuck in a traffic jam caused by a bicycle race around the Colosseum. The Roman Politizia had blocked off the regular route for the bus and kept directing traffic farther and farther toward the northeast—directly away from the Trastevere district in the southwest part of Rome. While trying to follow the confusing directions of the traffic officer, the bus driver was spewing flustered Italian phrases into his cell phone, begging the bus dispatcher for directions to get back on the route.

Bill and Candace laughed about how different this experience was from what would have happened back home. If there was going to be a bicycle race in downtown Minneapolis, then for days in advance the local newspapers would publish maps with alternate bus routes during the race. Bus drivers would be briefed on which detours to take to avoid the race area. But in Rome, no advance planning had taken place. The bus driver was left on his own to navigate eastward around the race site, circle back west toward the Vatican, find a bridge across the Tiber, and then work his way south toward the Trastevere district.

What a disaster! What should have been a thirty-minute evening ride turned into an hour-and-a-half night-time debacle as they sat in rain-drenched clothes on a sweltering hot bus crowded with annoyed passengers and a clueless bus driver.

But Candace didn't care. She was with Bill. And they were a couple now. She could not have been happier anywhere else in the world with anyone else.

FIFTEEN YEARS LATER, a continent away from Rome, and anything but happy, Candace and Bill came home together—if they could describe as "home" that newly rented condominium unit in downtown Minneapolis. They had spent only a couple of tumultuous days there together before Bill had been arrested. And most of the boxes of their household possessions moved from Eden Prairie remained unpacked and piled around the apartment.

It was an awkward homecoming, as Bill had been firmly instructed by his lawyer not to say anything more to Candace about the case. Now that Bill's attorney had been disqualified from representing Candace, the judge had warned that attorney-client privilege would apply only if Bill and his attorney Andy Dietrich maintained careful confidentiality. And that meant keeping Candace out.

For the first couple of days after his return, Bill was even more taciturn than before. True to his reserved nature, Bill hadn't shared much in the way of details. Still Candace gathered from stray comments that being jailed for more than two weeks had been a trying experience. She thought it best not to push too hard.

At the same time, Candace was increasingly convinced her failure to be more forthright with Bill and her willingness to accommodate his natural reticence had been the greatest mistake of her life—and the greatest weakness in their marriage. As an opening, maybe she could be the one to express her feelings, without pushing him to reciprocate at first.

Her first attempt at more direct and honest conversation went badly—very badly. And, to make it worse, she realized afterward that she should not have initiated her communications offensive by trespassing on the forbidden territory of the case against Bill.

But she could not refrain. She had to let Bill know about her crisis of conscience.

In the days since the court hearing, Judge Williamson's admonition that Candace had a moral and professional obligation to honor the grand jury subpoena and to testify had been gnawing at her. When Williamson had pointedly reminded Candace of her duty as an "officer of the court," those words struck her to the core of her professional identity.

In her professional responsibility class at the University of St. Thomas School of Law each year, Candace reminded students of the words of the great American jurist Justice Benjamin Cardozo. He had said that, by being "received into that ancient fellowship," a lawyer becomes "an officer of the court, and, like the court itself, an instrument or agency to advance the ends of justice."

A black-letter rule of lawyer ethics prohibited a lawyer from knowingly disobeying an obligation under the rules of a tribunal of justice. Judge Williamson had graciously refrained from imposing the punishment of contempt for that disobedience. But that was little solace to Candace.

She had become a lawyer because she was drawn to the highest ideals of the legal profession. She had accepted the invitation to join the faculty at the University of St. Thomas because they understood the practice of law as a vocation. By seeing the profession as a higher calling, Candace and her colleagues appealed to an ideal of professional responsibility that was so much more than merely avoiding discipline.

Candace had received Judge Williamson's rebuke personally. She had fully internalized the view of the legal profession as offering the opportunity to serve her fellow human beings and the system of justice with moral forthrightness and dignity. Now her personal pride in being a woman of moral judgment and of professional integrity was corroding.

Her own action—or rather her deliberate inaction—was alienating her from part of her own personality. She identified not just as a lawyer, but as a good person who was a lawyer, having always insisted there need be no contradiction between the two. But her continuing disobedience of the court order was at war with her professed ideals.

Struggling to reconcile her apparently conflicting duties to her husband and to the legal profession—having sworn oaths of fealty to both—she asked Bill if she could talk through her thinking on how to balance these competing demands. She suggested that, if she were to change course and volunteer to testify, she could help set the stage for a positive interpretation in Bill's favor. By coming forward, she could put their conversations about the missing explosives in fair context and thus ensure everything would be presented in the best possible light. Moreover, knowing in advance of her testimony, Bill and Andy Dietrich could readily respond and confirm that Bill's mistake in logging the explosives at the construction site was entirely innocuous.

Mistakenly taking Bill's initial silence as an invitation to press her point, Candace then went a step further. She argued that Bill should be the one to speak up now and publicly acknowledge the error in logging explosives. The whole thing would sound so much better coming from him. He would appear forthcoming and honest, even willing to admit a mistake and explain how it was an innocent one.

And if Bill would do that, it would spare her from having to testify. Or at least it would make her testimony beside the point and redundant, as she would have nothing then to add to what Bill had already disclosed.

Bill looked absolutely horrified. "God, no, Candy," he responded. "That's a terrible idea. I shouldn't be telling you this, I suppose, but you have to understand why we should not take that approach. Andy thinks there's a good chance the grand jury won't find enough probable cause to indict me on the federal explosives charge. You know, it's pretty clear that even Lieutenant Burton doesn't believe that I had anything to do with this. He's a pretty good guy, and I'd like to think he's a good judge of character—at least my character. If the cops aren't convinced, it is unlikely a grand jury will be.

"Even if there were an indictment and this case were to go to trial, the evidence is so weak that Andy says our best strategy may be to simply rest after the prosecution presents its case. We'd present no evidence. I wouldn't have to take the stand. As Andy puts it, we'd show our confidence in my innocence by demonstrating our conviction that the prosecution's case is so weak as not to even deserve a response.

"But if you were to testify, then everything gets complicated. At the very least, I'd have to take the stand and explain about the mistake in logging the explosives. That might plant in the mind of the jury the idea that I might have taken some of the TNT for, you know . . ."

Bill continued, in an anxious tone, clearly trying to convince her. "And, Candy, this is not just about me. If we can get past the deadline under the Speedy Trial Act without an indictment from the grand jury, the charge against me will be dismissed. And then we can try to get everyone to start looking harder for the real culprit. Remember, every day that's lost with these baseless charges against me is a day lost in finding who murdered our little boy."

Candace wanted Bill see how this moral quandary was eroding her self-confidence and undermining her sense of moral balance. "But what about me, Bill? If you aren't willing to give in a little, share some of this information publicly, then the whole burden rests with me. I'm the one who has been subpoenaed. I'm the one who's disobeying a court order. Bill, please understand. This is leaving me in an impossible position. You're forcing me to compartmentalize my life, to separate my loyalties to you and to the law and to betray one or the other. I take both seriously. Both define who I am. You should know me well enough to realize this is tearing me apart."

"Candy, I know it's hard, but we've got to stick together," insisted Bill. "This is my life on the line here. You've stood by me so far. I hope that isn't going to change."

"No," sighed Candace, settling back on the sofa. "I'm still with you."

"Good," said Bill with relief. "And, you know, we really shouldn't be talking about this."

So Candace acquiesced and retreated back into the silence between them.

For a while after J.D.'s death, she had sensed they were drawing together again. They'd been talking, like they had not talked in many months, years even. But now the law had come between them. The one thing most on their minds—the possible criminal charge hanging over Bill's head—was the one thing about which they could not speak.

Well, actually, the legal case was the second thing most on Candace's mind. No matter where her introspections began and how far they wandered, they always circled back to J.D. Whatever the topic of the moment or the matter that demanded her immediate attention, the wrenching loss of her boy was never far away in her thoughts.

In the early weeks after the car bombing, and before Bill's arrest, she had found growing comfort and had perceived restored intimacy with Bill by being able to talk about J.D. with him. Surely they could still talk about their son. That topic could not be, could never be, taboo. She would not tolerate anything that caused them to push J.D. into the past and leave him out of their continuing lives together.

She tried again to break the impasse between them by periodically calling up a treasured memory of J.D. Sometimes Bill would follow her lead and break through the wall of silence. But, frustratingly, within a few minutes, the barrier would seal up again. She could see in his eyes that Bill had become distracted and was no longer listening to the story she was telling.

She did, of course, understand. She could only imagine the stress he was under, being accused of killing their child, while the state's most notorious prosecutor was calling for his execution.

Nonetheless, she persisted in attempts to reach out to him. And her patient, loving efforts began to bear fruit. When she found Bill sitting forlornly in the apartment with a sad look on his face, Candace would sit down next him on the sofa and hug him quietly. She didn't try to intrude with words. She was content to simply let him know that she was there.

In response, Bill slowly became more attuned to her moods. One day when she disappeared into the bedroom for a solitary cry, Bill refused to abandon her to her sorrow. He followed her into the bedroom, and sat on the bed, quietly holding her hand, until the tears stopped.

As the days passed, Candace noticed that Bill alternated between being morose and exhibiting an energy she had not seen in him in a long time. Notably, Bill's episodes of reanimation arose in a conspicuous pattern. He appeared revived whenever he returned from one of his daily meetings with Andy Dietrich.

Especially given the prior episode, she knew better than to ask him about how the legal representation was going. Still, as this parade of enhanced vitality marched forward yet again, she decided she had to know more. So, with premeditated casualness, she asked in an roundabout way how Bill was feeling.

With a rejuvenated brightness in his eyes, he came alive to her. "Candy, what I'm feeling is very strange. I know I should be petrified, frightened out of my mind, thoroughly despondent. And, as you know more than most, since you've had to put up with me, I have been depressed. I really am scared. I'm very scared. Sometimes, I can hardly bear the weight of being subject to this criminal investigation, to know that people think I murdered my own child. But that fear, that anxiety, that humiliation is not the only thing I'm feeling.

"I'm also finding, oddly enough, that I've discovered a new purpose in life, something that I now realize has been missing for far too long. When I go to Andy Dietrich's office and work on my defense, I'm doing something that matters. I'm fighting for my freedom; I'm fighting for my name. As weird as it sounds, defending myself against these horrendous charges has given me a sense of meaning."

Bill looked Candace directly in the eyes. "Maybe it's just that I've been living without direction for so long. These past few years, working in that dead-end job for your father, has been draining the life out of me. Being without a purpose, without a calling, is . . . is, like feeling a part of your soul melt away every day.

"It's hard to explain what's happening to me. When I dwell on the accusations against me, I feel like I'm plunging into a long, dark, and endless tunnel. But when I focus instead on defending myself, on working to show my innocence, then I feel like I'm emerging from a long sleep. Then, there is hope."

Candace hadn't heard Bill talk with such animation since, well, since they had moved to the Twin Cities. Maybe, she thought, just maybe, the door was finally opening again. When this is all over, when the obstacles to communication are swept away, then they could really talk.

Bill's confession of intertwined fear and hope could not break down the barricade of secrecy. But his refreshing disclosure provided a new incentive to each of them to find and exploit holes in those fortifications. Because they were precluded from speaking on the subject of most immediate concern, Bill and Candace began finding clever ways to circumvent the imposed silence and to interact with each other in a personally meaningful way, while holding to the communications blackout. Precisely because such interactions were difficult and awkward, and thus demanded careful deliberation and planning, the delicate feints they made toward each were all the more appreciated and carried greater affectionate meaning.

One evening, for example, they were sitting in separate chairs in the living room area of the condo, watching an old horror movie on the wide-screen television, which they had hung high on the wall. The cat, Tucker, had always been rather sensitive to what he perceived as emotional tension, so he had become more and more fretful as the victims of the movie monster screamed through the speakers of the surround sound system.

When Tucker became confused, he often behaved in an ostentatious manner, trying to seize attention, in an attempt to be reassured of his proper place in the home. On this occasion, without any warning, the cat suddenly leaped up some four feet from the floor all the way up to the narrow upper edge of the wide-screen television attached to the wall. Then, perched on the top of the television, he hung his front paws over the edge and stared at them.

Simultaneously both Bill and Candace dissolved into laughter. Candace was laughing so hard she could hardly catch her breath and tears were streaming from her eyes. Bill had jumped to his feet, worried at first that the television might come crashing down, and then had fallen back toward his chair, missed his seat, and dropped to the floor. While wincing and grabbing his sore rear end, Bill looked over at Candace and laughed even louder than she.

For the rest of the evening, there was an easiness between them and a lighter mood. They made love that night for the first time since the tragedy.

During their long hours together in the condo, they frequently played music on the sound system Bill had set up to fill the silence and to lift their spirits. They alternated as to who would choose what music to play. When it was Candace's turn, she often selected a collection of Beatles songs, both because she had always loved the band and because most of the tunes were cheerful.

One of her favorites was John Lennon's anthem, "All You Need Is Love," which had been recorded live in 1967 with an orchestra for the first global television link by satellite. When the compact disc reached this song in the Beatles collection, Bill sang along at the chorus. Candace joined in. When the recording reached the chorus for a second time, Bill walked over to Candace, took her by the hand, and led them in a simple two-step dance. After swaying in each other's arms, they kissed.

For one brief moment in time and space, Candace could almost believe the words with which the Beatles ended the song—"Love Is All You Need."

AND THEN, ABRUPTLY like the needle of an old-fashioned record-player jerking off the platter, everything slipped back. And the cause of the retrenchment once again was Bill's alienated relationship with Candace's father.

Bill had not been back to the office at Insignia Construction since the day of the car bombing. Weeks now had passed. He never said anything to Candace about when he might return to work. And she had been afraid to ask him.

His paycheck continued to be automatically deposited into their checking account every two weeks. The very fact that the paycheck kept coming, while Bill didn't go to work, simply reinforced to her—and she was sure to Bill as well—that her father truly had been carrying him at the company, regardless of what Bill actually contributed.

Candace had seen her father a few times in the past several weeks, but always without Bill. She had gone to her father's house for lunch a couple of times. And, when she was working at the law school, her father had arranged to come by and see her once or twice.

Now that she and Bill seemed to be moving on an even keel again, even under the trying circumstances, she spoke for the first time about her father. One evening, she mentioned she would like to have her father visit them in their new home.

She saw that Bill was uncomfortable with the idea. When she pressed, he erupted.

"You know," Bill said, "I'm not as oblivious to what's going on around me as you and your father think."

"What do you mean?"

"I know that George keeps me on at the construction company just because I'm family. Or, more likely, as a favor to you."

Candace couldn't offer any rebuttal. Her father had never said so, but she had thought as much.

"And while you may be the one who balances the checkbook each month, it does all come out of the same account." Bill pointed to an old roll-top desk that had been placed in the main area of the condo. "And all of our financial papers are kept in that desk. Remember when that guy bumped into the back of my car at the intersection last year?" asked Bill rhetorically. "Well, I pulled our car insurance policy out of that desk drawer. And your 'secret' life insurance policy was right there as well."

Candace was astounded. "So you did know about the insurance policy when I sat there and told Lieutenant Burton you didn't know anything about it. You let me lie to the police!"

"It wasn't a lie. You thought you were telling the truth."

"But you didn't speak up and correct my mistake."

"No, I thought admitting I knew beforehand about the insurance policy might leave the wrong impression with the police."

"And maybe it leaves the wrong impression with me!"

"Now, Candy," Bill said, dialing back from his irritation and affecting a soothing tone. "Surely you don't mean that. You know I'm not capable of doing such a thing. We're all right, aren't we?"

"Yes. I know you didn't do it. We're all right."

But, once again, Candace was avoiding the truth. She wasn't all right. She was feeling queasy.

THE CURTAIN of silence had fallen back in place. Neither of them struggled to tear it open again. At most, one or the other peeked through the veil from time to time, without lifting it away. Their conversations deteriorated to contrived but tepid remarks about the weather, or a falsely enthusiastic declaration that the condo was starting to feel like home with the placement of a piece of furniture here or the unpacking of another box there, or a casual inquiry as to what the other might like for dinner.

The sharp edge of that last exchange about her father and the insurance policy had dulled quickly. Even during the darkest days of their marriage, Candace reminded herself, they had never been overtly hostile to each other. Nonetheless, what she had learned from Bill's outburst was not so easily forgotten.

As the days drew on, Bill did cast an occasional sympathetic look in her direction, which Candace faithfully returned. But what Candace had hoped was the first step toward a restoration of marital intimacy was over, at least for now.

The days passed. They were at home. Together. Alone.

~14~

ROBBY SHERBURNE was increasingly desperate, even frantic. He watched his political hopes melt away like a cube of ice tumbled out on a picnic table on a hot summer day. With each passing day and still no indictment of William Klein by the grand jury, Sherburne's reputation as a confident and triumphant crime-fighting prosecutor was steadily evaporating.

The members of the grand jury had been sternly warned not to read newspapers or watch the television news. Yeah, right. Sherburne knew that they knew. They weren't hermits, scrupulously avoiding any contact with the outside world. The grand jury members had not been sequestered away in a secret location, where they would have been under strict supervision.

So it didn't matter what they had been instructed, Sherburne fretted. The grand jury members surely knew that Judge Williamson had refused to force Candace Klein by penalty of contempt to testify before them. And they surely knew that Candace Klein was proclaiming her belief in her husband's innocence.

In the federal criminal justice system, a grand jury of ordinary citizens selected from the community must review the evidence and hear from witnesses to determine whether there is reason to believe that an individual has committed a crime. If the grand jury concludes there is probable cause, an indictment is issued against the accused. Historically, as Supreme Court Justice William Brennan once wrote, the grand jury was envisioned "as a bulwark for the individual citizen against use by officials of the powers of the Government in ways inconsistent with our notions of fundamental liberty."

In mundance modern reality, however, a prosecutor typically is in charge of the grand jury process—scheduling the grand jury meetings, deciding what evidence to present (and withhold), choosing which witnesses to call (and which to bypass). A New York state judge once remarked that any decent prosecutor could get a grand jury to indict a ham sandwich.

Well, Judge Williamson effectively had let the grand jury know that there wasn't much pork between those slices of stale bread served up by the United States Attorney's office. This grand jury was turning up its collective nose at the case against William Klein.

Trying to buy a little more time in the prospect that something new might turn up in the car bombing investigation, Sherburne had taken another run at Judge Williamson. He filed a motion asking for an extension of time to get a grand jury indictment, pleading "extraordinary circumstances." But to no avail. Andrew Dietrich had responded on behalf of William Klein that the only "extraordinary circumstance" present in this case was "the reckless disregard of the United States Attorney for the rules of criminal procedure." No joy for Sherburne was to be found before Judge Williamson.

The experienced hands in the United States Attorney's office had assured Sherburne that all would not be lost if no indictment was forthcoming in the next few days. The Speedy Trial Act directives were not so rigid. Even if prosecutors could not secure a grand jury indictment within the thirty days required by the Speedy Trial Act, the most likely consequence would be a dismissal for now of the federal charge—but a dismissal without prejudice. Federal prosecutors then could issue a new charge sometime later when they had more evidence in hand and thereby start the clock running again.

Even if a reproachful Judge Williamson insisted on dismissing the federal charge with prejudice, perhaps by finding that the government had engaged in misconduct by attempting to circumvent federal criminal procedures, a loophole almost surely could be found to pursue some type of charge in the future. To this point, the focus of the investigation had been on the allegation against Klein that he used an explosive that had resulted in the death of his boy. Thus, even a dismissal with prejudice likely would preclude only renewing that specific charge.

On a second go-round, federal prosecutors could reformulate the charge to focus on the attempted murder of Mrs. Klein. This reframed criminal complaint almost surely would be a sufficiently different charge in substance so as to fall outside of the Speedy Trial Act timeline that had been set in motion by Klein's arrest for murder.

And, in any event, nothing that happened in the federal criminal process would undermine the possibility of a state murder charge against Klein. Supreme Court case-law treats the federal government and the state government as separate sovereign entities. So a failed criminal charge at the federal level would not prevent the state from proceeding. Under this "dual sovereignty" rule, the bar of "double jeopardy" simply does not apply when the second charge, even if based on the very same allegations as the federal charge, issues from the state government.

The unfortunate developments in Judge Williamson's courtroom were not devastating to the case, insisted the senior assistants in the United States Attorney's office.

But they missed the point. The developments were most definitely devastating to Sherburne's political ambitions.

Judge Williamson effectively had laid down a challenge to Sherburne to get a proper indictment against Klein within two weeks. Even if one or the other legal strategies worked to salvage a federal case down the line, Sherburne's failure to meet the Speedy Trial Act deadline enforced by Judge Williamson would be a humiliating public defeat.

Last night on one of the local television stations, when ending a report on yet another day without a grand jury indictment, the news anchor commented that "this car bomb case has blown up in the face of United States Attorney Robby Sherburne." Sherburne wasn't laughing, but he had to admit that the anchor's pun summed up his situation pretty well.

And he was smart enough to know it was mostly his fault. He hadn't been patient. He had abandoned his "political percolation" strategy too early. He'd pushed too hard and too fast. He had taken a gamble to promote his incipient political candidacy.

And he was losing.

Still, he hadn't lost quite yet. Or at least he hadn't lost everything. Even complying with Judge Williamson's strict adherence to the statutory deadline, the United States Attorney's office still had three more days to secure that grand jury indictment.

Sherburne had called Alex Kramer of the ATF in to his office to send him out yet again to shake the bushes and see if something might fall out. If Sherburne could get some new concrete piece of evidence to bring to the grand jury, there was still a chance to turn things around. Even if a complete reversal of his fortunes was unlikely, given the pounding he was taking in the press, he needed something to fend off the jackals in the Department of Justice, who had never been happy to see him become United States Attorney in Minnesota.

Indeed, things had gotten so bad that Sherburne was willing to go the extra mile and accept help from any source. Like that old saying, Sherburne thought, "any port in a storm." When Kramer had told him he would do his best but remained shorthanded, Sherburne swallowed his pride. He told Kramer to make full use of that damn Eden Prairie cop who had insinuated himself into this case before and then had embarrassed Sherburne in court.

"Mel," Burton called his partner, Melissa Garth, over to his desk in the Eden Prairie police department. "I know we've been all over that crime scene, but I don't see any choice other than to go over it again. The evidence we've got, while consistent with Bill Klein being the culprit, just isn't enough to ensure a conviction. I'm still not convinced myself. And neither is the grand jury, which is resisting Sherburne's importuning."

"Sherburne's putting on a lot of pressure, huh?"

"Yes. But I'm not going along just to get along. I've got to see this one through myself and figure things out."

"So what do you suggest?"

"I think we need to go back to the Klein house for another look around. I know. I know. It's been weeks and the ATF forensics team was all over that place. But maybe a fresh pair of eyes—or two— might see something. After all, the two of us didn't do any digging around there ourselves the morning of the car bombing. We left it all to others. At least I'll feel better if I know we took a careful look ourselves.

"So let's give it a go. That place was a mess after the bombing. There's always the chance someone missed something."

◆　◆　◆

ON THE DRIVE from the police department to Dunnell Drive on the east side of Eden Prairie, Burton brought Garth up to speed on where things stood:

"Sherburne of course is completely fixated on Klein, especially now that he's been embarrassed at the court hearing. But Alex Kramer and I have been trying to follow up every possible lead. Unfortunately, the only other lead we have is that unidentified third person on the fast food drive-through security video. You know, there's that point on the video in which a third person other than Bill Klein and Olin Pirkle can be seen and appears to be alone in the vicinity of the van with the explosives."

"Has ATF technical support been able to further clarify the video?" asked Garth.

"No," said Burton. "You can only do so much with a digital video, notwithstanding what you see on TV crime shows. If the pixels aren't there and the distance is too great, you end up with a blurry, unfocused form, no matter how much computer-whiz-bang adjusting you perform."

"Anything else you could do?"

"We brought Klein's father-in-law, George Peterson, back again and had him take another look. That didn't help. He still couldn't make an identification.

"We even brought in every Insignia Construction worker listed as being on the construction site that day, not only to have each of the workers look at the figure in the video, but for Kramer and me to eyeball them and see if any of them appeared to resemble the unidentified person."

"Did any of them look like that guy?"

"Well, that's the problem. Sure, more than one of them did look a little like the guy. But that's because the figure is so blurry that a lot of people would look like him. Each one of them seemed pretty sure he had been busy elsewhere on the construction site and never alone at the truck."

"So, I guess that's a dead end."

"Worse than that, at least for Sherburne. The prosecutors are obliged by the so-called Brady rule to share any potentially 'exculpatory' evidence with the defense. Kramer tells me that Sherburne tried to argue with the senior lawyers in the United States Attorney's office that this video is not 'exculpatory' because the appearance of the third person is just a coincidence and there's no evidence whoever it was actually took anything from the truck.

"But even Sherburne knew that the career prosecutors in his office weren't going to risk being sanctioned by the court for misconduct in holding the video back. And, in any event, if the case gets to trial, the prosecutors are going to use part of the video to connect Klein to the explosives at the construction site. Then the defense is going to get the rest of the video anyway.

"And Klein's lawyer will have a field day with that video—arguing to the jury that it was this third person who is the real perpetrator."

ED BURTON and Melissa Garth stood several feet apart in the drive-way at 3732 Dunnell Drive, orienting themselves to what had been the crime scene, now nearly three months ago. The broken windows of the house had been replaced, the melted blacktop had been filled in and sealed, and the burned grass had grown back in along the yard.

Dark scorch marks remained on the trunk of the oak tree that had been near the center of the blast. The tree was mammoth, tower-ing well above the height of the two-story house. Several of the lower branches had been broken off by the force of the explosion. But the tree had survived remarkably well, with intact healthy limbs and green leaves further up the trunk.

Garth was exactly five-foot tall. When you're always seeing the world from such a low vantage point, you start at an early age to won-der whether you have really seen everything that might be up on the higher shelf.

Burton had told her that ATF had searched the tree. But there's a search and then there's a search. Maybe a short person's per-spective would add something here.

"Ed," she yelled. "Didn't I see a ladder around the side of the house? Help me carry it over here."

Burton and Garth set up the ladder next to the tree. Garth climbed up slowly, scanning every limb of the tree as she paused at each rung on the ladder. When she had reached a height that paral-leled the roof of the house, she still was only about half-way up the tree. The ladder had been extended as far as it would go. As Burton looked on anxiously, Garth grabbed a hold of the nearest branch and clambered still higher up the tree.

Then she saw it. Something small, thin, and dark. It was on edge to her viewpoint, stuck in a cleft where a high branch met the trunk of the tree. It probably was only a fragment of a decayed leaf lodged in tight in the groove. Still, she'd come up this high, so she thought she might as well take a closer look.

Garth balanced herself by leaning her abdomen against the tree, planting each foot on a separate lower branch, and grasping a higher

branch with her right hand. With her left hand, she took a pair of tweezers from her pocket. Using the instrument, she plucked out a small,
ragged, roughly square piece of what looked to be black fabric. Biting the
handle of the tweezers between her teeth, while being ever so careful not
to allow anything to touch the retrieved item, she then freed her left hand
again to remove a plastic evidence bag from her pocket.

And into that bag she dropped whatever it was she had found
in the tree.

"ALEX," ED BURTON said in an excited voice as he poked his head
into the office of ATF chief Alex Kramer. "Now I've always wanted to
say this." His voice took on a mock solemnity. "We've had a major
break in the case."

"What do you mean?"

"Well, Mel found a small piece of duct tape, which you know
was used to attach the TNT to the Klein car. Indeed, this piece had
part of the red protective coating from the TNT stuck to the sticky
side of the tape. It had lodged after the explosion in the upper part of
the big oak tree in the yard in front of the Klein house.

"Because this narrow piece was caught in a groove in the tree,
it escaped notice by anyone. And because the canopy of leaves from
the upper branches of the tree hadn't been blown off by the explosion,
that tiny fragment escaped most of the weather over the past three
months. It was almost pristine."

"Yes, yes," Kramer said impatiently.

"We got a print."

ON AN UNSEASONABLY mild week day in mid-August, Lieutenant
Ed Burton waited outside of St. Gregory's Catholic Church for Candace Klein to emerge after morning Mass. After she had clasped hands
with the priest, she spotted Burton. She turned away, as though she

intended to walk in the other direction. Then, after a moment's hesitation, she turned back and stepped over to him.

"Mrs. Klein, I have something important to tell you."

With a sigh, she said, "All right. I guess I'm my own lawyer now, so I can't fend you off with the 'no-contact rule' again. But I'll only give you a minute."

"Could we go somewhere private?"

Candace looked back at St. Gregory's and, seeing that everyone had exited, said, "We could sit in the church for a minute."

After they had taken seats side-by-side in a back pew, Burton turned toward her and said, "We found new evidence at the scene. A piece of duct tape from the car bomb was lodged in the oak tree and hadn't been damaged by the rain or water from the fire-hoses."

"And?"

"We found Mr. Klein's fingerprint on it."

She slowly dropped her head into her hands. She didn't weep. She didn't make a sound. She just sat there, covering her face. Had he really done it? she wondered. Had Bill really killed their son?

"I'm sorry," said Burton.

Candace looked up at Burton. Her face was expressionless.

"If I may say so," Burton observed, "you don't seem as shocked as I thought you might be."

"No," she acceded in a flat tone. "I'm just numb. Nothing shocks me anymore."

"You've been coming to this same conclusion on your own, haven't you?"

"No," she said, but her voice wavered.

"You really think your husband is still innocent? Even after I've told you we found his fingerprint on the murder weapon and at the crime scene?"

"I didn't say that. I honestly don't know what to think."

"Something has caused you to have doubts."

"Yes," she admitted.

"For other reasons?"

"Yes."

"Based on things we don't yet know about?"

"Yes."

"Are you ready to tell us now?"

"Are you sure it's Bill's fingerprint?"

"Well, it's only a partial print and there are limited points of comparison with the exemplar print we took from Mr. Klein when he was booked at the jail."

"What does that mean?"

"Well, we were only able to lift a partial latent print from the tiny piece of duct tape we found. As I understand it, the fingerprint experts believe they can declare a match with between eight and twelve points of comparison—you know, studying the ridge patterns in the print. Even with the print on the duct tape being less than a full print, the experts regard what they've seen as a match.

"I'm sure that a good defense attorney, and I know that Mr. Klein has hired a good one in Mr. Dietrich, will try to discredit the validity of the fingerprint match."

Burton looked directly at Candace and waited for her eyes to meet his. "Mrs. Klein, you know I've been pretty straight with you. I have to say to you now, that while I've had my own doubts, I'm having a harder time avoiding the worst conclusion here. When you put this fingerprint evidence together with everything else, it's pretty hard to give any further benefit of the doubt to Mr. Klein."

"I hear what you're saying," acknowledged Candace. "I'm not saying I've come to the point where you are, but I do understand your position."

"So are you at least ready to talk with us, now?"

"It's not that simple."

"This man tried to kill you!"

"That's what you say. And Sherburne's trying to kill him!"

"Well, maybe we can do something about that . . . arrive at some kind of arrangement."

◆　　◆　　◆

"SO THERE YOU have it, Mr. Sherburne," Lieutenant Ed Burton said. United States Attorney Robby Sherburne, Burton, Alex Kramer of the ATF, and Candace Klein were sitting at a conference table in the United States Attorney's office. "If you agree not to seek the death penalty, Mrs. Klein will testify before the grand jury—and at trial. She's not going to say she thinks her husband's guilty, but she's willing to obey the judge's order, respond to the subpoena, and tell what she knows. While she has been careful in what she's said to me, I'm given to understand she may know or have heard from Mr. Klein more about his handling of the explosives at the construction site and something more about the insurance policy on her life."

"All right," Sherburne said. "We'll go forward with that understanding."

He could promise her anything today, Sherburne mused. It's not like this would be binding on him, like some kind of contract. If the public later called for the death penalty when they got to a conviction, he'd put it back on the table, protesting that he couldn't ignore the public demand. By then, he'd have the testimony from Mrs. Klein he needed.

Sherburne started to rise from his chair. "Thank you very much, everyone."

"Not quite so easy," replied Burton. "We want it in writing, with your signature on it. In fact, I'm going to take a video on my cell phone of you making that very promise to Mrs. Klein. And I'm telling you right now, if you squelch on the deal, I'll be sharing that video— and maybe some additional tidbits about how you have handled this case—with every reporter who'll listen."

"So you'd destroy both of our careers?" Sherburne retorted, as he sank back down into his chair.

"Then I guess, for both our sakes, you'd better keep up your end of the bargain," replied Burton in a steely voice.

"And one thing more," said Candace. "Bill remains on release and is not to be taken into custody . . . at least until after the trial."

Now Burton looked surprised. "But, Mrs. Klein, this man tried to kill you. I honestly do think he killed your boy. We have to take him into custody."

Candace was not moved. "No, I still am not convinced. I'm willing now to do the legal thing—the right thing, I hope—and testify, as Judge Williamson ordered. But I'm not yet ready to condemn my husband.

"If the jury convicts him after a fair trial and based on all the evidence, I'll . . . I'll have to come to terms with that. But I'm not going to let him be hauled off to jail before he even gets a chance to make his defense. No, Bill remains on release . . . or no deal."

Damn it, Sherburne thought. He knew he was trapped. Even with the new fingerprint evidence, he wasn't absolutely certain he could move the grand jury to an indictment. And, even if he got an indictment, a conviction was no sure thing. Testimony by Mrs. Klein could be the key.

Without being able to impose the death penalty on a child-killer, as he had promised the public, he well knew that he was kissing goodbye to any chance of becoming governor. But, then, his political career was already in shambles after the courtroom debacle. He probably could not resuscitate a viable gubernatorial candidacy, even with a conviction and capital punishment.

And, for Sherburne, it was no longer just about the fading dream of ascending to higher office. His current job was now at risk as well. Whether he was able to secure a death penalty wasn't his most pressing concern any longer. If he failed even to get an indictment or lost the case at trial, he was in serious danger of being fired by the president and attorney general. With Mrs. Klein's reluctant help, he might salvage his tenure as United States Attorney, followed by a lucrative investiture in a major law firm down the line.

"Do we have a deal, Mr. Sherburne?" asked Candace.

"Yeah," he replied resentfully. "Yeah, you got a deal."

WHEN CANDACE RETURNED to the condominium after her meeting with Burton, Kramer, and Sherburne, she dreaded the inevitable encounter with Bill. She thought she was doing the right thing. She didn't know what else to do at this point except tell the truth. But she still felt like a traitor. And she knew Bill could only see it as a personal betrayal. And who could blame him?

Burton insisted on escorting her back to the condominium building. He became agitated when she refused to allow him to accompany her into the elevator up to the twelfth floor, where their apartment was. He told her he would remain in the lobby until he had heard from her that she was all right in the condo.

Candace realized that, perhaps oddly, perhaps foolishly, she wasn't afraid of physical harm. She still could not imagine Bill would hurt her. Even now, with all that had happened and all that she had learned, she could not picture him as the perpetrator of this violence against his own family. She had doubts, to be sure, but they had not coalesced into full-blown suspicion of outright guilt. To be honest to herself, she felt scattered and unsteady, not really sure what she thought any more.

When she came into the apartment, Bill was standing in the hallway to the bedroom. She had insisted that the United States Attorney's office immediately inform Andrew Dietrich she would testify. And, of course, she expected Dietrich would promptly contact Bill. Her expectations obviously had been met.

"Candace," Bill asked, "how could you ever believe I could do something like this?"

"I don't," Candace replied. "I don't believe it."

Bill looked at her expectantly and waited.

"But I don't *not* believe it anymore either," she said with defeat. "I just don't know what to believe. And I've learned I can't trust you. So I have to trust myself and tell the truth. It's my duty to the law . . . and to myself."

Bill said defiantly, "I never lied to you, Candace. I may not have told you everything, but I never lied."

She suddenly became aware that he was no longer calling her "Candy." She tried to remember when this transition had occurred. She sighed. Even though she had come to find the diminutive nickname irritating, she curiously felt a sense of loss with its suspension. It was but one more step along an increasingly long path away from each other.

In a sad voice she returned, "Keeping secrets is lying, especially in a marriage."

Bill shot back: "Then you're a liar too, Candace."

She felt like she had been slapped in the face. And what's worse, she felt that she deserved it.

"You're right. You're right. But my fingerprint was not found on the murder weapon!"

Bill stood quietly, looking deflated. "I don't know how to account for that. I do know how that looks. Maybe, somebody else . . ."

He was still again for a longer period. Then, in a barely audible whisper, he said, "It wasn't me."

A solitary tear leaked out of Candace's right eye.

"Bill, maybe I did lie. I lied to you about the insurance policy by not telling you what I was doing. I lied to you by never speaking up to you about what has been going on between us for too long. By avoiding the difficult truth, by letting things drift along, I wasn't honest with you or with me. I should have trusted you enough, trusted our marriage enough, to insist we talk about my father and your job with him. I know I've lost your confidence as well. Maybe that's one more reason I have to tell the truth now. I can't continue with lies, hidden secrets, false impressions, deception."

She tasted salt as the lone tear reached her upper lip. "I have to tell the truth now," she continued. "I don't know what will happen. Jesus said, 'The truth shall set you free.' I have to get free, Bill. I have to tell the truth."

"You do know what will happen," Bill said regretfully, but without any apparent rancor. "The simple fact you're testifying will destroy me in front of the jury."

"That's not what I intend, Bill," Candace assured him. "I have no intention of condemning you. But I have to do the right thing. I tried to tell you this before, but you didn't want to listen. I know I should have pushed harder. As difficult as it is for both of us, I have to do it now. I have to be a faithful witness."

"If you really still believed I was innocent, Candace, you wouldn't testify. You'd keep my confidence. You'd protect my secrets. You wouldn't let people think I was the murderer of our own child."

Candace said nothing. She had no answer.

Bill peered at her closely with sad eyes. And then he began to move from the hallway toward the door.

Only as he turned from the hallway did Candace see that a wheeled suitcase was trailing behind him.

When Bill reached the door, he paused and, without looking back, said, "I'm still free . . . for now . . . and I guess I have you to thank for that. Andy Dietrich has found a cheap place for me to stay until the trial. After the trial, I expect the government will give me another place to stay."

And he was gone.

Candace sank on to the sofa and wiped away the trace on her cheek of that single tear. She had no more to give.

~15~

ON THE NORTHEASTERN bend of central Minneapolis bounded by the Mississippi River, two monumental civic buildings dominate the city landscape—one gargantuan and medieval in character and the other glistening and contemporary in style.

Occupying an entire city block on the southwest side of South Fourth Street, the Municipal Building is most likely to be called "City Hall" by Minneapolis locals, although it contains offices for both city and county government. The exterior of the building was completed in 1895, on the site of the first schoolhouse west of the Mississippi River.

This colossal structure was assembled with russet-colored granite blocks, many weighing more than twenty tons. These massive rectangles of stone were quarried in Ortonville near the South Dakota border and carried to Minneapolis by horse-drawn wagons. The Romanesque architecture of arches, columns, and cylindrical spires brings to mind an impenetrable fortress from J.R.R. Tolkien's realm in *Lord of the Rings*.

Ascending over the green copper roof of the Municipal Building is one of the world's tallest bell towers, displaying a clock face larger than London's famous "Big Ben" and a minute hand that is fourteen feet in length. The tower also houses fifteen chiming bells, ranging from hundreds to thousands of pounds of cast iron.

Immediately to the northeast across South Fourth Street rises the United States Courthouse, a sleek, modern skyscraper of steel and glass that was completed in 1997. Federal courtrooms and judges' chambers are arranged inside the fifteen-story tower, which extends upward from a rectangular six-story block of administrative offices.

On the east side, the building is an escalating vertical expanse of glass. With a convex framework, narrower at the bottom and curving outward with the rise of each story, the eastern face of the building appears to be slowly toppling toward the Mississippi River a couple blocks away.

The west side of the courthouse is fronted by an expansive sea of concrete dotted with an archipelago of greenery. Designed to simulate glacial deposits left during the last ice age, the emerald islands form oblong hummocks embedded into the man-made moraine plain.

Each day for nearly two weeks in mid-October, Candace Klein navigated around the artificial glacial drumlins on her way into the United States Courthouse. The trial of *United States v. William Klein* unfolded over nine court days in the tenth floor courtroom of United States District Judge Sally Williamson. Although Candace's personal participation as a witness occupied but part of a single day of the trial, she faithfully attended every court session, from early morning to late afternoon.

Longtime court observers and self-appointed legal experts from the local law schools proclaimed that the outcome had been assured even before the jury had been seated. Given that these confident prognostications were shared only after the jury verdict had been announced, the percipience of these pundits might be impugned. Still, even Candace—as cheerlessly and intimately familiar with the matter being examined in court as anyone could be—found the proceedings to be peculiarly anticlimactic.

THE PROSECUTION BEGAN its case with forensic scientists from the federal Bureau of Alcohol, Tobacco, Firearms and Explosives, who described the timed TNT-fueled explosive that had destroyed the Klein vehicle and killed James Daniel. They explained their findings that, based on the composition of the TNT, the materials used in the device could be traced to a particular manufacturer which had sold the product to a couple dozen construction companies. One of those commercial purchasers of the explosives was Insignia Construction, where William Klein was employed as an engineer and supervisor.

Lieutenant Ed Burton of the Eden Prairie police department outlined the investigation from his arrival on the scene on the first day to his partner's eleventh-hour discovery of the tiny fragment of duct tape spewed into the air by the blast of the car bomb and lodged high above in the nearby oak tree. A federal crime lab scientist confirmed that the latent partial fingerprint was a match to Klein.

George Peterson testified about William Klein's access to TNT at the construction company, as well as the process for using and logging explosives. Peterson identified Klein on the fast-food restaurant's security video as one of the persons appearing alone next to the van with the explosives at the construction site.

THE MOST ANTICIPATED event, of course, was the appearance by Candace Klein—although the basic contours of her testimony had already been revealed when she had appeared earlier before the grand jury, which then had returned an indictment against William Klein. Without adornment, commentary, or conspicuous emotion, Candace described what she had seen and heard, including what she had learned from her husband.

Despite clumsy attempts by Assistant United States Attorney Aaron Isaacs to elicit an opinion from Candace as to her husband's guilt, and aside from the unnecessary objections interposed to such questions by the defense, Candace declined to impart any private impressions. She carefully narrated what had happened factually and described conversations with thoroughness, but did so dispassionately and without personal color.

Through an arduous exercise of self-control, Candace largely succeeded in draining any feeling from her voice (other than a slight quaver which only she could detect) and wiping any expression from her face. To maintain the necessary grip on herself when she was on the witness stand, she tightened her abdomen so firmly that afterward she felt as though she had done hundreds of crunches at the health club. Carefully hiding her exhaustion until the adjournment by Judge Williamson of that day's session, Candace went directly home and straight to bed. (But she rose early again the next morning, for her daily pilgrimage to the courthouse for the continuing proceedings.)

Two of the conversational topics with her husband that Candace related on the witness stand unfolded as both the prosecution and defense had anticipated. The third, which proved to be the most emotionally devastating, had not been expected by either side or by Candace.

Candace first outlined her conversations with Bill about the use of the TNT at the construction site and his acknowledgment to her that he could not account for and failed to timely log two of the TNT sticks. She next described her belated discovery that Bill had long been aware of the million-dollar insurance policy on her life.

Then came a moment of prosecutorial serendipity. Assistant United States Attorney Isaacs asked Candace to reconstruct that morning of the darkest day of her life. She explained how Bill had asked her to take his car, how James Daniel had missed the bus, and how she had returned to the house for her missing purse when the explosion occurred. Without any tactical cunning other than to impress the casualty of the car bombing on the jury, Isaacs closed this line of questioning by asking her to recall Bill's statements at the moment of the tragedy.

Candace hesitated for several long seconds, suddenly appreciating the appalling alternative interpretation of the words Bill had uttered on that awful morning. Before that query posed to her on the witness stand, she had accepted Bill's reiterated phrase that morning as nothing more than a horrified and guileless exclamation of a father's loss. With her voice briefly betraying the oppressive sadness that she had thus far well-concealed, she narrated how Bill had repeated, "J.D. was supposed to be on the bus. He was supposed to be on the bus."

Lest the jury fail to appreciate the impact of the testimony, the prosecutor recited the words again, slowly and with pointed emphasis: "So, Mr. Klein said, 'J.D. was supposed to be on the bus.'"

ALL OBSERVERS AGREED that attorney Andrew Dietrich mounted a valiant defense on William Klein's behalf. If it were possible to lead the jury toward reasonable doubt, Dietrich marked the most accessible path.

Under the circumstances, the defense had no option other than to put the defendant on the stand. William Klein proved to be a competent and reasonably sympathetic witness. He affected an appealing balance between composed insistence on his own innocence and heart-broken grief as to the loss of his child.

From the beginning of his testimony, however, and even more so when he came under sharp cross-examination by the prosecution, Klein was plainly on defense. He had to acknowledge, of course, that he had access to explosives, that he had failed to properly account in the log for two sticks of TNT, and that he knew that his wife's life was covered by a million-dollar insurance policy. And he had to admit that he had lied about both matters, falsely logging the missing sticks of TNT after he had left the construction site and misleading his wife about his awareness of the insurance policy.

Klein explained at some length he had not been forthcoming for fear that his actions would be misconstrued. He confessed he had been foolish in not coming clean earlier. Nonetheless, the contrast drawn with his wife's plainly forthright and honest behavior was not missed by any courtroom observer or by the jury.

Dietrich also presented an expert witness to challenge the crucial fingerprint evidence, which was the only evidence directly tying William Klein to the crime. The defense expert extensively questioned the scientific validity of any comparison of a fingerprint exemplar to a latent partial print. The expert argued that the federal fingerprint analyst had crossed the line from objective science to subjective opinion in finding a match.

This defense witness cast doubt on the supposed perfect reliability of fingerprint identification, re-telling the much-publicized story of the Portland, Oregon, man who had been accused of participation in the terrorist train bombing in Spain based on a fingerprint identification by the FBI's super-computer which then had been confirmed by FBI analysts. Only after the poor man had spent weeks in jail wrongly accused of the atrocity did federal authorities back away and begrudgingly admit that the fingerprint taken from a terrorist's bag in Spain simply did not match the Portland man.

Directly attacking the fingerprint match in Klein's case, the defense expert argued that the partial print found on the duct tape was too small and lacked sufficient clarity to make an accurate comparison with the fingerprint exemplar taken from William Klein. The expert accused the prosecution's witness of teasing out comparisons in the ridge pattern that were not there.

Consistently, through both cross-examination of the prosecution's witnesses and later direct examination of defense witnesses, Dietrich returned to the security video and the unidentified third person. Carefully building the case for another perpetrator, Dietrich regularly referred in his questions and asides to the blurry video figure as "the Mystery Man."

THE STRENGTHS, WEAKNESSES, and themes of each side's cause were well-capsulized in the closing arguments made by each attorney before the case was finally submitted to the jury.

Assistant United States Attorney Isaacs was first to present a closing argument:

"William Klein had it all planned out. He had found a way to collect a million dollars, end an increasingly troubled marriage, and escape from being trapped in a dead-end job with his own father-in-law as his boss.

"Klein would steal explosives from work, where he had easy access to TNT in his construction job. He would wire the TNT into a timed bomb on the vehicle his wife would drive, to which he also had easy access.

"And, crucial to his plan, Klein would blame it all on a fellow at work, Olin Pirkle, who had been caught stealing construction supplies and who thus would be the perfect patsy. Klein already had called the police to report the theft by that worker, cleverly making sure that Pirkle had already been brought to the attention of the police. When the car bomb exploded, Pirkle would immediately be suspected of trying to kill Klein in retaliation for having cost him his job and then reporting him to the police.

"There was a challenge, however. Klein had to make it look like Olin Pirkle was trying to kill him, of course, so that the events would neatly fit his story of the disgruntled former employee seeking revenge. That meant that the car bomb had to go on Klein's red-painted Honda coupe, which everyone knew he drove. So Klein then had to manipulate his wife into driving his car on that fateful morning. And that's exactly what happened. To Candace Klein's surprise, her husband asked her to drive his car—a car he otherwise jealously protected and wouldn't let anyone else in the family touch.

"Klein did not plan on two things, however. He didn't plan on getting his own son killed. James Daniel took the school bus to school each day. Klein assumed the boy would be well out of the way by the time his wife started the car rigged with the bomb. Sadly, J.D. missed his bus and wound up being where he wasn't supposed to be. Remember Mrs. Klein's testimony, that her husband reacted to learning his son was in the bombed car by repeatedly saying, 'He was supposed to be on the bus.' In the shock of the moment, William Klein revealed the first thing that had not gone according to plan.

"The second unexpected event was that Pirkle would travel to Las Vegas after being fired and, lucky for Pirkle, appear repeatedly on casino security video during the very time the car bomb was placed. Klein's plan to pin his wife's killing on Pirkle fell apart.

"All that was left to William Klein then was to rely on misdirection. He misled everyone, including his wife. Klein knew his failure to properly log the missing TNT could no longer be explained by saying Pirkle must have taken the TNT. So Klein now hoped his failure to properly log the missing TNT would not be noticed. He acknowledged to his wife that he had not properly logged the TNT, assuming she would keep his secret. He hoped the TNT would not even be tied to the Insignia Construction company.

"Klein also knew he wouldn't be suspected of trying to collect on a life insurance policy if everyone thought he was unaware of it. Without any knowledge of the policy, collecting a million dollars could hardly be a motive. Only later in an incautious moment when he spoke in anger about his father-in-law—and only when he thought his wife would maintain her refusal to testify—did Klein reveal that he had known all along about the million-dollars on his wife's life.

"Then, through good police-work by Lieutenant Ed Burton and his partner, Officer Melissa Garth, it all fell apart for Klein. Klein's fingerprint on the duct tape used in the car bombing tore away the veil of secrets. While the defense has worked hard to undermine the fingerprint evidence—a reliable method of identifying criminals that has been used effectively for more than a century—the evidence cannot be dismissed. Klein has no explanation for how his fingerprint came to be found on the murder weapon. So he has to argue it away, pretending it was not really there.

"But Klein's fingerprint was on the car bomb. And his fingerprint was there because he was the one who had taken the explosives from the construction site and created a murder weapon from it. He cannot escape from his responsibility. The evidence demands a verdict of guilty."

Andrew Dietrich responded with his closing:

"This is a case of random unconnected dots that only seem to link Bill Klein to this horrific act because the prosecution has invented a clever story that draws the lines together without any regard for complicated reality. But the dots need not be seen as connecting Bill Klein to any wrongdoing.

"And there is another dot—a big, fat, round dot—that the prosecution wants you to ignore. Remember that "Mystery Man"? They want you to ignore that dot because no line can connect that dot to Bill Klein. But this is not just a dot, not some flyspeck that can be ignored. It is huge, round, bouncing ball, which now is flying across the court at the prosecution. And the prosecution is trying to duck out of the way.

"Yes, Bill Klein had access to explosives at the construction company. There's nothing nefarious about that. Thousands of Americans use explosives for perfectly legitimate purposes—like construction.

"Yes, Bill admits that he logged the two sticks of TNT afterward, rather than contemporaneously when the TNT was used at the construction site. He shouldn't have done that. But let's be clear. That's just a bureaucratic error, resulting at most in a fine for the company.

Of course, maybe those two sticks of TNT were missing because someone else had helped himself to the TNT when Bill wasn't looking. More on that in a moment.

"Yes, Bill had learned his wife had purchased a million dollar life insurance policy on herself. Bill didn't buy the policy or encourage his wife to get it. She did that on her own and without confiding in Bill. And for many Americans, and especially for professional couples like Bill and Candace, a life insurance policy with a million dollar face value is not unusual. And professional couples with life insurance policies are not scrambling to kill each other to collect on the proceeds.

"The prosecution tells you that Bill's fingerprint is on the proverbial murder weapon. That's simply not correct. Weeks after the murder—after the crime scene had been left unattended for three months—the police found a piece of tape scrap with a fragment of fingerprint on it. The fingerprint was a partial print. If the government would be strictly accurate about this, they can only say the partial print *might* have come from Bill Klein. But maybe not. And, even if it was Bill's fingerprint, the TNT may have been stolen from Insignia

Construction, which might explain how his fingerprint was transferred from the TNT to the adhesive substance of the duct tape.

"Which brings us back to the biggest dot of all, the one that can't be connected to the story drawn by the prosecution. This is not a small dot or even just a dot at all. It is an asteroid-sized object that crashes down and destroys the prosecution's theory.

"Olin Pirkle and Bill Klein were not the only people with access to the TNT in that van at the construction site. You've seen the video from the nearby restaurant. There was a third person—other than Pirkle and Bill Klein—who was alone at the back of that van. George Peterson, who owns the construction company and hires the workers, couldn't identify this person.

"Who was he? What was he doing there? Who is this 'Mystery Man'? And why aren't the police doing more to identify him? Why isn't the prosecution focusing its attention on finding this person?

"We don't know who he is. The prosecution doesn't know either. The prosecution wants you to pretend it doesn't matter.

"We still don't know why someone was targeting—not Candace Klein or her dear boy—but Bill Klein. Someone tried to kill Bill Klein. And it was almost surely that 'Mystery Man' who could not be identified at the construction site.

"Bill Klein was not the perpetrator of this atrocity. He was the intended victim. And until Bill Klein is acquitted, the police won't even be looking for the true criminal.

"Where is that 'Mystery Man'? By your verdict of acquittal, you can tell the government to look harder."

IN REBUTTAL, ASSISTANT United States Attorney Isaacs had the last word:

"The defense would have you believe that someone else committed this act, some other unknown person, supposedly caught on the video tape of the construction site. As George Peterson testified, there were a dozen workers at the site that day, any one of whom might have been near the van for a moment and thus caught on the security video. It could even have been a random person passing by.

"And the defense would have you believe this unknown third person, for no apparent reason, without any motive, attached a car bomb to the very vehicle that would be driven by the defendant's wife. So the defense would have us imagine this third person happened to be an expert in explosives—just like William Klein and Olin Pirkle.

"The cold reality is that only two people had any motive at all to do this horrible thing.

"One of those two people was Olin Pirkle—if we were to speculate that his anger about being caught stealing and then being pursued by the police could harden into murderous intent against the man who reported him to the police. So, it might have been Pirkle. But it wasn't. It simply was not. That we know for a certainty. Even the defense does not try to argue that Olin Pirkle had anything to do with the car bomb.

"The only other person who had any plausible motive was the man who stood to receive a million dollars in life insurance proceeds if his wife died. That man was William Klein.

"He had access to the explosives. He admitted to his wife that he had fudged the log records on the explosives. He admitted to his wife he knew about the million-dollar insurance policy. And his fingerprint was later found on the duct tape used to attach the bomb to the car. Yes, it was a partial print, but the experienced experts at the crime lab found sufficient clarity to make a solid match.

"The defense tells us that William Klein was not the kind of man who would kill his own wife. Perhaps he hadn't been that kind of man. But the chance to score a million dollars—and simultaneously escape an unpleasant work and family situation—can change a person.

"In any event, this is truly a case in which the evidence speaks for itself. A million dollars in motive. A man who had easy access to explosives and to the car on which the car bomb was installed. A man whose fingerprint appears on the device that killed a child. That man is William Klein."

◆　　◆　　◆

AFTER ONE AFTERNOON and evening of deliberation, the jury informed the judge that they had reached a verdict. When the parties had been recalled to the courtroom the following morning, with Candace faithfully looking on as before, the jury foreman announced, "Guilty."

Before anyone else could react, Bill turned from his position standing behind the counsel table, looked for Candace in the gallery, and then said in a voice that carried through the courtroom: "Candace, you told me that Jesus said the truth will set you free. I really do pray you now have been set free." In a tone that sounded more resigned than bitter, he added, "It hasn't worked out that way for me."

Candace winced, but said nothing. Had Bill now told the truth? she wondered. Or has the truth continued to elude him? And, if he at long last had been forthright, did the truth come too late for him to find salvation?

Judge Williamson pounded the gavel and waited for the room to fall silent again. "While formal sentencing will be scheduled later, with the death penalty not being sought, the sentencing guidelines plainly call for an extended term of imprisonment. So I'll ask the Marshals to take Mr. Klein into custody immediately."

As Bill Klein was led out of the courtroom, Candace was tempted to drop her head. Instead, she firmly instructed herself, she must remain resolute, see the matter all the way through, and not turn away.

Even as Bill was taken down the aisle of the courtroom, she realized she had come to another resolution, without being fully conscious of her deliberation. This would be the last time she saw her husband.

She had faithfully attended every minute of the trial. She had refrained from offering even a hint as to her opinion on her husband's guilt. She had seen it through. Now that the answer had come, or at least the jury's verdict on events, she could not bear to continue. She would not attend the sentencing.

~16~

THOSE ANGUISHED months from the morning of the bombing to the evening of the jury verdict would be forever chronicled in Candace's personal history as the "Summer of Loss." She had lost her boy. She had lost her husband. She had lost her home.

Determined to abate her time of mourning, however, Candace Klein resolved that the undeniable Summer of Loss would not slide inexorably into an Autumn of Grief that drifted fatefully into a Winter of Sorrows. She could not change the past, but she could control her own future.

Shortly before classes for fall semester began at the University of St. Thomas School of Law, Dean Colleen Ordway had again invited Candace to accept a one-year paid leave of absence. Candace had once again declined. Descending into a year-long bereavement—separated from her work and its life-affirming purpose, and isolated from the benevolent community at St. Thomas—would leave her destitute and emotionally impoverished.

Fortunately, Candace also had no need to accept any extension of the calendar on which she would be considered for tenure on the law faculty. The tragedy had fallen on her shortly after the end of her third year on the faculty at the University of St. Thomas. By that point in time on the "tenure track," she already had published three major law review articles, while receiving the highest peer and student evaluations of her teaching.

The formal written tenure standards set three articles as the quantitative minimum that must be submitted by a candidate for tenure. Candace already had satisfied that minimum expectation. However, Candace well understood that St. Thomas held to the highest standards of scholarship, which was one of the reasons she had come to the Twin Cities. Three articles was the floor, not a ceiling, and by itself was no guarantee of receiving tenure. The tenure committee would look to her portfolio for evidence of a pattern of scholarship that promised future productivity. A faculty member who worked steadily on research and writing during the untenured period would be judged more likely to continue scholarly activity, than the faculty member who was inactive for long periods of time.

For obvious reasons, Candace had made no progress on a fourth scholarly article during the previous summer. Still, with the fourth and fifth years on the tenure track ahead of her, she had ample time to finish at least one more article before she would be evaluated for tenure. Each of the two semesters consisted of thirteen weeks of classes, to which should be added about one week of pre-semester preparation, one week for a fall or spring break in the middle of the semester, and one week (maybe two) to grade exams afterward. That allowed her nearly five months each year—including three uninterrupted months each summer—to devote to scholarly writing. Accordingly, Candace admonished herself, she would have no excuse for not maintaining a writing schedule designed to produce at least one and maybe two more major articles before the tenure clock ran down.

Candace did accept one accommodation offered by Dean Ordway. She had been scheduled to teach first-year Civil Procedure in the fall, a task she had relished for the past three years. She regarded it as a distinct privilege to teach beginning law students and guide them in discovering a love for the law and for learning—and to do this in a course like Civil Procedure that most students initially found daunting.

However, with Bill's trial being set for October, which would mean that she would miss two weeks of class right at the middle point of the semester, Candace worried she would fail to meet her obligations to her students. Moreover, she also feared she would struggle unsuccessfully to maintain composure in front of a classroom of new and unfamiliar people, during the period when her personal pain would be paraded before a jury and highlighted on the nightly news.

Dean Ordway generously agreed to take over the section of Civil Procedure, on top of Ordway's other considerable duties as head of the law school.

With reluctance but sober recognition of her own limits, Candace acceded. Given the sad if unsurprising outcome of the trial, as well as Bill's sentence to life in prison shortly thereafter, she was very glad she had been able to keep a lower profile in the law school during that period.

By spring semester, when Candace was scheduled to teach Professional Responsibility, the worst of the events would be past. And she then would be teaching to upper-level students she previously had in other classes—a congregation of friendly and familiar faces, many of whom had been at her house in June generously assisting in the unexpected move from suburban Eden Prairie to downtown Minneapolis.

During the fall semester, Candace would continue her work with Sharon Tipplett in the Veterans Clinic. With Candace added as a supervising attorney, the clinic was able to enroll a larger group of students and provide legal representation to more of those men and women who had served their country so heroically and sacrificially in the armed forces.

In late October, Candace had learned of the gratifying success of the appeal she had briefed for the veteran with crippling back pain, who had been denied disability benefits by the Department of Veterans Affairs. Receiving financial assistance through restored veterans disability benefits, and with the family's debt payments to other creditors restructured, this veteran and his family were seeing the answer to their faithful prayers.

For an interval, Candace worried that this family's legal victory would be overshadowed by their own personal hardship. This veteran's young boy was afflicted with chronic leukemia. In early November, he suffered an alarming relapse. With the malignancy impairing the infection-fighting function of white blood cells, the boy contracted a respiratory infection which was not responding to antibiotics and threatened his life. As the boy fought back against the infection, Candace sojourned to the hospital every evening to sit with the parents.

Acutely aware of the loss of Candace's own boy, these parents leaned heavily on her and drew considerable comfort from her presence. Candace was overjoyed and much relieved when the young boy recovered. She was not confident she could weather another loss of a young innocent, even if the child was not her own.

DURING THE AUTUMN months, as Candace continued to work with veterans and their families, including those who had lost family and friends in military service overseas, she perceived an exceptional openness to her counsel and realized that others derived extraordinary comfort from her personal attendance in their hour of need. As she had with the veteran's family and the young boy suffering from leukemia, Candace apprehended that she was so gratefully embraced because her own tragedy had become a matter of widespread public knowledge. Her empathy was accepted as genuine and her words of consolation were especially valued because others understood she had been well acquainted with sorrow and yet had persevered.

Although pleased she was able to offer meaningful solace to others, Candace also experienced a nagging disquiet about the source of her ameliorating counsel.

Sensing she was troubled, Father Alexander Cleveland inquired one day in early November after morning Mass.

Candace explained to the priest that she felt tremendously blessed she had been able to bring healing to others out of her own pain. And yet she had been burdened by the perverse notion that her tragedy somehow had been pre-ordained so that, through affliction, she would learn to serve the afflicted. Apologetically acknowledging that her discernment had become distorted, she confessed it had had crossed her mind that her own son's death might have been divine will.

"No, no," said Father Cleve emphatically. "You must not think that. You should not feel that. What you're feeling is a form of survivor's guilt. When a person survives an accident in which others perish, she often feels guilty, believing that somehow her own survival was achieved at the cost of others. That's irrational of course, but a natural emotional response.

"You have a gift, Candace. You are able to offer genuine comfort to others who are afflicted. To be sure, you draw upon the reservoir of your own experiences in offering that comfort. And one of those personal experiences is your own struggle to overcome tragedy. Because your heartfelt empathy grounded in your own loss draws others to you, you are tempted to believe your tragedy was a sacrifice demanded from you by God. You're troubled by the thought that the loss of your son was the price exacted by God to mold you into an instrument of healing.

"God indeed is forming you and strengthening your gift of comfort. But that's because of His mercy and saving grace, not because He sacrificed your son.

"It was not God's will that your son should die. It is not God's wish that any one should perish. Death comes into the world through our collective sin, our rebelliousness as human beings. Because of that stain of original sin, death comes to the good and bad, the innocent and the guilty. We are broken people living in a broken world.

"But God's love for us, even in our sinful brokenness, is so strong, and God's divine and eternal purpose is so powerful, that He is able to take these broken people in this broken world and make something holy and good from it. As Jesus said, 'Behold, I make everything new.'

"Candace, your refusal to drown in your pain and your willingness to serve others is a testament to your love for J.D. Because of your faith, God has redeemed the evil of J.D.'s killing. When you serve others, J.D. is resurrected in your heart. Treasure that. Never doubt it."

CANDACE WAS NESTLED comfortably on a recliner chair, placed next to the large picture window of her twelfth floor condo unit in downtown Minneapolis. As she read through the Sunday newspaper on this morning after Thanksgiving, she occasionally paused and gazed down at Loring Park. The trees were now mostly bare, offering only a tantalizing taste of the apricot and cherry that had garnished the park even into late October. Here and there a solitary orange or red leaf still clung to a branch, resisting the onset of winter.

Technically, Candace remained a tenant of the Zuazos. Not for long. The house in Eden Prairie had sold sooner than she expected and at a price that left enough for a down payment on a new residence, even after paying off the line of equity that had covered Bill's legal defense. Having settled comfortably into the condo and appreciating its convenient location across the street from the University of St. Thomas law school, Candace had approached the Zuazos about purchasing the condo and becoming a permanent downtown Minneapolis resident. With some financial help from her father, and what she suspected was generosity by the Zuazos, her initial low bid was accepted. Closing on the sale would come within the next couple of weeks.

Having returned from early Sunday Mass at the nearby Basilica of St. Mary, Candace had planned to relax until lunch-time by reading the *Minneapolis Star Tribune*. Tucker apparently approved of her plan, as he had immediately jumped up and draped himself across her upper legs for a nap.

In the weeks and months since they had left Eden Prairie, the cat had become more and more affectionate toward her. It wasn't like he had many options for human companionship, she reflected. Still, Candace allowed, there was something most comforting about the perfect trust of a feline, purring contentedly as he rests in your lap.

The buzzer sounded at the intercom near the door, signaling that someone was trying to contact her from the front desk down on the first floor of the condominium building. Almost without thinking, she said out loud: "I can't answer the door. I've got 'cat privilege.'"

"Cat privilege" had been something of a family tradition in the Klein household. When the cat had chosen to curl up on someone's lap, that fortunate person was immune from being asked to answer the phone or the door or to run an errand inside the house. Given Tucker's preference for J.D., the little boy usually had been the one claiming "cat privilege" to avoid a chore.

Thinking about that piece of family lore caused a shiver of emotional pain to shudder through Candace's heart. But the pang was followed by a light laugh, as the silliness of the custom struck her.

The buzzer sounded again. "Well," said Candace to Tucker, "there's no one else to answer the door." She started to sit up, which jostled the cat out of her lap. He jumped down to the floor, stalking away with ostentatious irritation at having been interrupted in his nap.

Answering the intercom, Candace was connected to the security guard at the front desk. He told her that a police officer named Burton was asking to come up to see her. With reluctance, as she couldn't imagine that Lieutenant Ed Burton would be carrying good news, she told the guard to send him up.

Burton came immediately up the elevator to the twelfth floor and down the hall to the condo. Candace met him at the door and invited him in to sit down in the living area.

"There's been some news about Mr. Klein," said Burton without any preliminaries. "I thought I ought to pass it along to you, just so that you would know."

"What's happened?" asked Candace.

"Mr. Klein was being transported by the U.S. Marshals Service from a medium security facility in Oxford, Wisconsin, where he was being evaluated, to a high security correctional facility in Terre Haute, Indiana. The transport van was involved in an accident on the highway. The driver of a truck had fallen asleep, crossed the median, and struck the transport van head-on. Both drivers were killed and the van was overturned. One of the two guards in the back was seriously injured. The other guard was overpowered by some of the other inmates being transported. After they got the key and unlocked their shackles, they escaped."

"So you're saying Bill has escaped from prison?" she asked incredulously. While she was startled by this turn of events, she realized she was not anxious. Even now, even after all that had happened, even after the jury's guilty verdict, she still could not conceive of Bill as a violent and malicious man. It never occurred to her to be afraid for her personal safety, to worry that he might come after her.

"No, Mr. Klein was still in the transport van when the police and then Marshals Service personnel arrived at the accident scene. Mr. Klein had given some basic first-aid to the seriously injured guard. And he had put a blanket under the head of the other guard, who had been knocked unconscious by the escaping prisoners. He was just sitting there in the back of the over-turned van waiting when law enforcement arrived.

"The police and marshals were so surprised, since Mr. Klein was the only one of the six prisoners who had remained behind, that they asked him why he didn't run away as well.

"He simply said, 'I don't have anywhere to go.'"

On hearing this, Candace felt . . . sad. Unutterably sad. She felt no anger, no hatred, no bitterness toward Bill. The man she had loved and with whom she had built a life and family for more than a decade had been sitting there alone in a prison transport van, with nothing left and nowhere to go. How heartbreakingly sad.

Then she became angry, although the target of her indignation was not Bill. She was irritated with Burton. By intruding into her Sunday morning with this depressing news, he had unsettled that fragile equilibrium she had worked so hard to reach in the past several weeks.

"Why did you tell me this, Lieutenant?" she inquired with exasperation. "What am I supposed to do with this information? How does this help me? How does this help me get on with my life?"

Burton was taken off-guard, not expecting that Candace would be displeased. He immediately but belatedly realized he had been insensitive, not considering how she might react to this development. While he felt he had a duty to share the news with her, he could have done so differently.

Candace abruptly stood up, leading Burton to rise to his feet as well. In a formal tone as though addressing an unwelcome stranger, she said, "Well, then, good day to you, Lieutenant."

She went directly to the door and held it open for him to depart. As soon as he had passed through, she immediately pushed the door tightly shut, not with a slam but not gently either.

Before the door had latched, Candace already regretted treating Burton so coldly. The poor man was only doing his job, she realized, keeping her informed about something he reasonably assumed she would want to know. Her sense of unbalance reflected her precarious emotions, that she was not yet fully recovered. It was not attributable to his behavior.

She jerked the door back open, just in time to see Burton turn the corner down the hallway toward the elevator bay and pass out of her sight. She opened her mouth to call to him, thought better of it, and stood quietly one small step outside of her condo.

Well, she thought with a mental sigh, that's one more person that I'll probably never see again. J.D. Bill. Now Burton. Each one had forever passed from her life.

Candace retreated back inside the apartment.

She closed the door.

~17~

EVEN IN THE TWIN CITIES of Minnesota, snow in April was not common, although it wasn't exactly rare. As was typical of late spring flurries, very little crystallized precipitation had accumulated on the ground. Rather than reshaping the landscape by burying sidewalks, streets, bushes, and yards in fleecy drifts, only a thin layer of snow had been pasted on the ground and on every uncovered object.

The dusting of snowflakes had washed away the color of the setting without changing form. A nearly transparent veil of white covered the earth, concealing nothing that lay underneath. The suburban panorama had been visually transformed into an old-style black-and-white photograph.

The startling exception to this achromatic scene was the bright splash of scarlet that stained the frosted ground next to the head of the man lying near the driveway. The only other color standing out in this ivory and ebony world was the darker red of the luxury automobile parked in the driveway, which had not yet been enveloped in snow.

◆　　◆　　◆

"HIS NAME IS . . . *was* Maik Pnommavongsay," said police investigator Melissa Garth to her partner, Lieutenant Ed Burton, as she stood next to the nearly headless body. "In Laotian gang circles, he was known as 'M.P.' He was reputed to be the head of one of the biggest drug-dealing gangs in the Twin Cities."

"Yeah," said Burton. "I've heard of M.P. Every Eden Prairie cop has heard something about him, ever since he slithered out here to live in a house away from the chaos to which he contributed in the inner city. He supposedly did his best to keep his criminal activity in the city separate from his suburban lifestyle out here. But he could hardly keep the gang rivalry neatly confined to one part of the Twin Cities.

"In fact, Mel, just before you joined the Eden Prairie police force—about a year-and-a-half ago—rival gang members pulled into this driveway and sprayed the house with bullets. No was one hurt that time."

"Isn't this the place that Alex Kramer of the ATF talked about, where the feds experienced their biggest embarrassment in this state in years?"

"You remember right, Mel. That infamous ATF raid was conducted on this very house. Informants had told their federal law enforcement handlers that M.P. and his gang were setting up a cache of illegal weapons out here in Eden Prairie. So they all showed up one day, kicked down the door, and turned everything inside out. The ATF came up empty. Either there were never any weapons out here or they'd been moved before the feds could get here."

Garth gestured back to the body. "When the first responders arrived thirty minutes ago, it was obvious M.P. was dead. Looks like he was hit squarely in the face. Must have been a high-caliber weapon, as it darn near blew his head off.

"M.P.'s buddies thought the shot came from over there." Garth pointed toward a wooded hill about two hundred yards to the southwest, across the street. "One of M.P.'s crew even boasted to a patrol cop they'd fought back by emptying a couple of magazines in that direction. Patrol officers are canvassing the area to see if there's anything over there, beyond bullet holes in trees."

Mel then glanced at the maroon Jaguar XF with alloy wheels and a trunk spoiler. "I'd guess M.P. was hit just before getting into his car. Nice ride," she said admiringly. "With these accessories, this car must have set him back at least a hundred grand."

From his crouching position next to the body, Burton looked up and stared thoughtfully at the car for several moments. Then he stood up and looked up and down the driveway. He swung to his left and examined the house. Then he walked back down the yard, slowly scanning the driveway yet again.

Burton returned back to where Garth was standing near the body and car. He asked, "Do you notice anything unusual about this scene? Like something out of the past?"

Garth surveyed the area, looking all around. "Not really, boss. What's grabbed your attention?"

"I can't quite put my finger on it. I'm having one of those déjà vu moments. I just feel like I've been here before."

"Well, maybe you have been," suggested Garth. "This isn't the first time the Eden Prairie cops have been called to this location."

"No, no, that's not it," said Burton. "I certainly knew about M.P. and his presence in Eden Prairie. But I've never been asked to investigate him. I know I've never been here before."

After a pause, he muttered to himself, "But it certainly feels like I have been here."

Burton stood silently for a long time, continuing to look over the yard, gaze back at the house, and contemplate the long driveway.

He felt that something important lay just outside of his range of vision.

Then it came to him.

"I know, I know," he said excitedly. "Doesn't this driveway and even this house look an awful lot like the Klein scene? Same Tudor style of house. Same long and winding driveway down toward the street."

"Yeah, yeah," acknowledged Garth. "I see what you're saying. But it's not really the same. This driveway curves to the right instead of to the left like the Klein driveway did.

"And, as you well know, Ed, I got up close and personal with that gigantic oak tree in the Klein yard. The big tree in this yard isn't an oak. It's an elm, I think. And this style of house isn't that unusual. There must be dozens —"

"This is Eden Prairie," interrupted Burton. "Murders out here are rare. And to have two high-profile, carefully executed killings in just twelve months. What are the chances of that?"

"It's just one of those coincidences you dislike so much, Ed. Random chance. And besides, it's not like there's anything in common between these two cases. Klein turned out to be a bad guy, no doubt about it. He tried to kill his own wife and ended up killing his boy. But there was never any hint that he and his wife were involved in other criminal activity. By contrast, this M.P. was thoroughly criminal. And this definitely was a gang hit. On top of that, the murder weapons weren't even the same. Klein used a car bomb. One look at M.P.'s body here, and you know it was a gunshot—probably a high-powered rifle shot—to the head."

"Something doesn't feel right to me," insisted Burton. "Two murders. Two assassinations. In a single year. In Eden Prairie! That's too strange."

"Strange things do happen. Eden Prairie isn't so isolated from the criminal element that troubles the rest of the Twin Cities, whatever people out here like to think."

Burton looked over at the body, lying next to the Jaguar sports car. "Do you remember the color of the Klein car, you know, the one destroyed by the bomb?"

"It was pretty much all black by the time I saw it, boss," said Garth in an attempt at gallows humor. Seeing that Burton wasn't smiling, she continued on a more sober note, "Yes, I do remember. It was red."

"Just like M.P.'s car," observed Burton.

"Hardly," countered Garth. "This is a high-end Jaguar, a genuine sports car. Klein had a Honda coupe, which only looked like a sports car."

"Both red," noted Burton.

"Well, Klein's Honda had been painted fire-engine red. This Jaguar is more, well, dark burgundy in color."

"Burgundy is still red," insisted Burton.

199

"You're reaching for parallels, Ed," responded Garth. "And what's the point anyway?"

Burton didn't answer. Other than deepening his frown, he made no move and uttered no sound for several long minutes.

"Say," as he finally spoke, "wasn't the Klein house also on Dunnell Drive? What are the chances of both of these killings happening on the same street?"

Garth shrugged.

Burton then asked, "How close by is the Klein house?"

"Not very close. A couple of miles at least." Garth pulled out her iPhone and pulled up a map of Eden Prairie. "Yeah. This house is on the west side of Eden Lake. Dunnell Drive is interrupted when it reaches the lake. On the east side of Eden Lake, Dunnell picks up again and runs all the way east into Bloomington on the other side of Highway 169. The Klein house is way over there on the east edge of Eden Prairie."

Things started to click into place for Burton. "What's the address here?" he asked in a tight voice.

Looking up to the porch of the house and then flipping open her notebook, Garth said, "3132 Dunnell Drive."

"What was the address of the Klein house?"

"I've hardly got it committed to memory," protested Garth. Burton threw her an annoyed look. "Okay, okay," she said. Garth walked over to their car, called dispatch, and asked them to look up the Klein address.

After a moment, she shouted back, "3732 Dunnell Drive."

"It can't be," whispered Burton, as his stomach lurched. Then speaking more loudly as he came over to where Garth remained at the car, he said, "That's identical to this address, except for the second number."

"You know, you're right," Garth said, shaking her head. "I do have to admit that's kind of odd. Yet another coincidence."

"I don't think it's a coincidence at all," replied Burton. "I'm starting to think it is something much worse. I'm thinking there's been a terrible, terrible mistake. A fatal mistake."

Burton pulled out a pad of paper from his pocket and jotted several series of numbers on it. He showed it to Garth. "Think about it, Mel. Suppose you write down the number '1' with a short line slanting to the left that is added at the top of the longer vertical line. And suppose you write it in a sloppy, hurried manner. Then you pass the handwritten note on to someone else, who writes the number down yet again, and then passes it to still someone else. See how the handwritten '1' slides into a '7'?"

"I suppose. But what are you getting—" Garth halted. Burton could see the lights turning on in her eyes. "Now, wait a minute. Surely, you're not suggesting this is all an accident?"

"Not an accident," replied Burton. "There's nothing accidental about either of these killings. But perhaps someone got the wrong address."

Burton's radio crackled to life. "Lieutenant Burton," came the voice of one of the patrol officers exploring the wooded area southeast of the house. "M.P.'s idiot followers told us they shot off their guns in this direction after M.P. was shot. Well, they managed to hit somebody. We've got a blood trail, which stands out pretty well in the snow. We haven't followed it very far. But we found a rifle that someone had ditched into the bushes."

Garth ducked into the car to answer a call from police dispatch. She turned back to Burton. "Ed, one of the neighbors down the street says, looking out his window, he sees a strange man hiding in his back yard. The caller says that it looks like the man is badly hurt."

A NURSE FROM the station on the seventh floor at the Fairview Southdale Hospital in Edina, Minnesota walked over to Lieutenant Ed Burton, who was waiting outside the suspect's hospital room with another police officer from Edina. "The doctor says you can talk to him now. He'd lost a lot of blood, but he's had a transfusion. And the bullet wound to his leg wasn't that difficult to treat. He's going to be just fine. The doctor says there's no medical reason to deny you access to his hospital room."

Officer Garth came down the hospital corridor. "Ed, we just got a call from the chief. He says the fingerprints came back to a Toby Boreo, formerly of New Jersey. Turns out the FBI has been looking for him since the 1980s. They say he's an old Mafia hit-man who used to be known as 'The Rocket.' I guess he was pretty fast with a gun. He's still wanted on several federal charges of interstate murder-for-hire. The fingerprint check must have alerted someone in D.C. The chief already got a call from the FBI asking where we're holding him."

"Oh, no," said Burton, thinking he had done enough bidding for the feds to last him a lifetime. "I'm not going down that road again. We're in charge here."

Burton glanced over at the Edina police officer who had joined him in keeping watch over the suspect's hospital room. Burton said to his fellow suburban cop, "This guy shot someone in Eden Prairie. We caught him, dead to rights, in Eden Prairie. He's in my custody. And, at least for now, that's where he's going to stay."

"You'll get no argument from me," said the Edina officer. "As far as I'm concerned, you can play this game however you think best."

I thought I'd already played this game, thought Burton. *I played it all the way through to the end.* Now it's looking like the last play is going to be overturned on further review by the referee and the whole thing is going into overtime.

◆　◆　◆

BURTON OPENED THE DOOR to the hospital room, went in, and stood at the foot of the bed.

"Hey, it's about time you cops showed up," said the gray-haired, clean-shaven man. He tried to wave his hand, but it was securely fastened by cuffs to the metal frame of the hospital bed. "I was just going for a walk this morning, minding my own business, and out of nowhere I got hit by a bullet. I hope you're going to catch whoever did this to me."

"You can drop the act, fella," responded Burton. "We've already confirmed that the identification in your wallet is fake—good fakes, though. And we've run your fingerprints. Mr. Toby Boreo."

The slightly built elderly man simply shrugged.

"While you were sedated as the docs fixed your leg, we tested you for gunshot residue on your hands and clothes. Positive. And we found the rifle you ditched after you got shot. You spilled blood all over the rifle too, which we'll have no difficulty confirming with a DNA match. So we got you cold for the murder of Maik . . ." Burton struggled with the last name. "Pnommavongsay."

The man chuckled. "That's a mouthful, ain't it?" He sighed and said, more to himself than to Burton, "You should never get mixed up with Laotian gangbangers. I had to learn that the hard way."

"I think we have everything we could ever want to tie you to this morning's killing," Burton said.

As Burton read him his rights, Boreo said nothing, but kept smiling.

Then Burton changed course. "Now I want to ask you instead about another killing, the Klein boy."

The grin remained plastered on Boreo's face, but Burton thought he saw the smile slip just a little.

Boreo responded: "Don't know nuthin' 'bout that."

"Oh, come on, Boreo. You know we got you for this shooting. The FBI's coming for you. And you know, you'll probably get the death penalty. Even a city cop like me knows there's a federal death penalty for murder-for-hire."

"So they're going put a needle in my arm, is that what you're saying?" sneered Boreo. "You think that's going to scare me? I'm seventy-five years old. Not gonna live forever."

"No, honestly, I'm not trying to scare you. I'm just saying that you're already going down on the M.P. shooting. So, then, it doesn't matter whether you admit to the Klein bombing too."

"Don't know nuthin' 'bout that."

Burton persisted. "The poor kid's family deserves to know what happened."

Boreo shrugged again.

"His father's sitting in prison for the rest of his life."

Boreo repeated: "I don't know nuthin' 'bout that."

Garth pounded on the glass window to the room. When Burton looked back, she gestured to him to come out.

When Burton stepped back into the hall, she said, "Chief called again. A Special Agent Darren McCormack of the FBI is at Eden Prairie headquarters asking about this Boreo guy. The chief is stalling him, but he doesn't promise he can keep it up for too long. Looks like the feds are going to get this case too."

Burton replied, "Well, not yet, anyway. Tell the chief to hold them off as long as he can. I'm doing the best I can here. But I'm getting nowhere. I should have realized right away you can't appeal to the morality of a guy who left that behind decades ago. I'll have to try another tack."

Burton went back into the hospital room. "The FBI's asking after you. The word is they've been trying to find you for years, that you were a true professional, quite the worthy adversary for the FBI."

Boreo smiled and nodded.

"You're a legend, I guess."

"Don't I know it!"

"It's funny. They call you 'The Rocket,' or at least they did back in the days of the crime families on the east coast. I'm told that's because you were known to be fast and true as a missile when you took someone out."

Boreo continued to smirk.

"But this time, you couldn't even hit the right guy at first, could you? Hey, you couldn't even put a bomb on the right car. 'The Rocket'? Seems like you really should have been known as 'The Clown.'"

The smile dropped, and Boreo's eyes flashed angrily. Then he leaned back in the hospital bed and put his hands behind his head.

"Clever, clever," said Boreo. "I see what you're doing, cop. First you question my morals. Now you question my manhood. You hope I'll lose my temper and talk."

"Well," Burton responded. "I guess that proves you are a professional. Nothing gets past you. But you still ended up as a genuine clown in the end."

Boreo smiled and said, "You'll have to do better than that, cop."

Burton again was interrupted by a knock on the window of the room. Outside the room, Garth was holding up and pointing to her cell phone.

As Burton stepped out into the hall, Garth told him, "The chief says to expect the FBI here in about an hour. He's making them go through the formality of making an official request from Washington, D.C. But that's the best he can do. He can't stall them any longer than that."

When Burton returned to the hospital room, he dragged a chair over near the bed. He was tempted to check to be sure the cuffs attached to the man's wrist and metal frame were secure, but then decided that would contradict the more friendly and candid approach he now wanted to take with the suspect. So, without further ado, he simply sat down right next to Boreo.

"I'm going to be straight with you, Boreo. This is the last chance I'll have to talk with you. In about an hour, the feds will be here. They're going to take you into custody."

Boreo shrugged again.

"So, to use language that an old wiseguy like you may better understand, 'I want to make you an offer you can't refuse' . . . or at least one that you shouldn't refuse."

Boreo rolled his eyes at this reference to *The Godfather*, but he afforded a quick chuckle.

"Once the feds take you into custody, my guess is they'll put you away so far deep inside some maximum security prison way out in the middle of nowhere you'll essentially have disappeared from the face of the earth. Oh, yes, they'll have to let you talk to a lawyer once in a while. But they'll get a gag order from a judge preventing your lawyer from talking to the press or anyone else until your trial. And then once you've been convicted, back you'll go into the dungeon until your execution."

"Still trying to scare me, huh, cop?" said Boreo with contempt.

"No, no. Hear me out. I'm just setting the stage here, making sure you understand the background. You see, you're an embarrassment to the feds. You've been on the lam for some thirty years. They've never been able to catch you. Even now, they'll just hate it that it was a suburban cop like me that got lucky and nabbed you. So now you've gone and killed a young boy—"

"I don't know—"

"Yes, yes, I get it. You don't know 'nuthin.' But just hear me out. You've gone and killed a young boy—by accident—and my guess is your drug gang employers are the ones who screwed up, not you. But the feds aren't going to care about that. They'll still be embarrassed because none of this would have happened if they'd just caught you years ago. And now they'll be even more humiliated because the feds have sent someone else to prison for the crime you committed.

"Now maybe they won't be able to pin the car bombing on you, at least not right away. But you know they're going to shake down every gangbanger in the Twin Cities. Don't you expect one of them is going to talk? So if the story does come out, it will come out in dribs and drabs. And you can be darn sure it isn't going to come out in a way that makes you look like anything other than an idiot.

"So here's what I can offer you, Boreo. I don't answer to the feds. They can't tell me what to do. In fact, I don't much like the feds, because they've burned me too in the past. I can't stop them from taking you. But I can make sure they don't take you before you've had your say. So if you tell me the real story right now, I promise you this. I'll give your story to the press. Your story, in your words, will be at the top of the TV news reports tonight and on the front page of the paper tomorrow."

Boreo looked intrigued. "Really? You'd do that? On your honor?"

Geez, thought Burton. *On your honor? Come on.* Oh, well, he had to play along with this misanthrope. "Yes, on my honor." Burton couldn't resist embellishing, "Cross my heart and hope to die."

Boreo laughed agreeably. "Hmm. Well, you know, I'll just have to think about it."

"You'll have to think fast," pressed Burton. "We don't have much time. This offer only stays open until the feds get here and take you away. Then you'll never get your story out. And, I can sweeten the pot."

"Oh, really," responded Boreo skeptically. "What else could you possibly offer?"

"I'm guessing you're the kind of guy who would get a real kick out of throwing a monkey wrench into the feds' game-plan. If you tell me all about the car bombing and how it all went wrong, I can practically guarantee you that when the public learns about it, heads will roll at the FBI. When people learn that the FBI dropped the ball with you, and then a boy got killed all these years later, they'll be outraged. The talk shows will highlight how the feds screwed it all up. In fact, the first guy to lose his job will probably be the United States Attorney here in Minnesota, once it becomes clear he wrongly convicted a grieving father of killing of his own child.

Burton waited a beat, then added, "So, Boreo, you'll be famous. You'll be the man on the top of the news for days, as first the United States Attorney and then those FBI officials who failed to catch you all these years are roasted alive by the press."

Boreo grinned broadly, showing all his teeth and looking like a shark ready to swallow a most satisfying meal.

TRUE TO HIS MONIKER, once the Rocket blasted off with his mouth, the sky apparently was the limit. With very little further prompting, Boreo began to tell his story.

He knows he'll never be out of prison again, realized Burton, *so now he'll want to settle scores and point the finger for his mistakes at someone else.*

"So," asked Burton. "How exactly did you end up here? In Minnesota, I mean?"

"Bad judgment. Worse luck, I guess," said Boreo. "Retirement for a wiseguy like me didn't prove as easy or as permanent as I had hoped. I suppose everyone thinks us old Mafia types had hidden away huge stacks of cash from the good old days when the families ran every-thing. When it all changed a couple of decades ago as the new ethnic gangs took control of the street life and when the feds started cracking down even harder on the rackets, I actually did have a pretty good nest egg. I hoped I could just slip away somewhere and keep my head down. But money runs out. Old habits die hard."

As Boreo told the story, an old contact of his from back in the day in New Jersey had kept his hand in some things, mostly drugs, and still did some supplying to the new groups, including some out in the Midwest. He somehow heard that one Asian gang in Minneapolis wanted to eliminate the leader of some other Asian gang. These sad char-acters just couldn't seem to get close enough to their enemy to take him out. Instead he gathered they did stupid things, like shooting up his house. So they were looking for someone a little more . . . professional.

"Seemed like a simple job and easy money. So I was pretty sure I'd get away with it real easy. It sure didn't turn out that way."

"What do you mean," asked Burton.

"Well, I don't pretend that all of us in the old days were ge-niuses or something. But these gangbangers really aren't going to win any awards for intelligence. To begin with, they gave me the wrong ad-dress for this M.P. character. The wrong address! Can you believe it? How hard is it to write down the correct street address?"

Boreo became still and looked down. When he continued, his voice was softer. "You got to understand, I'd never blow up some little kid. Not on purpose. The gang that hired me said this M.P. guy lived out in the suburbs but only with other gangbangers. There weren't supposed to be any children around. How could I have dreamed they'd send me to the wrong house, for crying out loud?

"But that's what happened. When the group that hired me found out this M.P. guy was still alive and the bomb had gone off somewhere else, they refused to pay me. Come on, it wasn't my fault. They were the ones who screwed up. At first, I thought it was best to just get far clear of it all. So I went back home to . . . well, wherever I was living then. I should have stayed there.

"But I still needed the dough. And I guess my ego was bruised, since I'd screwed it up the first time, even if it wasn't really my fault.

"So I decided to come back and finish the job. Surely I wouldn't be unlucky twice. I figured I'd use a good old, simple rifle this time, so that I could stay far clear of the house and could eyeball the target through the scope—make good and sure it was the right guy this time.

"I guess this M.P. guy and his buddies were wise that something was up, because as I soon as I picked him off with the rifle, all of these other guys came running out of the house and looking around. And, would you believe it, these goons start shooting everywhere. It was crazy. I was this close to getting away, but then I took one in the leg."

"What about the car?" asked Burton. "How did you pick the wrong car? You know, on the first attempt."

Boreo grimaced. "The rival Laotian gang in St. Paul that hired me for the job said that M.P. was notorious for riding around all high-and-mighty in his red sports car. When I suggested that taking him out in his own car would be the perfect hit, they loved the idea."

"But what about putting the bomb on the wrong car?" persisted Burton.

"I'm not an idiot," protested Boreo. "I know the difference between a Honda and a Jag. But I guess I did think these gangbangers were idiots. Of course, I knew right away that the Honda I found at the house they sent me to wasn't a real sports car. I just figured these dummies didn't know any better. It was a red car after all. And it sorta looked like a sports car, as much as a Honda could. I assumed it was the car they meant."

Boreo paused again. "I assumed wrong."

"Mr. Boreo, ever since I started to put two and two together after this morning's events, I've been wondering how in the world it happened that you stole TNT from Bill Klein's construction site and then ended up attaching the bomb to Klein's car. That just seems fantastic to me."

Boreo gave Burton a condescending look. "What makes you think that's what happened? Come on, do you really think this Klein guy's luck was so bad that, in addition to everything else, the TNT used in the car bomb belonged to his own construction company? I don't know where you got that idea. I certainly didn't steal any TNT from that Klein fellow."

"Surely you didn't bring the explosives with you from New Jersey."

"I never said I came from Jersey," replied Boreo. Then he smiled again and continued, "With all the security and inspections of things and records at the airport, I couldn't fly here. So I drove."

"So that you could carry the explosives in your car?"

"Oh, hell no. The chances that a cop will pull me over on the highway are pretty small. And the risk is even smaller that he'll search the car. Still, the risk of having explosives in the car is just too great. Some bomb-sniffing dog could find me out. Or explosives could even go off. I want my bombs snuffing out someone else, not me.

"Besides, whether it's guns or TNT, I know how to find what I need at the job site, if you know what I mean."

"I'm not sure that I do. Enlighten me."

"Well, once I got here to Minnesota and my 'employers' had endorsed the plan of a car bomb, I checked out information on the Internet about local construction companies and what jobs they were working on and so forth.

"So, yes, I stole the TNT. And, yes, I stole it from a construction site. But I didn't steal it from Klein's construction site up north somewhere. I certainly didn't need to spend hours traveling out of town to find some TNT that wasn't adequately secured. I stole it right here in Minneapolis."

Of course, thought Burton, now feeling foolish. Things had been happening so quickly since that morning, and he was feeling so rushed knowing that the FBI was on the way, that he hadn't thought it all the way through. He had gotten carried away, assuming a more complex set of connections between Boreo's crime and Klein's misfortune than comported with a simpler reality.

He now appreciated that the chances that Boreo would have stolen the TNT from the Insignia construction site and then turned around and accidentally attached Klein's own TNT to Klein's car would be astronomical.

With an ironic shake of his head, Burton realized this also meant that Klein had been right from the very beginning in thinking that the TNT he had not logged had indeed been detonated at the construction site. There never had been any TNT missing from Insignia Construction.

And that also meant that the third unidentified person on the restaurant drive-through security video truly was nothing more than an innocent bystander. That figure probably had been another of the workers on the site. In any event, whoever it was had nothing to do with the car bombing.

Recognizing that he was being served a huge helping of humble pie today, Burton suddenly apprehended that his finding of the security video, which he'd been so proud of as great police work, actually had led everyone in the wrong direction. At the trial, the prosecutor had used the video as additional evidence to tie Klein to the explosives. And the defense had focused on the unidentified third person, suggesting he was the real culprit. And both had been wrong.

Not only had there been nothing nefarious about that third person's presence, likewise no meaningful connection to the case had been shown by the presence of both Olin Pirkle and Bill Klein alone in the vicinity of the explosives van. In finding the video tape, it now dawned on Burton, he had brought a classic red herring into the investigation.

"Yeah," allowed Burton, sheepishly, "now that I think about it, I guess it was a big leap to go from Klein using explosives at that construction site near St. Cloud to the assumption that was where you'd found the TNT."

"Ya think?" said Boreo in a snide voice.

"But there's still one thing that I don't understand. We did find Klein's fingerprint—or at least what we thought was Klein's fingerprint—on a piece of the duct tape used to attach the bomb to the car."

"Oh, that," acknowledged Boreo. "Now that is something I suppose I am responsible for. When I arrived at the house where I thought I was supposed to be, I waited until all the lights in the house had gone out. I'd brought with me some equipment to rewire the keypad outside the garage and then open up the electric garage door. But when I scouted it out, I found there was a side door to the garage. And it wasn't locked.

"Once inside the garage, I had planned to attach my bomb to the undercarriage of the car using a magnet. Well, either the metal and plastic on the Honda Accord didn't take well to a magnet or the magnet I had brought wasn't strong enough for the weight of the bomb or something else was wrong. I just couldn't get the bomb to attach securely with the magnet.

"Then I spied a roll of duct tape hanging on a nail right there in the garage. I pulled off several pieces of it and improvised with that to attach the bomb. I was wearing gloves, so I guess the fingerprint belonged to whoever had last used that duct tape roll."

"And undoubtedly that person who was last to use the tape was Bill Klein," completed Burton, "since you found the tape roll in his garage."

Boreo nodded. "I guess a powerful string of bad luck did attach to Klein after all. The TNT may not have come from his construction site, but the fact that he had any connection at all to explosives in his job sure made him look suspicious. And then the fact that his fingerprint was on the duct tape I used to attach the bomb made him look pretty damn guilty."

Boreo looked up at the ceiling and said, "I'd say that was more than enough bad luck for one guy. You just gotta hate coincidences like that."

"Yes, you do," agreed Burton. "Yes, you do.

~18~

[ONE YEAR AFTER THE TRAGEDY]

CARRYING A SMALL suitcase holding his meager belongings, Bill Klein walked out of the front gate of the federal prison camp in Duluth, Minnesota. He ambled toward the public bus stop nearby, clutching in his hand a bus token given to him by the prison administration upon his release.

As Bill's innocence had become more than merely apparent, the Bureau of Prisons had moved him from a maximum security correctional facility in Indiana to the minimum security prison camp in Duluth, anticipating his imminent release in his home state.

Bill had asked the Bureau of Prisons not to give the media his release date or the information that he had been moved to Duluth. He further asked that his family be notified, but only a few hours in advance. In that way, he was assured his elderly mother in Florida wouldn't learn of the "where" and "when" of his release in time to make the trip. He didn't want his mother to see him at the gates of a prison. There'd be plenty of time for a reunion later. But not here.

Candace was only a couple of hours away from Duluth, of course. So even with a last minute notice, she could get here . . . but Bill could not indulge any sentimental expectations that such a meeting would happen.

The Bureau of Prisons accommodated each of his requests, a surprising generosity for an agency not known for transparency with prisoners or their families.

213

After only a few steps toward the bus stop, Bill heard a voice call out his name. His heart leaped . . . until he realized that it was a man's voice he had heard.

He turned to see Lieutenant Ed Burton walking toward him.

"So, feeling a little guilty today, are we?" Bill asked with some bitterness. "Quite a turn-about, huh?"

"To be honest, yes," said Burton, "I do feel guilty, and more than a little. I'm sure I'm the last person you wanted to see today. But I had to be here anyway. It was only right that I would be willing to face you. I owe you that much."

Bill sighed. "Well, I must confess yours is not the face I had hoped to see. But I'm still glad to see a familiar face. And, to be fair, you were only doing your job. I do know that, while you helped put me in prison, you're also more responsible than anyone else for getting me out. I never had the sense that you had it in for me—not like that damn Sherburne."

Burton nodded and said, "Well, this whole matter turned on him in the end, didn't it?"

"I hate to take satisfaction in seeing someone else go down," replied Bill. "But I couldn't help but smile when I saw on the prison television that he had resigned as United States Attorney.

"So, Burton, I suppose I should not be too resentful. You did right by me in the end. Besides, if even my own wife turned away from me, I can hardly hold a grudge against you."

"So, how are you?" Burton asked.

"Fine."

Bill was willing to be fair to Burton, but that didn't mean he was about to confide all of his feelings to him.

"Did they treat you all right inside?"

"It was tolerable."

That wasn't a lie, but hardly the complete truth. The bruises on his face and ribs from the beating Bill received during his second week in prison had long since healed. Even in the unsavory company of the drug dealers and weapons traffickers who populated a maximum security federal prison, child murderers occupied the lowest rung on the ladder.

Bill had quickly developed a sixth sense about when violence was likely to break out. By being ever so cautious, and when necessary acting out in front of a prison guard so that he earned a trip to the segregation ward, he'd never again gotten more than the occasional push or punch.

Adding up all the days, he must have spent the equivalent of two full months in the segregation ward during the six months he had spent in prison. It was lonely there, which wasn't all bad, given his mood.

Still, there was the smell in segregation. You never got used to the smell.

Days in segregation did give him time to renew a habit of daily prayer, which like so many people he had lost in the years since Catholic high school. To be sure, he hadn't felt much like praying in the first month or so behind bars. If anything, he harbored a real grudge against God. But slowly and eventually with genuine commitment, he had turned back to prayer. And he had achieved a more powerful communion with God than ever before in his life. He knew he wasn't the first person who found a stronger relationship with God in prison.

The nineteenth-century conception of prison as a "penitentiary"—in which wrongdoers would have the opportunity to repent of their sinful ways and be reformed—no longer held sway with policy makers or prison officials in the modern world of criminal corrections. Nonetheless, Bill had been given plenty of time to think in prison—and, even though he had committed no crime, he was afforded all the time in the world to repent his sins. Indeed, time to think was about all he could really call his own during those long days—and especially the interminable nights. With all that time to think, he had come to understand and accept his pronounced liability for his own plight.

The slide downward had been propelled by a cold and professional killer who had murdered his boy and left Bill to take the fall.

And Robby Sherburne with his political ambitions definitely had greased the skids. But by hiding his mistakes, concealing his troubles, and breaking faith with Candace, Bill had put himself at the top of that steep chute for the fateful ride to the bottom.

Bill had never been able to sustain anger toward Candace at any point in their marriage. Not even after she had become the prosecutorial key to his indictment and conviction could he carry animosity. But he had felt abandoned. Like many husbands, he had regarded his wife as his best friend, perhaps his only real friend. Losing her trust had been a devastating emotional blow. Only when she was no longer there had he appreciated how alone he had become. And, much too late, he realized he had removed himself emotionally from his wife long before he had removed himself physically.

Over the months in prison, his sense of betrayal by Candace's testimony had faded—but it had never disappeared. He had to admit he had unfairly and unfaithfully withdrawn from her many months, even years, before the tragedy. He had come to regret his deplorable and selfish act in leaving his wife torn between her identity as an officer of justice and her loyalty to a husband who no longer had merited her confidence. He appreciated his unfairness in expecting her to remain perfectly reliable, without being reliable himself.

In sum, he could not justly blame her for the difficult choice she had made. But assigning fault to himself did not draw the sting from his memories of her words in court.

Although he no longer could remember the title of the book or its author, he recalled an often-quoted passage in a French romance novel that had been assigned in his college "lit" class: "To know all is to forgive all." He was not persuaded. He did know why Candace had agreed to testify at his trial. He did understand that she had chosen the only course left to her under the circumstances. Yet it was still so very hard to forgive.

After his conviction, he initially had refrained from trying to contact her because of his pain and, in all honesty, because of his resentment. Even when he had received legal papers from Candace's lawyer, which formalized in legal terms their separation, he had signed the documents immediately without reading them closely and sent them back directly to the lawyer.

Later, when the bitterness had receded even as the heartache lingered, he had abstained from contact with Candace because of his own guilt in having also caused her pain. And given that he thought he'd be locked up for the rest of his life, he had felt an obligation to release her to move on with her life.

Now he too had been released. Now he too had a chance to move on with his life. But the very fact that the pain endured was ineluctable evidence that he still loved her. And, God knows, he was lonely. He truly missed her.

He could not reasonably and fairly have hoped she would come.

But hope he had.

◆　　◆　　◆

"CAN I GIVE YOU a lift down to the Twin Cities?" asked Burton, interrupting Bill's unhappy reverie. Burton pointed over to his unmarked police car parked near the bus stop.

Bill hesitated and then gave in, as he had no other prospects.

"Only if I get to ride in the front seat this time," he said, in a lame attempt at humor.

"Of course. Of course." And, reciprocating the weak comedy, Burton added, "And we'll leave the hand-cuffs off this time as well."

"Ha, ha," replied Bill dryly, as the two walked over to and got into the car.

As the car entered the freeway toward Minneapolis, Burton asked, "What are your plans? Where in town can I take you?"

"I don't have any plans," said Bill in a flat voice. "To be honest, you may as well leave me off at the homeless shelter downtown. I obviously can't go home. After Pirkle broke in and held Candace hostage that night, we left the house in Eden Prairie for good. I think Candace has since sold it. And I had left the condo in downtown Minneapolis even before the trial. So I don't really have a home any more. And what little money I have left I'd rather not spend on a hotel room."

"Sorry, man. I figured that might be the case. Well, I've got you covered. There's an apartment in Savage, Minnesota, a few minutes south of Eden Prairie, that we use on occasion for witnesses or informants or someone who needs a safe place to stay. I pulled some strings, and under the circumstances, no one is going to say no. So the apartment is yours for a while. I can only let you have it for a couple of months, but at least it gives you a place to lay your head while you think about your next step."

"I'll take it," Bill said instantly, surprising himself with how quickly he seized on any courtesy. How hungry he had been for human kindness!

Burton's cell phone rang, and he flipped it open. "Burton here." Burton listened intently. "You don't say! Well, well, well. We're turning around and will get back there right away."

Closing the phone, Burton opened the window, placed a police beacon on the car roof, and turned on flashing lights and sirens. He veered to the left, crossed over the median of the highway, and headed back in the direction from which they'd come. "Back to the prison, pronto," Burton explained.

Bill's first reaction was raw, heart-pounding fear. *Oh no,* he thought, *they're taking me back to prison. My release was some kind of mistake.*

Bill remembered reading in the Minnesota papers about a former sixties radical who had been captured in Minnesota in the early 2000s and then imprisoned in California after pleading guilty to plotting to assassinate a cop in the 1970s. (Ironically, it suddenly occurred to Bill, the radical group's plan had been to use explosives to bomb a police car.) This woman had been released to her home in Minnesota at what the California prison warden thought was the end of her prison term. Then she was re-arrested a few days later and sent back to prison in California because the prison administration had made a mistake in calculating her release date.

Seeing Bill's face turn pale, Burton interceded, "No, no. You're not going back inside."

Because they hadn't gone very far on the highway from Duluth to the Twin Cities, and the car now was traveling a higher rate of speed on the return, they pulled back up to the front gate of the prison camp within only a few minutes.

Candace.

She had come.

There she was, standing by the front gate, holding her cell phone.

Bill vaulted out of the car and sprinted toward her. Then he jerked to a stop and pulled up short of her.

After all, he thought, this was no movie-style ending, in which the boy and the girl jump into each other's arms and kiss deeply as tears run down their faces.

This was the woman who believed he had tried to kill her. This was the woman who believed he had murdered their son.

This was not the romantic climax to a love story.

Still, Candace did move closer to him. After a brief but noticeable hesitation, she put her arms around Bill for a short embrace.

There were tears on her face. And she was trembling.

"I GOT HELD UP by a construction detour on the highway," she said. "When I got here and they said you'd already left, I didn't know what to do. Then someone said they'd seen you leave in an unmarked police car. I called 9-1-1, not knowing what else to do. They said they'd check into it. Thank God, they got through to Lieutenant Burton."

Turning to Burton with a smile, she said, "Thank you, lieutenant, I owe you more than I've ever told you. And now I owe you so much more. But I'll be taking Bill home."

As these words left Candace lips, she wondered whether her home could ever be Bill's home again. Was she being too impulsive?

Was her feeling of guilt at misjudging Bill prompting her toward precipitous action? And, yet, was guilt really so bad? If it prompted one to do the right thing, to correct a past wrong, was guilt not to be embraced?

This man, who had been her college sweetheart, her husband, her partner in life, the father of her child, had mutated into a monster in her thoughts. And then, all of a sudden, she had learned that she, and everyone else, had been wrong. So terribly, unjustly, unforgivably wrong.

Candace knew now, of course, that Bill had always been innocent. But just as the heart often leads the head in love, the heart may lag behind the head in moving beyond resentment.

She never had descended to hate. But, God forgive her, she had turned away. She had abandoned him to what she thought were his just desserts.

Even though she now knew that her enmity had been so badly misplaced, the feeling of . . . disquiet . . . persisted. She couldn't turn off her emotions like a water faucet.

And yet, Bill would always be her husband. Not in the eyes of the law any longer, but perpetually in the view of the Church. Shortly after Bill's conviction, Candace had filed for and been granted a legal divorce. For purposes of property ownership, selling the house in Eden Prairie, planning for the future, and even such mundane things as preparing annual tax returns, she had needed to become a separate and self-sufficient person.

Some well-meaning friends and acquaintances, as well as busybodies who approached her after Mass in church, had urged her to petition the Catholic Church for an annulment. Some even argued that "annulment" was simply "Roman Catholic" for "divorce."

She didn't believe that. Petitioning for an annulment would be a lie. Whatever else might have been true or false, and despite what had later occurred, she had been married to him. It had been a genuine marriage. "What God has joined together, let no man put asunder." That wasn't just Catholic doctrine, it was Candace's belief. The sacrament of marriage was forever.

Under Catholic teaching, a grant of annulment meant that no genuine marriage had ever existed. It meant that the parties hadn't understood what marriage was or one of the two had deceived the other into agreeing to marriage. But there had been a real marriage between her and Bill. They had been a real family.

As she often had said to herself, and sometimes to others, the monster who murdered her child could not be the same man she had married.

And, now she knew, the monster who had murdered her child was not the same man standing before her.

With a civil divorce, then, Candace had resigned herself to being alone for the rest of her life. Well, not so much alone, but with a different vocation for her life. Her family would henceforth be her father, brothers, and their wives and children. Her family would be her colleagues at the University of St. Thomas School of Law who worked side-by-side with her and supported her without question or doubt.

What now? she wondered.

Candace walked toward her car, with Bill trailing close behind. An awkward silence prevailed between them.

Then Candace tripped over a crack in the pavement. Bill reached out. "I've got you, Candy," he said. He took her arm firmly and steadied her against falling.

"Yes, you do," she replied. "You do have me. Again. If you still want me."

Did she mean it? Could Bill be her husband again, not just in church doctrine but in her heart? Or, if not by romantic emotion, at least at first, by custom of daily life? Could they share a life together again, despite the animosities, real and imagined, that had defined them for the past many months?

No one else in the whole wide world could understand her experience of losing her beloved son, seeing him killed before her own eyes, learning that her own husband was the author of that tragedy . . . and then learning that he was not.

No one. Except for Bill. His pain in being labeled as a child-murderer and seeing his own wife deny him was directly parallel to her pain. Or, to be truthful, Candace admitted, his pain, though likely greater, overlaps with my pain. I cannot know what he has suffered in being disowned and discarded, left alone in a prison cell.

They say that you cannot build a lasting relationship out of shared pain. They say that people who come together in tragedy are unlikely to succeed in a subsequent romantic relationship. But what other foundation was there for them?

There was another foundation. There was still James Daniel. He remained the strongest tie between them.

If staying together in marriage for a living child would have been right and appropriate, perhaps the same could be true for a child who has passed on. By building a new life together, J.D. would always be remembered as part of a living and continuing family.

Who knows if such a relationship, such a revival of their marriage could work? God knows.

More Information

For those wishing to further explore the history and nature of places and institutions mentioned in this novel, here are on-line sources:

Basilica of St. Mary: http://www.mary.org/index.php?option=com_content&task=view&id=89&Itemid=102

Eden Prairie, City of: http://www.edenprairie.org/

Good Shepherd Catholic Church, Golden Valley: http://www.goodshepherdgv.org/

Loring Park and Johnson's Lake: http://www.mpr.org/www/mnmonthly/9806_lake.shtml; http://reflections.mndigital.org/cdm/ref/collection/mpls/id/190; http://www.hclib.org/pub/search/mpls photos/mphotosaction.cfm?subject=Johnsons%20Lake

Municipal Building, City of Minneapolis: http://www.municipalbuildingcommission.org/Building_Information.html; http://en.wikipedia.org/wiki/Minneapolis_City_Hall

United States Courthouse, Minneapolis Building: http://www.mnd.uscourts.gov/Courthouses/courthouse_minneapolis.shtml; http://www.gsa.gov/portal/content/101158; http://skywaymyway.com/blog/index.php/2010/05/17/drumlins-of-federal-courthouse-plaza/

University of St. Thomas School of Law: http://www.stthomas.edu/law/